PRAISE FOR
AUDREY CARLAN

*"FIVE STAR REVIEW! I recommend this book
to anyone looking for a sweet, fierce love story.
It takes a lot to write an original story that takes
twists and turns you won't see coming."*
~Abibliophobia Anonymous Book Reviews Blog

*"DAMN! Audrey did it again! Made me smile, made
me laugh & made me cry with her beautiful words!
I am in love with these books."*
~Hooks & Books Book Blog

*"A sensual spiritual journey of two people
meant for each other, heart and soul.
Well-crafted and beautifully written."*
~Carly Phillips, *New York Times* Bestselling Author

Silent Sins

A LOTUS HOUSE NOVEL: BOOK FIVE

Silent Sins

A LOTUS HOUSE NOVEL: BOOK FIVE

AUDREY CARLAN

WATERHOUSE PRESS

DEDICATION

To my soul sister Nikki Chiverrell
The day I thought of the idea of this story,
I knew it would be for you.

You are the epitome of a woman driven by the throat chakra.

The life you live, the hardships you've overcome,
are a testament to your strength and beauty.

I named my character Honor because
it is an honor to have you as my chosen sister.

Though your story isn't the same as hers,
I think you'll find a kinship to her journey.

With sisterhood and love.

NOTE TO THE READER

Everything in the Lotus House series has been gleaned from years of personal practice and the study of yoga. The yoga positions and chakra teachings were part of my official schooling with The Art of Yoga through Village Yoga Center in Northern California. Every chakra fact and position description has been personally written by me and comes from my perspective as a Registered Yoga Teacher and follows the guidelines set forth by the National Yoga Alliance and the Art of Yoga. If you want to attempt any standard yoga positions detailed in any of the Lotus House novels, please consult a Registered Yoga Teacher.

The aerial yoga positions listed in this particular book have been from taking classes and hours of research. Do NOT attempt any of these positions without having first been taught by a credentialed aerial yoga teacher. To teach this particular type of yoga, a teacher should have a separate credential.

I suggest everyone take a yoga class. Through my yoga schooling and teaching the gift of yoga to my students, I have learned that yoga is for everybody and every body. Be kind to yours, for you only get one in this lifetime.

Love and light,
Audrey

CHAPTER ONE

THROAT
CHAKRA

The throat chakra, known as the Vissudha in Sanskrit, is located in the neck. Located between the head and the heart, it is the chakra that maintains the integrity between what is thought and what is felt.

HONOR

White-hot searing pain followed by a euphoric rush and the instant crush of extreme relief soothes and calms the war raging within me. I don't want the pain...I *need* it. For long moments, I sit quietly, enjoying the seconds of peace and serenity surrounding that first initial piercing of skin. Each rip of flesh eases the fear, the anxiety, the sheer loathing I have toward myself and the world around me. A world that he is no longer a part of.

I dig the blade deeper, requiring more...searching for

something that I can never find.

It works for a while. Small moments. The only beauty I have to look forward to anymore. Memories of happier times cascade through my mind like a pinwheel spinning in a gust of wind.

Running through the woods, him hot on my heels, me squealing in delight.

I press the razor blade deeper. More pain.

Him shunning the mean, popular girls who picked on me in school.

Shivers ripple through every nerve ending with each new blessed slice.

Movies. So many movies. Every Sunday, sharing a bowl of popcorn, laughing at the same parts as the images on the screen flickered by.

My mouth waters as sourness hits my tongue. Acid curls and burns inside my gut.

Nights long ago, cuddled up with one another as if the entire world had disappeared and there was only the two of us.

I dip my head back against the wall, close my eyes, and allow the full-body flush of heat and adrenaline to fire its way through my system as I flick my wrist, until I feel something... *anything*.

For me, pain is the only acceptable substitute for love and loss.

Once the blood drips and pools down around my forearm, congealing into thick, maroonish globs, I glance around, blinking away the regret and tears. I've finished this session and huddle in the corner where the tub and wall meet. My toes are freezing, curled in, pressed against the cold tile I'm sitting on. I sigh, my stomach rolling with nausea as the self-deprecation and disgust weave into my mind.

Hannon wouldn't approve.

He didn't approve back when we were kids when he caught me doing it at sixteen. He most certainly wouldn't now in my midtwenties. Except it doesn't matter, because he's not here to scold me.

To hold me.

To love me.

To save me.

A dry laugh leaves my lungs as I stand, trembling and leaning against the vanity for purchase. My newest cut throbs and aches, the two-inch-long line marred with slowly drying blood. I didn't go too far this time. Not as far as I wanted to go.

Coward.

The single word wreaks havoc on my psyche, taunting and prodding the loser within. I furl my fingers around the razor blade, wondering if I could just do it. End it all. No one would miss me. Certainly not my parents or the high-society brats who call me friend when I know we're anything but. Those gold-diggers use up everyone in their path until there's nothing left. They are friends by status alone, not by choice.

A sob tears through my chest as I think once again about how much Hannon would detest what I've done, what I've become in his absence. I snarl and growl at my image in the mirror.

"You want me to stop, Han, come back and make me!" I smack the counter hard, dropping the razor blade. It falls, clinking its way into the sink, where drops of blood smear along the white ceramic surface.

No response. Not even a flicker. There's only my reflection in the mirror, and what a sad sight that is. Blonde hair, almost white for how light it is, long and unruly beachy waves I've done nothing with. My eyes are two hollow ovals, gray and lifeless. Suits my mood. Chapped, dry lips I used to think were pretty curve into two bows meeting in the middle. I *used* to be pretty. Now I'm just here. Walking through each day, wishing I could be wherever he is.

The ache to be near Hannon hammers against my heart, like it always does, a nagging beat I can't escape. Turning on the faucet, I wash away the blood and rinse the new cut, noticing the others near it are fading nicely. The henna art covers them well, much to my parents' displeasure. Another reason to keep using the earthy dye to cover my sins. I'll have to reapply to make this newest mark disappear, but that will be easy enough. Still, the new mark doesn't take away the urge to flee, to run, to be close to him.

With a speed I'm used to after one of my "sessions," I fly into my bedroom, pull a hoodie from my closet, and throw it on, the icy claws of despair prodding my haste, aiding every movement. I step into my tennis shoes, the laces already tied, and am out the door. Once I reach the hallway, I tiptoe my way down the stairs that lead to the grand, main entrance of my parents' mansion. The black and white marble floors have been shined to perfection, nary a speck of dirt to be found. Mrs. Judith Gannon-Carmichael would never stand for anything less.

I hear loud voices, swollen with pompous righteousness, as they echo through the receiving room off the entryway. The door is open, so I do my best to slither along the opposite wall, hiding in the shadows in the hope I can get to the kitchen and off to the garage without being detected. Mother would look down upon my casual attire and be horrified in front of her friends, many of whom she and my father are currently entertaining.

The sounds of haughty laughter and clinking glasses echo through the open door as I skate by the evening gathering without notice. Thank goodness for small favors. If my luck sticks, Sean will also be home tonight. The last couple times I escaped to his house, he wasn't altogether welcoming. Loving, yes. Welcoming, no. There's been a hint of frustration in his demeanor when he's spoken to me recently and an overall weird sensation that I can't quite pinpoint when I visit. Regardless, I need to be there *right now*. Nowhere else will do. Not tonight, when I'm raw and twitchy.

Making it to the gigantic garage, so large it could double as a football field, I pass by an endless array of my father's obsession: cars. From classic American brands to European sports cars, my father has it all. With enough money to buy Queen Elizabeth out of her position in Buckingham Palace, he can afford the best, and he proves it in every shiny, new purchase.

I hop into my black, somewhat modest Mercedes S-Class coupe, probably the cheapest car in the entire garage and still considered luxury. For one full minute, I sit and just breathe, attempting to calm the swirling devastation that threatens to swallow me whole.

Just a little longer and you'll be closer to him, I remind myself until I hear his voice. Like in a dream or a memory that's just too hard to grasp.

Hold on, Bunny. Be still...find your peace.

Hannon's voice is a whisper over my senses. Those were the last words he ever said to me. My heart tightens as if being held in his strong hands.

For you, I will, Han. I promise.

I smash the button for door number six. The moment the heavy metal door rises high enough for my ride to fit under it, I shoot out into the bleak darkness of the night. I've taken this drive many times over the last two years, and each and every trip feels as if I'm driving toward heaven, only to remember once more I'm living in utter hell.

The miles fly by, my thoughts a mixture of memories and the crawling, aching desperation within me.

I take the steps two at a time at the front of the bright blue and white row house in downtown San Francisco. The Bay Area wind bites at my back as I ring the bell several times in quick succession. The lights are on in the living room, so I know he's here. He just *has* to be. If not, I'm going to use the emergency key Hannon gave me years ago. I haven't had to use it recently. I've tried to stay away, knowing each time becomes harder than the last. For both of us.

The door opens, and a tall man I don't recognize stands in the doorway. The warm tones of the light inside cast his face in shadow, but I can see he's attractive, lean, and a nice dresser based on the slacks and cashmere sweater he's wearing. On his nose is a pair of tortoise shell, square-shaped glasses.

"Hello. Can I help you?" His voice is as genuine and lovely as his corresponding smile.

I swallow, my throat suddenly dry as the Mohave Desert. Tears threaten at the back of my eyes. What's going on? Who is this man? Why is he *here* at this late hour?

"Who is it, love?" Sean calls out from farther in the house.

Love.

A word often used as a term of endearment. A term that's being used by Sean and directed at the nice-looking, late twenty- or early thirty-something man standing in front of me, currently wearing an assessing expression.

"A darling blonde with big doe eyes and a sad smile," he calls back. He tips his head to the side. "You lost, sweetie? Do you need help?" the man asks as I stare mutely.

Incapable of speech, I stand there like the lost little girl he thinks I am. I damn near feel that way until suddenly Sean puts an arm around the man's waist and nudges him aside to see who's at the door. The instant his eyes meet mine, his laughing smile turns into a frown. I hate it instantly. He used to look at me with laughter and joy.

"Honor." He says my name low and deep, as if it is a plague brought down upon his house. In front of me is not the same man who used to pull me in for long hugs and intense conversations about the world and, most importantly, sharing how much we both loved my brother.

I shake my head and place my hand over my mouth, a fresh bout of unease and loathing streaking up my spine. "No," I whisper.

He inhales visibly, his chest lifting up and going back down as if he is preparing to give one of his patients bad news.

Sean pushes past the man standing at his side, wraps his arms around me, and pulls me into the house. The man behind us shuts the door, keeping out the chill. All of a sudden, I feel too hot in my jeans and hoodie—scaldingly so.

Sean cups both of my cheeks and stares into my eyes. "Honor, it's good to see you. But honey, it's very late, and you didn't call first." A shiver ripples through me, and he continues dropping his arms to his sides. "I'm sorry if what you are seeing surprises you. I wanted to tell you first."

I choke out a sob, the next words leaving my mouth

agonized. "When? How long?"

Sean clenches his teeth, making his jaw look even more chiseled and fierce. "A few months. I couldn't keep him away from the house any longer. It's not fair to him or to me. Hannon wouldn't want that."

The mere mention of Hannon sears through me. The session earlier was nothing compared to the pain whipping through me, wanting to burst free as Sean locks his arms around me.

I can't stop the trembling, which starts at my teeth and flows through my insides like a bucket of snakes being poured into a small body of water.

The words leave my mouth before I can contain them. "How could you?"

His arms drop from around me, and he grasps my biceps loosely. "He's been gone two years, Honor. You have to move on. We *both* have to move on. The torch you're holding, forcing me to hold...it's unhealthy."

I clench my teeth. "Does he know?" I tip my head to the side, gesturing to the man standing near and listening in. "Does he know you told my brother you'd love him forever?" My voice is accusatory and scathing as I practically spit out each syllable.

Sean's features harden, and he scowls. "And our forever was cut short!" he grits through his teeth. "No one knows that better than me." His lips curl into an expression of disgust. "And that was Hannon's *choice*. Not mine. He made that all on his own. I've spent long enough being alone and a year in therapy getting past *his* betrayal. Now it's your turn."

I ignore the blame game he's playing. "You were everything to him." I'm barely able to speak through the thick fog of emotion coating my throat.

Sean's pretty brown eyes close as if he's letting that soak in for a minute. His dark hair is tussled. A few paces beyond, the man who answered the door stands, not intruding but staying close. I'd probably like him if he wasn't dating Sean. He doesn't look like a bad guy. His face is kind and honest, though he looks nothing like my brother. This guy is geeky chic and a little reserved. Hannon was blond and blue-eyed, filled with life and joy that exuded through his pores into every person who entered his orbit.

I close my eyes, the truth dawning on me in one tragic realization. Pain. Like me, Hannon was in pain. Only he chose to hide it from the two people who mattered most. And without so much as a heart-to-heart, he went his way alone, backed up into a corner where he made the ultimate sacrifice.

Tears leak down my face, and my lips quiver as I wish he'd reached out. Just once would have been enough to talk him out of it. Every day, I love and hate him for not giving me that chance to change his mind. To be there for him the way he was always there for me.

"Honor, no man loved Hannon more than I did. For five years, we were happy. He was in the closet, unable to share in our love publicly, but I didn't care because he was mine, and that's all I ever wanted and needed. Until he took that choice away from me. I would have taken what your parents were going to dish out. I'd have done anything to make him happy, change the past, make him believe we could suffer it all, as long as we had one another." Tears form in Sean's eyes, and the man near him places a hand on his shoulder.

I close my eyes tightly, not wanting to see another man giving him comfort.

"Hannon made his choice all on his own. We had no idea what his plans were, and for the past two years we've suffered, and for the rest of our lives, we're both going to suffer for it. But I'm not going to stop living."

I lock my arms around Sean and hold him as if it's goodbye. He returns the hug, keeping me close. He turns his head and whispers into my ear. "You are the only other person in the entire world who loved him and feels the loss as deeply as I do. As his twin sister, you have to know that better than anyone."

And I do. Oh, how I do. The day I buried my brother was the day I buried half of my soul.

For long minutes, I hold on to Sean, knowing this has to be the last time. "Me being here is hurting you."

His grip tightens. It's an answer without words.

"I won't come again."

"Don't say that, Honor. I couldn't live knowing I lost you too." His chin falls against my neck, where he places a kiss. "I love you, but you remind me of Hannon, and I need to let him go. Let him be free. You do too."

I shake my head. "I can't."

"You can, and you will. Eventually, thoughts of Hannon will make you happy, not sad. That's where I'm at. I love talking about him, thinking about him, sharing stories. And it helps. Promise me you'll do the same. Start the process for healing."

Healing. What's that?

Instead of lying, I give a noncommittal nod. "I'm sorry I was mean."

"Honor, baby girl, you're family. Always will be. I want you in my life. I just want you to be healthy. Hell, *I* want to be healthy."

On that we can agree. At least as it pertains to Sean. As

my brother's life partner, he became my family too. He is one of the only people I have left I can trust. He cares about *me*, not my money or what kind of status I can give him.

"Will you meet my friend? It would mean a lot to me to have your acceptance. I can't move on until I know you're going to be okay with it."

Dread fills my heart, but for Sean, one of the best guys in the whole entire world, I can push aside my selfish need for him to never move on from my brother and be a true friend. I nod and step back, wiping at my wet eyes.

Sean takes a full breath, staring at me before nodding succinctly. He maneuvers us around and gestures to the tall man, whose eyes are also watery behind his glasses.

"Honor Carmichael, meet my boyfriend, Chad Schilling. Chad, this is my best friend, Honor, Hannon's twin sister."

Chad smiles, revealing a beautiful set of white, even teeth. He presses his glasses farther up the bridge of his nose in an endearing way before extending his hand for me to shake. I take it, and he clasps it between both of his. "Lovely meeting you, darling. Sean has told me endless stories about you and Hannon, and I just want to say, I love Sean, and I'm so sorry for the loss you both endured. I look forward to spending time with you in the future and getting to know you."

I choke back the tears that want to spill out when I hear he's in love with Sean. It's a hard pill to swallow because I'd always believed that Sean and Hannon would go the distance, growing old together, the three of us being a family. Now I'm the outsider in this trio, regardless of the bittersweet sadness in Sean's eyes right now.

No matter what, this introduction changes everything. I can no longer escape to what used to be Hannon and Sean's house, looking for Sean to talk me through the overwhelming grief that sometimes engulfs my entire being.

"I'm sorry I stopped by unannounced. I won't do that anymore. And it's very nice to meet you, Chad." I focus my attention on Sean. "I love you, Sean. I want you to be happy, and you're right. Hannon would want you to be happy too."

Sean rushes forward and embraces me. "I love you. Promise me you'll get help. See someone to work through this? Promise me."

Knowing there is no way he's going to let me leave this house until I've promised, I concede. "Okay. I will."

He pulls out his wallet and removes a card. "Call this woman. Her name is Monet Hart. She's incredible, and I think you'll like her a lot."

I glance down at the white business card and nod.

★ ★ ★

"Honor, you seem a little lost today. Why?"

I stare out the window and watch the clouds roll by and then shrug.

Dr. Hart's voice is gentle when she replies. "You know, I can't help you if you don't talk to me. We've gone through this for two months now. It's time you were more forthcoming."

I inhale slowly and turn my head toward the woman sitting in a chair across the room. She's incredibly beautiful and a dead ringer for Lucy Liu, the actress. Long, cascading black hair, almond-shaped, coal-black eyes, and a long, athletic figure. She's wearing a white blouse with a cowl neck, a beige pencil skirt, and a pair of matching Louis Vuittons that make her legs look a mile long. She looks expensive because she is.

Not only is her hourly rate off the charts, the woman is a genius with getting me to spill my guts without me even realizing I'm doing it. She's incredibly good at her job.

When I committed to Sean that I'd attend therapy, I figured why not? I had nothing to lose. My life is filled with doing what my mother forces me to do. Mostly, I attend countless charity functions so she can groom me to take on the lead role of Mrs. Carmichael, the best charitable planner there ever was. None of which I'm interested in participating in. All the events and charity work... All a smokescreen, created to make her look like a saint, when she's anything but a good person. The only benefit is I'll happily give any amount of money needed to a good cause. I have zero attachment to the money I have because I didn't earn a single cent of it.

I'm a trust-fund baby. Money is something that will never disappear in my world. I'm already worth a few billion dollars, and I didn't do a thing to get it besides being born. My parents, grandparents on both sides, and their grandparents before them were all trust-fund babies. The money keeps coming. I barely know what we own anymore.

I have an Ivy League education and a degree in business I haven't used and have no interest in using. I'm walking through life with absolutely nothing to show for it. No goals, desires, talents, or skills to speak of. Basically...I'm nothing.

Knowing that Dr. Hart isn't going to let me mull over my response for much longer, I admit what's hurting me today. "It's Hannon's birthday."

Unexpectedly, the doctor laughs. Loudly. The sound coming from her lips mimics ringing bells. Lovely, just like the woman doing it, though I find her laughter hurtful because she knows anything involving my dead brother guts me. Honestly, it doesn't hurt as much as it pisses me off.

I narrow my eyes and strut over to stand near her chair. I place my hands on my hips, the ire her laughter brings burning against my flushed skin.

"Why are you laughing!" I demand on a growl.

My response only makes her laugh harder, so much that she fans her face with the yellow legal pad she keeps on her lap. "Sit down, Honor. My goodness you're funny."

I stomp over to the couch across from her, sit down softly as my ingrained manners require, and cross my arms over my chest. "Why?"

Dr. Hart blows out a breath of air and tucks an arm around her belly protectively. I noticed she's been gaining weight since I started coming, but I didn't think much of it. Now that I see her cup a section gingerly, it hits me. She's pregnant.

"You're pregnant!" I blurt out.

She grins. "Yes, just entering my fourth month. Did you think I was just getting a little fluffy?"

I lift my shoulders defiantly once more. "Not my business. What is my business is why you think me telling you what's got me down today is so funny? Frankly, Dr. Hart, it hurts my feelings."

"Honor, I'm sorry you took my laughter the wrong way, but do you even realize what you said?"

I shake my head.

"You're sad because it's Hannon's birthday."

"Yes, I know that. It's what I told you," I grumble.

"Did it not occur to you that, as twins, it's *your* birthday too?" She blinks a few times and curves her lips into a soft smile. "Happy birthday, Honor."

Her words smack me across the face without warning.

Stupidly, I didn't realize that it was *my* birthday, so focused on the fact that Hannon would have been twenty-six today, but he's not here, so there was nothing to celebrate. We always shared our birthdays. The two of us would plan an entire day of fun just for us. No parents. Not that they ever remembered. Even Sean, when he came along, would allow us our day and celebrate the night with Hannon privately.

Tears prickle at the back of my eyes. I glance at the clock, noticing the short hand about to reach the five and the little hand the twelve. It's just about the end of the workday. And that saddens me more as I give her more honesty. "You're the first person today to tell me happy birthday."

Dr. Hart leans forward and places her hand on mine where it rests over my knee. "And how does that make you feel?"

"Alone."

CHAPTER TWO

Flying Lotus Pose (Sanskrit: Padmasana)

This is an aerial lotus pose. Typically, beginners start with the hammock cushioning the buttocks, back, and legs as though you are sitting in the hammock longways. Place your legs into the hammock with the soles of your feet touching. An intermediate student can take the position farther by easing the silks behind the shoulders and biceps. The silks are then wrapped around the outsides of the feet so that you have a delicate push/pull of the upper and lower body to create balance.

NICHOLAS

"Ma! I'm here. What smells so damn good?" I holler while setting down my gym bag and keys and kicking off my sneakers. "Watch your tongue, boy!" my mother yells back.

I make my way through my childhood home, along the hallways filled to the brim with family pictures of my five sisters and me, my mother and father, and our extended Italian clan. I come from a big family. Not only did my parents have six children, but they each came from six themselves. That makes for some roaring family get-togethers. It's a good thing my parents built their home long ago when the market outside of Berkeley in the Bay was still affordable. The house may not be huge—my sisters had to bunk up all their lives—but it has an enormous backyard that backs up against a small river. One we've taken advantage of more times than I can count with gatherings, birthdays, and celebrations.

Like tonight. Family dinner nights are Sundays—no exceptions unless one of us is out of town. My mother would have my hide if I blew her off. And if I said I was sick, either she'd be banging down my door, checking in on me, bringing homemade chicken noodle soup, or one of my sisters would. My family is close. Very close. It's just our way. Sometimes it can be a pain in the ass, but most of the time, it's the best feeling in the world. I've never felt alone or out of touch because there is always someone at the ready to hold my hand and lift me up, support me and my goals and dreams. And I do the same for them. Family is everything to the Salernos.

I get to the kitchen and find my tiny mother slaving over several pots simmering on the stove. Homemade marinara steams up the room with a mouthwatering scent that equals happiness and home. Nothing better. Getting close, I wrap my arm around my mother from behind and kiss her temple.

She lifts the free hand not holding the ever-present wooden spoon and embraces my arm. "My Nicky."

"How you doin', Ma?"

My mother pats my forearm. "I'd be better if my boy would speak like a gentleman."

I grin, knowing my mother hates profanity of any kind. Even a simple "damn" grates on her nerves. Squeezing her tight, I kiss her temple again. "Sorry, Mama. Won't happen again," I lie, playing the game we always play.

She chuckles. "Liar. Be a good boy and get your mother a glass of vino."

"You got it." I give her one last squeeze and head to the small cellar off the kitchen where we keep the endless supply of our family's wine. My father's side comes from a long line of vintners, which allowed us to afford this house and enabled my mother to stay home and raise her family. Be a wife and a mother. Her claim to fame, as she puts it.

Not worrying about the varietal or vintage, I just pull a bottle off the shelf. In my opinion, they are all amazing because they were made by my dad and uncles. Food or drink made with love is the best there is.

Taking the stairs two at a time, I reach the landing back in the kitchen and find my sister Dawn. Her long dark hair is pulled back off her face in a ponytail, highlighting her high cheekbones and rosy cheeks. I grab her from behind, lift her up, and spin her around while she squeals in delight.

After I've made a full spin, I drop her down, where she turns around and hugs me tightly. "Hey, bro. How's it hanging?"

"Heavy and to the right," I joke, and she crinkles up her nose and punches my chest.

"Gross!"

It's our standard greeting, one that never gets old. Dawn and I have always been close, being a year apart, but I'm pretty tight with all my sisters. Behind me, Dawn's husband, Lorenzo, or "Lo" for short, claps me on the back.

"Nick, bro. How's business?" He lifts his hands into two fists and weaves from side to side as I playfully duck and punch his hands.

"Gym's good. Can't complain. Of course, we need new equipment, a new ring, an overhaul of everything really, but it pays the bills. That and the classes I teach at Lotus House."

"That aerial shit you do is crazy, man."

I grin. "What? You not man enough to give it a try?"

He shakes his head. "Hell, no. Dangling from silk over a hardwood floor. I'd like to keep my balls and bones in perfect working order, thank you very much!"

I grip his shoulder lovingly. When my sister married Lo, my mother got down on her knees and thanked the good Lord above for the miracle. He's the perfect son-in-law. Tall, dark, handsome, a family man, loves my sister to insanity, and most importantly...he's *Italian*. Lo comes from a good family and has recently taken an interest in winemaking. My father, Sal, couldn't be happier. Neither could I, since his interest in the business, along with my second sister, Angela, takes the pressure off Sal's only son not wanting to participate.

It's an endless argument, me not going into the family business, but one I've been winning lately. After I opened Sal's Boxing Gym & Fitness Center, my father eased off the winemaking lectures. I'm sure the day I named the gym after my dad—well, technically, after both of us, since I'm Nicholas Salvatore Salerno Jr.—he understood why I needed to do it. It was me going after my own dreams, being my own man. Do I love wine? Absolutely. You're not Italian if you don't love wine. I think they slip it into our genetic makeup when we're in the womb. Do I love what the Salernos have built? Hell, yes. I'm damn proud of my family. We aren't rich, but we're damn sure not poor. We're all living the lives we want to live, and that's all anyone can ask for. Me included.

My dad enters from the back deck, holding a plate of steaming grilled sausages. Ma may have made the marinara and pasta, but my father appreciates a nice grilled sausage instead of putting it in with the sauce. "Nicky! How you doin'?" he asks with that Italian flair.

"Good, Pops. Can't complain." I grab a few wineglasses as the rest of the brood makes their way into the kitchen.

Angela shows up with her boyfriend in tow. Ma has not shown him the love yet, mostly because he's quiet and Latino. It's not that she's racist; she just really loves being Italian and wants her children to have a horde of Italian babies. Still, Javier is wearing her down. He's been living with Angela for a solid year, and I expect a ring on her finger any day now. Once he makes that intention known, Ma will switch over to doting future mother-in-law in a second flat. All Ma wants is for her children to marry good, preferably *Italian*, men and have lots of babies. If he marries Angela, she'll accept him with open arms. Until then, no one is good enough for her children.

Cara, my third baby sister, breaches the kitchen with a new beau and, shockingly, a little girl who couldn't be more than three or four years old. *Oh, damn.* Shit is about to get *real*. One thing my mother loves more than being Italian is children.

I walk over to my sister and pull her into my arms. The man next to her braces visibly, locking his jaw tight and narrowing his eyes. Seems protective and/or jealous. I can relate to the first; the second will earn him time in my ring, meeting my glove-covered fists.

"Hey, care bear, you look good. Who's this you have

holding your hand?"

She gives me a wobbly grin, her brown eyes shining bright as she looks down. "This is Kaylee and my boyfriend, Scott." Scott is not an Italian name. And neither is the blond-haired, green-eyed guy putting an arm around my sister. This ought to be fun.

I offer my hand, and when Scott shakes it, I squeeze it hard enough for him to know I'll mess him up if he so much as hurts one hair on Cara's head. "I'm Cara's brother, Nicholas. Boxer." I tip my chin up and flex my muscles in what I consider my signature boy-scaring move. "You should come down to the gym sometime. Would be good to get to know you a little better, wouldn't you agree?" I squeeze harder and grin.

He pulls his hand away and shakes it while wincing. "Uh, I'm not thinking that would be good for my health."

I grin wickedly. At least he's smart.

Cara shoves my shoulder. "Nicky, be nice."

My mother turns around from the stove when she hears Cara's admonishment. Her blue eyes smile when she sees Cara and then turn hard as she takes in Malibu Ken, aka Scott. I hold back a snicker. One thing my mother despises is a Richie Rich, and this boy reeks of money from the tips of his Ferragamos up to his dress slacks and Ralph Lauren polo shirt.

Ma believes if you didn't till the ground yourself and work for every dollar you've ever received, you're likely not a good human. I guess my mother is a bit judgmental. Until, of course, she sees the curly haired blonde girl tucked behind her daddy's leg.

She leans down instantly, her rounded form balancing perfectly as she crouches. "And who is this angel baby?"

Scott tugs his daughter's hand, bringing her out from

behind him. "Introduce yourself, sweetie," Scott tells his daughter. I glance up at my sister, and she's biting her lip, not doing a very good job at holding back her obvious love of the child.

"I Kaylee," she mutters and walks over to my mother, swinging her skirt.

Another thing about Ma: all children love her. No matter how many twenty-something men my sisters have brought home, men who cower in fear of her and her legendary wooden spoon, children don't have that same fear.

"Aren't you the prettiest girl I ever did see? Do you like spaghetti?" Ma asks Kaylee.

"It's her favorite dinner," Scott blurts.

I grin. Good one. Point for Scott.

My mother's gaze flashes to Scott approvingly before going back to Kaylee. "Would you like to help me cook, angel?"

The little girl's eyes light up. "Ohh! Fun!" She giggles, and my mother scoops her right up, puts her on a rounded hip as if she did this every day, and hands the little one her own wooden spoon. Well, that was easy.

I turn toward my sister, who's got her hands clasped in front of her heart and a giant smile.

"Dodged a bullet on that one, care bear." I tap her nose like I always have with my sisters.

"You're telling me." She lets out a long breath, and Scott puts his arm around her, reminding me that a new man is all up in my sister's space. A man with a child.

"You and me." I point to Scott's chest and then my own. "We'll be having words. Soon. Feel me?"

Scott swallows but firms his spine and holds my sister closer. Point two for Scott. Afraid but willing to put himself out there. Of course, there's no way I'm giving him that inch of satisfaction when he needs to have the fear of her big brother put into him.

"Not a problem, uh, Nick." He forms his words, trying to sound confident but failing.

"Nicholas," I correct him firmly. He hasn't earned the right to use my informal name.

"Nicholas." He clears his throat. "You'll be seeing a lot of me from now on."

"Reeealyyyyy?" I draw out the word. "Then you'll need to have some wine. Meet the family. We do dinners—"

Scott jumps in. "Every Sunday. Got it. Feel honored I've finally been invited."

I frown at the word "finally."

"Care bear, how long you been hiding Malibu Ken?"

Cara squints. "Not nice, Nicky. And not *that* long." She looks away, diverting her gaze. That's her tell. A poker player she is not. That slip of the eye means she's lying through her teeth.

"Carrie, tell the truth," Scott admonishes.

Carrie? Special nicknames. *Fuck.* This is serious.

"Uh, maybe we kind of sort of already live together." She twirls her hair and shuffles her feet.

I'm certain my eyes about pop out of my head at this news. Cara's been hiding a man. "You are in so much trouble. This is going to be fun to watch." I grin, knowing my mother and father are going to lose their shit when they find out.

Cara grabs my biceps, holding me in place. "Don't tell them. I want them to fall in love with them both the way I have first..." she rushes to say.

"Love? Fuck, Cara. You love this guy and his kid, moved

in with him, and have been hiding this from your family? How long?" I whisper-growl closer to her face, my big brother hat firmly in place.

Scott pulls my sister back protectively. Another point for Scott, but this surprise is going to douse any hope they had of easing the family into him.

Right then, Gracie and Faith enter the kitchen, arms locked. Being the babies, the two of them have always been close, both hitting their twenties and still living at home.

Gracie's gray-blue eyes, similar to my own only with blue versus my green tone, lock on to mine. Grace and I look the most alike with our near-black hair and super-light eyes we got from our mother. She has a mixture of the blue-green-gray combo. The rest of the family have the dark, cappuccino-colored hair and brown eyes. She's also the baby, and I'm the eldest, so we have that oldest and youngest sibling connection.

"Girls." I let Cara off the hook for now and open my arms. Both rush into me. The scent of their strawberry shampoo hits my nose, reminding me of home. I breathe them in, my heart feeling at peace, being around my entire family. "How's my girls?"

"Great!" Faith laughs, hugs me once more, and jets off to talk to the rest of our sisters.

"Good, Nicky," Gracie answers, keeping an arm around my waist. "I got the job at Lotus House teaching Vinyasa Flow while I finish up my internship with Chef Jean Luc."

I grin. "See, I knew Crystal and Jewel would hook you up. You're a Salerno, and I taught you everything you know."

"Didn't hurt that I already had my registered yoga credential prior to that." She laughs, but I ignore it and nuzzle her close.

"How long are you going to be the right hand for the amazing, the talented...Chef Jean Luc!" I joke, rubbing her hair and making the top pouf up.

She pats it down and pushes the loose sides around her ears. Her cheeks pink up at the mention of the chef like they always have. I think she has a crush on the man, which is not good. Not only is he French, he's also ten years her senior. Mama would have a fit.

"He's perfect." She sighs dreamily.

I roll my eyes, lock my arm around her shoulder, and whisper in her ear. "You gonna tell your mother that?"

She cringes. "No way. He speaks French as fluently as she speaks Italian, and never the two shall meet."

"Uh-huh. And when he realizes you're sweet on him? What then?"

Her body goes stiff, and she turns to me. "He wouldn't. Jean Luc doesn't even know I exist."

My sister is sweet, innocent, and so gorgeous I had to beat up so many smarmy suitors in high school, my fingers were constantly bloodied. These girls have put my father and me through our paces with the boys sniffing around. Now that they're twenty and up, there's not much I can do but threaten their boyfriends or suitors into being respectful. I also do what I can to bring them to the gym so I can put them in the ring with a pair of gloves. Beat the fear of God into them. I know for sure, there's no way on God's green earth a hot-blooded male wouldn't see the beauty in our Grace. She's stunning.

"Well, if Mr. French doesn't notice you and your beauty, it's his loss. Besides, he's too old for you."

"Age is only a number." She pouts.

I tip my head back and laugh. "Tell that to your mother,

and see how well that goes over."

"No need. And what about you? You haven't brought a girl around in ages." She nudges my arm with her elbow.

I lift the glass of wine I poured and finally take a long sip, holding it in my mouth like my father taught me, allowing the wine's true essence to permeate my taste buds. I shrug. "None worth bringing home to all of you."

"What's that I hear? My boy finally find a sweet, young, *Italian* woman who can cook to bring home?" Ma butts in, setting the little girl down. She scrambles to her dad with a spoon slathered in red sauce running down the wooden surface.

"No, Ma, no woman." I groan and scowl at my sister for calling me out.

My mother bats my shoulder with her potholder. "Why not? You're a handsome man. You stop playing the field, and a good Italian girl is going to knock you off your feet!"

I chuckle and shake my head. "Ma..." I go over to her and wrap my arm around her shoulder. Her head barely reaches my sternum. "No woman could be as good as you. But I promise, when I find her, you'll be the first to meet her, yeah?"

She smacks my belly this time. "You better not be kidding around. I'm not getting any younger. I want bambinos running around this house again. I need laughter while I'm cooking or I'm unhappy. When are you going to give me some grandbabies to spoil?"

I sigh and let my head fall. "Ma, we have this conversation all the time. When I find the right woman."

"If you don't keep your Italian sausage in your pants and your eyes open, you never will."

That has all my sisters and me laughing hard. Even

scaredy cat Scott chuckles. Javier doesn't say a word, quietly sitting in the corner—the same one he has for a year. Watching it all go down. From what I understand, he has a big family, so ours couldn't be too far away from his.

"I'm going to die an old woman with no grandbabies. I just know it. Salvatore...you bury me, and my headstone will say... died alone with no grandbabies." She lifts her head and hands to the sky, feigning agony.

"No, you won't, Mom. I can promise you that." Dawn smiles huge as her husband, Lorenzo, loops an arm around her.

The way Dawn and Lo are grinning means they are about to drop a big surprise on us. One I suspected was coming. My mother wipes her hands on the towel over her shoulder, flicks off the burners, and stands in front of Dawn and Lo. My father grabs Ma's hand and holds it to his heart. "Dawn baby, you have something to tell your mama and papa?" His voice shakes as tears hit Dawn's cheeks.

My sister nods excitedly. "We're pregnant!" she says, and the entire room explodes in squeals of joy.

"Jesus, Mary, and Joseph! My baby is having a baby! Thank you, Lord!" Ma cups Dawn's cheeks and kisses her on the mouth. "I love you. I love you so much. You're going to be a mama!" Dawn cries and my mother cries with her. "I'm going to be a grandmother!" She kisses my sister again.

My father tugs Lorenzo to his side and puts out his other hand. Lorenzo holds on to it. "Made us really happy, son." He claps Lo on the back, his voice lower than normal.

I watch it all go down, happy that my parents and my sister are getting everything they've ever wanted. A pang of sadness pierces my heart that I wasn't the first one to announce a grandbaby. Being the firstborn—and the only son—there's some pressure to carry on the Salerno name, but I'm thrilled for Dawn and Lorenzo. It also gets the heat off me for a while. Added bonus.

When my sisters are done gaggling over one another like a bunch of hyenas, I nudge my way in front of my baby sis. I cup her cheek and swipe away a tear with my thumb. "You happy?" I ask, needing to see her eyes when she responds.

Her chocolatey gaze lifts to mine. "This is what I always wanted. A family. My own family." Her voice conveys nothing but awe.

"And you're getting it. So, I'll ask again. You happy, sunshine?"

"More than I ever thought possible," she whispers back, and I lean my forehead against hers.

"Proud of you. Going after what you want. Finding a good man in Lo. Making a home. And now you're building a family." I lay my hand over her stomach. "My baby sister is having a baby. Blessed. We are so blessed."

She nods against me and wraps her arms around my neck, and I hold her close.

"Can't wait to spoil him or her rotten."

Dawn laughs into my neck. "And I'll let you."

Yeah, she will.

Lorenzo taps my shoulder. "Can I have my wife back, bro?"

I flinch off his hand. "Back off. Getting some love. Get your own."

"She is my own; you back off," he jokes in return.

Pulling away, I smile as Lorenzo pulls my baby sister into his arms. Can't blame the man for loving my sister. She's the best, and now they're growing their family.

"You good?" Lorenzo leans into Dawn's face, capturing all of her attention. That's how it's always been with them since day one.

That's the kind of love I want. The kind where everyone in the room disappears when my woman is near.

"The best. I love you," she tells my brother-in-law.

He says it back and kisses her. The entire room breaks out cheers.

"We've got a baby on the way!" Ma announces proudly. "Go get the old vine reserve, Sal. We're celebrating tonight!"

I gulp my wine and take stock of my family. I was not kidding before. Blessed is what I am. Got a great set of parents, though nosey and intrusive. My five sisters are all happy and healthy. I've got my boxing gym and Lotus House. The only thing I don't have is a woman to share it with.

A heaviness breaches my chest. Regardless of what my ma thinks, I have kept my eye out for a good, honest woman to share my life with. Dated plenty of them. There's just always been something missing. Either I've got too much going with work and the yoga studio to keep them happy, or they want more than I'm willing to give. And forget about the ones who want a man with money.

The Bay Area is chock full of trophy wives. Bitches up on their high horses who think as long as a man has a large bankroll, he's marriage material. I need a woman who doesn't care how much money I bring in. Which isn't much right now. The gym is only in its first few years, and I bought it off the last owner who let it get run down, so the equipment is not new. I just started getting a regular membership growing, which is why I work regularly at Lotus House. The only reason I can live in the pricey area is because of the apartment on top of the gym. The place came with it. Pretty much the only real thing of monetary value I own is the gym and my 1969 Chevy Camaro Z28 302 in stunning Daytona yellow with black racing stripes. I love that car almost as much as I love my dick. And that's saying something.

Outside of working my ass off and that car, I don't have much to offer a woman. However, I'm building up the membership, getting regular fighters in for the league, including my Lotus House buddies, pro baller Trent Fox and his trainer Clayton Hart, as well as my buddy Dash Alexander and my old colleague Atlas Powers. Over the past few years, I've become pretty tight with the crew and have kept an eye on their women, whom I respect and care for like my very own sisters. Though, lately I've been hanging back now that all of them are paired up. No one likes to be odd man out or a fifth wheel. Still, I need to get back out there and play the field a little. I haven't seen any action with the ladies in a long while, although that's not for lack of interest.

Hell, every day it seems like I've got a new clinger in one of my yoga classes. The women come out in droves, but I don't tend to dip my stick where I eat. Meaning no Bettys from the studio. Then again, there haven't been any worth breaking that rule for. I come across beautiful women every day in my classes, but I've never felt that spark, that sizzle that makes me look twice at someone.

My pops always said I'd know it when it happens. When he met my mother back in high school, he was playing football, and she was a cheerleader for the opposing team. He said it was like he'd been hit upside the head by a linebacker the second his eyes landed on Josephine Ricci. After the game, he hunted her down and asked her out every day until she said yes. According to him, a woman may not know it's right, but it's up to us men to show them the errors of their ways.

I want that. I want to look into a woman's eyes and see my future, though at twenty-nine years old, I am starting to lose hope.

CHAPTER THREE

THROAT CHAKRA

The fifth of the seven chakras is all about willpower, making good choices, and the right to speak and be heard. A healthy throat chakra will empower an individual to always speak and tell the truth in all things. It is through this chakra that we manifest what we want in life. If it is blocked, the person is lost, lacking drive and motivation.

HONOR

Hannon,

Doctor Hart says I need to find ways to deal with my grief and anger toward you. She suggested I journal it all down. I tried. It didn't work. So, I'm trying something else. If I write to you, it's like you're still here. Makes me feel like maybe, just maybe, the words will make it to you.

Come back to me.

Over the past two years, I haven't been me. I don't even know what me looks like anymore. I've got a degree I don't use and money I don't know what to do with. I still sleep in the same bed I have my entire life. Maybe I should get my own place? But then I would really be alone. Utterly alone. At least with Mom and Dad and the staff, someone is always here.

I'm scared to be by myself. Scared of change. Scared of who I am without you.

What should I do?

How can I live without you?

All my love,

Honor

As I close the journal, I stare out the window. His voice comes to me.

Bunny...I'm always going to be with you. Just be still...find your peace.

Again, his last words haunt my thoughts.

"What does that mean?" I blink back the tears and wipe them away while staring out the window.

The grounds of our estate are lush and green. Perfectly trimmed bushes surround multiple flower gardens, though we're not allowed to pick the flowers. They're just for show.

Everything in my life is for show. Mother would go on a rampage if I picked a few to have in my room. She'd tell me to order them from the local florist and have them delivered, not pick them off the bushes and make them unbalanced.

A knock at my door is promptly followed by the devil's entrance.

"Honor, you're not dressed? The fundraiser is in one hour." My mother's voice needles my eardrums like nails on a chalkboard. "We need to show up in advance, give our support of the charity as their highest donor. We're receiving an award this afternoon for our continued commitment." She tuts.

I sigh, stand, and walk to my closet, where one of my mother's staff has left a dress. I didn't pick it out or try it on; though, I'm sure it will fit perfectly. It has long sleeves as my mother wouldn't want anyone to see the henna I've added to my body. Not that she cares what's under the designs.

In the past, my mother saw the scars, before I got too clever at hiding them. She didn't do anything then, and she hasn't since they started reappearing after Hannon's death. Judi Gannon-Carmichael would rather push the skeletons *into* the closet and provide me with long sleeves than bring light to a situation that's obviously harmful. The point is she doesn't care. Never has, never will.

I pull my tank over my head and push off my yoga pants before stepping into the silk garment. The dress is black with a high neck and long sleeves. The bottom flares out from the nipped-in waist in an A-line that ends just above my knees. There is a pair of black Louis Vuittons sitting near my closet, so I slip my feet into them.

My mother offers a small smile, as if she likes the way I look, but doesn't offer a compliment. I can't remember the last time she complimented me on anything. Not even when I graduated college with a perfect GPA. Likely because, as with all things, perfection for a Carmichael is expected.

Mother bustles to my vanity, where she pulls out an ostentatious, black diamond necklace they purchased for me as a gift for my twenty-fifth birthday. It's huge and hideous. Looks exactly like something my mother would wear.

"Not that one," I say, finding my tongue against the wicked witch's stare.

"Then which would you like? You must wear something with that neckline. It's too simple as it is."

"The strand of pearls." The one my brother gave me when I graduated college just before he took his life. It's the last thing he gave me and the one item I will cherish for the rest of my days.

Mother rolls her eyes, which, coming from her, is shameful. Showing emotion goes against the training of a tried and true blue blood. Rolling one's eyes would be frowned upon in her familial lines.

"Always with the pearls." She walks over to me and loops them around my neck.

I double them and allow them to hang prettily. There is one pink pearl hidden in the midst of the long strand. My brother said that was added on purpose. He wanted something unique to show me nothing in life is perfect and to remind me that being different is the same as being as pretty and lovely as a single pink pearl.

With my brother's pearls around my neck, I feel a bit more at ease. "What is this charity?"

"As if you care," Mother scoffs.

I frown, realizing that I don't usually care. I go to these

events because I'm told to, forced there by my family and our obligations. It's high time I actually participate. As Dr. Hart says, be present in the day-to-day. Find things that give me joy in each day, and it will be easier to feel as though I'm taking charge.

"I would like to know." I clear my voice and stand taller.

Mother grabs a ring she deems appropriate for my outfit, along with a handbag, and brings them both over to me. I hold out my first finger, where she slides on a large, black, oval-shaped ring made of real onyx. It's my favorite ring, and for a brief moment, I wonder if she chose it because she knows I favor it.

Mother ushers me to the chair near my mirror. I sit properly and cross my legs as she grabs the hairbrush and pulls my hair into a complicated series of twists. She then plucks one bobby pin after another from the gilded box I have and pushes them into my hair. Each pin scrapes painfully along my scalp, but I don't so much as grimace. Mother would hate that. If she takes the time to do my hair, I must sit still and accept what she considers a form of affection. It feels more like torture, but I'd never admit to it. Not since the day she spanked me black and blue with the metal handle of the brush when I was ten. Never again did I cross her when she had a mind for something.

While she finishes my hair, I silently put on my concealer to hide the dark circles under my eyes, sweep on a little eyeshadow, blush, and mascara until my mother tips her chin in approval. I gloss my lips with a pink sheen and glance at my appearance.

In the mirror is the same sullen girl I saw the other night, only this one is prettier, wearing a mask to hide the sadness for another day while her parents give money to charity.

"You'll appreciate this event, Honor. It's for the Suicide Awareness Foundation of California. Our last donation of five million dollars funded a new suicide hotline to be opened in the Bay Area. I thought you might like that."

My mouth is dry when I try to speak, emotion clouding the words I want to say. "That's...really wonderful, Mother. I love it. Hannon would love it." Tears fill my eyes, and I sniff them back.

"Oh, pish posh. Don't mess up your makeup. You're finally starting to look alive. Besides, don't think too much of it. We have to be mindful of the scandal your brother left us with. Our PR specialist said this was the best way to do that."

PR specialist.

Scandal.

A renewed sense of loss collides with my stomach like being punched. "You're donating to charity as a PR spin on Hannon's death?" I gasp and swallow down the bile lurching up my throat.

Mother, oblivious to the torment I'm experiencing inside, carries on with her plan as if she's done and said nothing wrong.

"What kind of monster does this?" I gasp.

She turns on her perfect Jimmy Choos and narrows her gaze before storming to my side. She swings her hand back and then forward. She slaps me. Hard.

A blast of heat blazes across my cheek. I hold the tender side of my face as her ire burns against my palm.

"Don't you ever talk to me like that again. I raised you better. Now, freshen up. We're leaving in fifteen minutes. I want you nothing but smiles as we give the society pages a photo opportunity that will leave all that your brother brought down on us behind us for good. You don't know this, but your father is planning to run for office."

"What!?" I blurt once again, not being the lady she expects me to be. I stand up quickly, making sure I'm not in striking range. It's been a while since my mother put her hands on me but not so long that I've forgotten how to run.

My mother flattens her hand over her hair and then down her skirt, making sure everything is in place. "Your father's going to announce in the coming weeks that he's running for governor of California. Get that hack of a liberal Democrat out of office and back on his farm in the Valley. Let a real politician take care of the state from now on."

Oh no. Poor California. Maybe I should move. Once the idea forms, a seed is planted. I only hope I have the power to go through with it.

"Now, grab your shawl and bag. It's time to give some money to some suicidal losers." She straightens her shoulders and marches out of my room.

Suicidal losers.

Hannon.

I close my eyes and send him love and all the good and kindness I have left in me. "I love you, Hannon," I whisper.

"I'll always love you, Honor." I imagine his voice in my head as I grab my things and follow my family to an event where they will be honored for being generous, when in reality they are just politicking and using their dead son to do it.

I make it as far as the meal before I'm rushing to the ladies' room, where I vomit up the rubbery chicken and the two glasses of champagne I was able to force down during my parents' award acceptance.

★ ★ ★

"Hello, Dr. Hart." I enter and sit down in my usual spot across from her leather chair.

"You can call me Monet, you know. I've told you that every time you've come over the last two months."

"Okay. Thank you, Monet."

My doctor smiles, and I can't help but think how genuinely beautiful she is. Makes me wonder how a rich woman can be so happy. In my experience, people with money are all unhappy. I glance over at her desk. On the corner is a picture of a handsome, blond-haired, blue-eyed hunk holding a little Asian girl with her mother's coloring on his shoulders. Ah, that's why. Sexy husband would do it.

"Is that your husband and daughter?"

Dr. Hart's gaze goes to the picture on her desk. "Yes."

"They look happy." I grab a lock of my hair and pick at the split ends.

"We are. Are you happy, Honor?" She asks the loaded question, and I finally decide that if I'm not going to tell her everything, there's no reason to come.

"No. I haven't been happy in a long time. More than that, I don't know if there was a time when I was truly happy. When Hannon was alive, I found moments of joy, but only if we were alone. Now I have nothing."

"Okay, let's start there. What do you like to do?"

I shrug. "I don't do anything. All of my time is spent hiding in my room, going to Mother's charity functions when she tells me to, or reading."

"You like to read?" She picks up on the one thing I actually consider my own.

"Yes."

"Why?"

"Because I'd rather live inside of a book than live in real life."

Dr. Hart's nose crinkles, and she tilts her head. "May I ask you a very serious question? One that may be hard to answer, but I need an answer and hope I've earned an honest reply. You know I can't help you unless you're honest with me."

My palms start to sweat, and I clench my teeth. *She knows.* I don't know how she knows, but she does. I can see it in her black eyes. The depth to which she sees inside me is startling. I fidget in my seat and think about what her question could be and how I want to answer it. Again, I have to remind myself I'm here for a reason. She's not going to lock me up in some insane asylum against my will. She may have the power to do so, but for some reason, I trust her. Trust her to guard my secrets.

"Ask me." I swallow and wait.

Monet taps her pen against her legal pad and stares at me. Her eyes seem calculating, deducing the truth she's seeking to confirm.

"Have you ever tried to harm yourself?"

My gut reaction is to lie.

No one is going to help you unless you help yourself. Hannon's words from the first time he caught me cutting rush back to the surface, giving me strength. My head is a two-ton weight when I give an affirmative nod.

"How?"

With that simple request, there is no judgment, no accusation, just a simple question that deserves an honest answer. But can I tell her? The only person who knew was Hannon, and when he found out, I stopped. For a while. I didn't need to hurt myself all the time. Sometimes but not *all* the time.

Tell her, Honor.

Hannon's voice slams into my consciousness as if he's right here, urging me, holding my hand while I war with the decision to bare all. Admitting my sins is one thing. Showing them is another.

"Honor, I'm not here to judge you. I'm your doctor. I'm here to help you deal with Hannon's death and the sadness I see in your eyes every time you enter that door." She points at the entrance to her office. "I'm here for you. Only you. You have the power to share as much or as little as you want. Though, I'm asking you to share with me. To trust in me. I'm not going to hurt you more than you already have been. I can promise you that."

"Oh, I know you won't." The snide comment slips from my lips. "No one can hurt me as much as I hurt myself."

Right then, something in me just cracks. The ooze of pity and my own self-loathing spill out as I unbutton my cardigan and pull it off my arms. Then I rest my hands palms up on top of my knees so she can see the henna covering my sins. Tremors wrack my frame as I sit there and wait for her to see through the intricate swirls, down to the disgusting evidence hidden beneath.

Dr. Hart stands up, places her legal pad on her chair, and sits next to me on the couch. She grips my hand. "May I?"

I nod, not capable of saying anything as she lifts my arm and pulls it into her lap. She runs the tips of her fingers over the art until she feels the raised areas of skin. She traces a finger from left to right along each line. About twelve or so on this arm, fewer on my right. Sometimes I just open an old one so I don't have to hide another one.

"Why the henna?" Her voice is gentle, like a soft breeze on a sunny day. There is no judgment or harsh accusation. Nothing but solidarity, genuine concern, and something else I can't decipher.

I wipe away the tears that have fallen unchecked down my cheeks. All I do is cry anymore. When am I going to stop crying?

Be still...find your peace.

My brother's words weave through this revelation, and I close my eyes to find my voice. "The ink covers the sins."

Dr. Hart pets my arm as she would a child. Lovingly. "I understand hiding scars. I've been in a situation in my past that I wasn't proud of and felt the need to cover them. But some of these are new, Honor. Recent." Her dark, questioning gaze meets mine.

"Yeah," I admit. "Sometimes it gets too hard."

"What does? What gets too hard?" She holds my hand, and I grip hers tightly, not wanting to let go. It's as if she's the only lifeline I have right now.

I close my eyes and let go. Let her in. "The nothing."

"Explain what the nothing is so I can understand better."

"I'm nothing. My life is nothing. Without Hannon, I have nothing."

My first expectation was that Dr. Hart was going to contradict what I said. Alas, she's smarter than the average doctor. I've been to therapy before. Well-intentioned counselors who supposedly had my best interests at heart. My mother hired a horde of them to come to the house and speak to me regularly because I never fit in. Never followed normal society rules or the mandated conduct of a blue blood

Carmichael. I've been found lacking my entire life. The only person who ever made me feel special, made me feel *anything*, was my twin brother. And he destroyed that when he ended his life.

"Honor...why do you cut yourself?" Dr. Hart asks the million-dollar question. The one I wouldn't even admit to Hannon when he asked all those years ago.

Why do I do what I do?

This is my last-ditch effort at finding the peace Hannon spoke of. I look up from my lap and trace one of the bigger cuts across my inner forearm. "I need the pain."

Dr. Hart pushes a lock of hair behind her ear. "Why do you need the pain?"

Once more, I close my eyes and think back to the other day when I pierced my flesh with the newest cut. My mother had told me she was going to introduce me to a man, a business associate of my father's. One with a long history of good standing with the one percenters and a family name that preceded him. She said if I was worth anything to our family, I'd go out with him and let him woo me, eventually marry me, and combine our families. For the greater good of the Carmichaels, she'd said. After she forced me to agree to an assigned date in the future when the man was available, I'd gone straight to my room and dug deep into my skin. The rush of endorphins skittered along every nerve ending, carrying me into a state of tragic bliss.

"I need the pain." I mumble again, tracing the scar of that particular transgression.

"Why, Honor? Tell me. *Trust me*. You've gotten this far. I can help you, but only if I understand." Her words are a plea for me to give in. To believe. And I do believe that this woman, with her kind eyes, small pregnant belly, happy family, and designer clothes, in her swank downtown San Francisco office, genuinely wants to help me. I just don't understand it. No one ever wants to help me. Truly see things from my eyes.

"Why do you help people?" I ask her in return.

She leans back, places her arm on the back of the couch, and toys with a loose thread on her couch. "Because I know what it feels like to be alone. To have very little hope for a good life. I want to change that for people who are lost."

"For people like me?"

"Are you lost?" She uses her MD Kung Fu to boomerang that back on me.

"I think so."

"Why?" Again with the whys.

I shake my head hopelessly. "Because I don't know who I am. I have no clue what I want from life. I have nothing tethering me to this world."

Dr. Hart places her hand on top of mine and squeezes. "Do you want me to help you figure those things out?"

I'm stunned silent by her response. In my twenty-six years on this earth, no one, not even Hannon, has ever offered to help in such a way. It may be her training, her innate knack for dealing with broken people, or perhaps she sees something in me that she wants to fix. Whatever it is, the question spurs the same reaction as throwing a raft into shark-infested waters where I'm barely treading water. It gives me hope.

I lick my dry lips and focus on her face. A small smattering of freckles are splayed across her nose like a fine dusting of glitter. Her eyes are black as night but sparkling with the light of the stars. Her cheeks are high on her wide face, and her black hair tumbles around her golden-colored skin, making

AUDREY CARLAN

her a striking beauty. I can see how she's captured the eye of the blond superhunk.

"Do you want me to help you find out what you like and who you are, Honor?" she asks again.

"Yes." The word slips from my lips as if it's a prayer, and maybe it is. Where I'm at now, Dr. Hart may surely be my savior.

"To do that, I'm going to need you to be honest with me and tell me why you need the pain."

Without thinking, I blurt out my secret, allowing it to coat this session with its hideous stain. "It's the only way I can feel anything. At least when I'm hurting myself, I can *feel* something."

Dr. Hart pats my hand and squeezes it. "Okay. Now *that* I can work with."

CHAPTER FOUR

Downward Facing Dog
(Sanskrit: Adho Mukha Svanasana)

Start with legs straight and feet to the floor. Center the silk along the hips. Place both hands to the floor and hinge forward. When you feel comfortable, try to balance your weight and lift your feet a foot or two off the floor. Follow the instructions from a certified aerial yoga instructor and only go as far as you are capable.

NICHOLAS

Lotus House is alive with energy when I enter, my baby sis, Gracie, hot on my heels. She's wearing a bright smile and the new yoga outfit I bought her to celebrate her first day.

"Hey, Nick!" Dara waves from the front desk where she's helping a blonde customer sign up for classes. Luna, the owner's daughter, is behind her, filing something away in the cabinets.

"Ladies, bringing in my baby girl Gracie to teach her first Vin Flow class. You pumped, Grace?" I ask, knocking her shoulder playfully.

"So pumped!" She squeals and does a little touchdown jig.

Dara smiles huge. "Girl, you know you got this. I've taken your substitute classes. Just remember, when you lose your place, breathe through it and go into tree, warrior, or child's pose, depending on if you have them standing or on the mat."

Grace leans into the counter, bumping the petite blonde next to her. "Oh, sorry."

The blonde looks up, but all I can see is her profile. And what a damn fine profile it is. Classic, proud chin, a small, straight nose, and bee-sting-reddened lips. Her skin is so pale I can see the light-blue veins running just under the surface of her long, swan-like neck. Her blonde hair is a golden platinum that's bundled up on top of her head, making her look more like a ballerina than a yoga student.

She mumbles something and then tips her head down, just as I round over to Gracie's side so I can see her more clearly. Long, black, fanned eyelashes meet the top of her cheeks as she focuses on the initial new client paperwork in front of her.

Smoothly, or not so smoothly, I encircle Gracie's bicep and ease her around behind my body and to the other side so I can be next to the willowy creature who's yet to look up. Something about her is calling to me, forcing my hand as I touch her shoulder.

Her gaze flashes up, eyes a foamy, see-through gray, like a cloudy white quartz. With a mere glance, I'm lost. Gone.

Sorrow. Sadness. Pain. All those emotions flash behind

her gaze before she licks her lips and looks back down. She drops the pen, her hand shaking when she picks it back up.

A barrage of images parades across my vision like a mini-movie. Looking at her eyes over dinner. Watching those eyes twinkle as I make her laugh. Staring into them, lust-filled with desire, as I press into her naked body. Sharing past sadness and helping her find peace while holding her in my arms. Her tears falling as she bares her soul.

For the first time ever, I've looked into a woman's eyes and seen my future, and it centers entirely around me being the man for her.

I stand there like a numbskull while she finishes her paperwork and enters the main entrance with her new lotus-shaped entry card.

"Fuck, did that just happen?" I whisper under my breath and press the palm of my hand against my forehead.

Dara places her hand over my fisted one on the counter. My entire body is strung tighter than a drum, and I have no idea why. "Loosen up. She's taking your class in fifteen minutes." She chuckles.

I turn my head and focus on my friend. She's an exotic, stunning woman. Her brown skin and ocean-blue eyes are startlingly unusual and nothing like those of the delicate blonde I just blanked out on after a single gaze.

"Hmmm, I'm guessing that rule you've got about not dating clients..." she hedges.

"Out the fucking window," I growl, staring at the closed doors, wishing I could see through them to catch one more glimpse of her.

Dara laughs hard, followed by Luna, who snickers and wiggles around doing a little dance. Christ, these women are as bad as my own sisters. Speaking of which, I do a three-sixty and realize that Gracie is gone. "Where's my sister?"

"Cool your jets, man. She's setting up for her first class," Dara offers.

I hunch over and shake my head, trying to clear it of the woman I've just seen. "I meant to take her to her class." My big brotherly duty is feeling neglected as I stand stupidly, my feet stuck to the floor.

"Oh, how sweet. Like she's in kindergarten and she needs her big brother to walk her in and protect her from the big bad yogis." Luna jabs me in the chest with a pointy finger.

"Ouch!" I rub at the spot and realize what she's said is the truth. Gracie doesn't need her big brother hovering. "Just wanted to make her feel supported. I'm proud of her."

Luna nods. "Then show her that by proving you know she can handle herself. No helicopter brothering at Lotus House. Got it?" Her words are firm and brook no argument. I swear, if I had a dime for every time I was bossed around by a beautiful woman, I'd be rich as hell.

I toss my towel over my shoulder. "Fine. You sure the blonde is taking my class?"

Dara nods. "Yep. I offered Gracie's Vin Flow, but she chose Introduction to Aerial Yoga."

"Did you warn her that it's a lot of hanging from silks above a mat?"

Dara grins. "Yep. She said something like, 'it sounds dangerous' and promptly signed right up."

"Huh. Maybe a risk-taker. I like it." Definitely wouldn't have assumed that from her hunched shoulders and lack of eye contact. If anything, she seems extremely shy and introverted. Guess I'll have to figure her out.

"What's her name?" I ask Dara.

"Dara..." Luna warns in that motherly manner from over her shoulder.

"Seriously, Luna. I know you're vying for boss lady when the moms retire, but I'm just asking what the woman's first name is, not the code to the safe."

Luna purses her lips as her red bangs fall over her forehead. "Maybe she wants her name to be private?" She blinks innocently.

"Give me her freakin' name, or payback is a..."

She waves her hands as if she's ringing off bad juju. "Okay, okay. Her name is Honor, but that's all I'm giving you. The rest you can find out the old-fashioned way. By asking her!" She looks down her nose at me.

"Honor." I let the name ping around in my head as I wave over my shoulder and head into the hallway leading to my assigned room. Good grief, if that isn't the perfect freakin' name for an angel like her.

★ ★ ★

The room is quiet as I walk through the lines of dangling, royal blue silks. Several regulars are in attendance, even though they should be taking the intermediate class. I make a mental note to have a chat with a couple of them, give a gentle nudge toward moving up in their study. I find a lot of yoga patrons are comfortable in a certain class or need that small vote of confidence from their teacher in order to take the next steps. It's my job to see their progress and push them out of their comfort zone and into new possibilities.

I stop at my personal yoga hammock at the front of the

class. It's a brilliant green so the students can easily see my movements through the silks as they attempt to mimic with their own placements. My yoga mat is leaning against the mirrored wall, and I grab for it and spread it out with a quick *snap*. Across the room, one set of shoulders jumps at the noise. I zero right in on her as she scrambles to place a mat on the floor under the silks above her. Though, she's way too far away for my liking, having picked the last spot farthest from the teacher. That will never do.

First, I choose a chill jazz playlist. Louis Armstrong's "What a Wonderful World" is the first song on the track. I feel the need for a bit of soul for this session. The easy music pipes through the room; the telltale violin strings wisp through the air, Lou's throaty timbre setting the mood. I kick off my shoes and socks before removing my tank. I don't always teach class bare-chested. Often, I wear a simple, black, ribbed tank and my standard black, knee-length, fitted shorts. Today, though, I aim to get one doe-eyed blonde's attention if it's the last thing I do. A smart man uses all that's in his arsenal, and when I pulled off my tank, a couple of girls in the corner giggled. Mission accomplished. Now it's time to see if I can catch Honor's eyes the same way she's caught mine.

I walk over to where she is fighting with the silks, trying to figure out how to mimic what the woman in front of her is doing. Only she's never taken a class, so she doesn't realize that the woman in front of her comes every week at the same time. She's one of the members I need to nudge into the next level. While that client practices inversion, Honor places her hands on her hips and scowls at the offending straps.

"What did these silks ever do to you?" I chuckle and hold out my hand. "I'm Nicholas Salerno, the teacher of this class, but you can call me Nick."

She glances at my hand as if it frightens her. Interesting. I nudge my hand closer. "Nick. And you are?"

Honor straightens her shoulders and clasps my hand. The second our hands touch, a sizzle of electricity zaps through the center of our palms. She tries to let go, and I squeeze harder. Her doe eyes snap to mine searchingly. "Honor Carmichael. I'm just Honor."

She tugs her hand away from mine and clasps it with her other one, ringing them together. I'd bet every last dollar in my bank account she felt the current of electricity between us at the single handshake. I can only imagine what it would be like body-to-body. A shiver rushes down my spine at the thought of embracing her. Holding her close. Kissing her.

I close my eyes and take a slow breath in and let it out. When I open them again, her eyes are on my bare chest. She swallows and lets her mouth fall open in a tiny gasp, one I feel all the way to my toes. The hair on my arms stands at attention as I pick up the mat between us and drag it up to the front where I can see her at all times.

"Um, excuse me, Mr. Salerno. Uh, Nick." Her voice is small and hesitant. "I don't want to be in the front. I don't know what I'm doing." She follows behind me, tugging the sleeves of her hoodie over her hands. She's wearing a pair of skin-tight, black yoga pants I cannot wait to see the back of, but from the front, her curves are slight but still kicking. Not gonna lie; I love a petite little thing I can toss over my shoulder like a caveman and take straight to bed. Honor isn't petite in height, but there's not a lot of meat on her. Nothing my mama couldn't fix with a few Sundays of her home-cooked meals.

Shit, Nick. Slow your roll. You're ready to bring her home to

Mama, and you haven't even kissed the woman or taken her on a date yet. I let out a breath of air and cross my arms over my chest. Her gaze follows the movement. She licks her lips and bites down on the bottom one. Christ, what I wouldn't give to bite her. *Anywhere*. Hell, *everywhere*.

"Honor, that's exactly why you need to be up front. You're brand new. I need to be able to instruct you directly and know that you are safe. Aerial yoga is a bit riskier with inversions and body placement. I wouldn't want you to get hurt. You being front and center means I can keep my eyes on you." *All over you*, I want to add but don't. Wouldn't want to scare her off.

Her head falls forward. "That's what I'm afraid of," she grumbles under her breath.

"Excuse me?" I grin, having heard every word.

"Uh, I'm okay. Thanks, Nick. I'll follow along."

"Is this your first time taking yoga?" I ask her, wanting to hear the breathy, sultry timbre of her voice.

Except she doesn't speak. She nods and looks down.

"Eyes up here, bunny," I say low enough so she's the only person who hears me.

Her gaze shoots up, but instead of uncertainty, I again see pain.

She gasps and frowns. "What did you call me?"

"Bunny?" I jerk my head back, just realizing what I'd said.

"Yes. Why did you call me that?" Her voice is needle thin and just as sharp.

I place both of my hands on my hips and bend a little closer—not too close. I might scare her away, because I'm getting the vibe this woman is seriously skittish. Still, I lean in enough that we have a bit more privacy.

"Honor, you're acting like a scared little rabbit. Bunny

fits."

"Please don't call me that." She speaks softly, looking at her feet.

"Fair enough. Now, I have to start class, but I'd like to talk to you more, after. Clear the air." Without waiting for her answer, because she very well may have reached her quota of words for one conversation, I step back and up to my mat.

"Everyone have a seat, sit bones flat to the mat in lotus position, only this time, let's place the feet together so that we're creating a circle of energy within our own body. Hands to heart center, close your eyes and set your intention for today's practice. What do you want to get out of it? What do you want to let go of? Breathe into that intention and exhale...letting go of everything that does not serve you."

I take the class through a series of floor routines to loosen up their spines and joints before having them stand and bring the largest silk loop behind them.

"Now, once you've got the silk settled along your back comfortably, I want you to bring your feet out in front of you and ease back against the silks. When you find your sweet spot, bring your feet out another foot forward and point the toes. Arch back and lift your arms over your head, allowing the silk to help you go farther into your stretch. Breathe in and exhale."

Once the class is in position, I pop out of my hammock and go straight to Honor. She's finally removed her oversized hoodie and is situating the silk along her lower spine. The pale-pink, ribbed tank she's wearing stretches across her breasts enticingly. Being a tried and true boob man, I am pleasantly surprised to see she's got a hefty rack, much larger than I expected on her slight frame. My hands are large, and her breasts will spill over them quite nicely. I groan, reminding myself to tamp down the images of squeezing her tits before my dick catches up with my brain and gives the class a show they won't soon forget. As it is, I've had to readjust my semi several times in reaction to her beauty.

"Here, let me help you." I wrap one hand around the silk above her body and grind my teeth as her fresh flowers scent reaches my nose. I bite down, unable to curb the urge to suck in one more long breath. The smell of wildflowers and tall grass surrounds me, taking me to a place of calm and peace unlike any other. Being near her soothes the chaos within my being. Every woman I've met before her does the opposite. Strokes the discord, when that's the last thing I need. As an Aries alpha male, my element being fire, I don't need a woman to goad me. Quite the opposite.

Honor's fingers turn white as they tighten around the silks above her. I grab the smooth, stretchy fabric behind her and expand it so it covers half of her lower back and a bit of her fine, heart-shaped ass. Once she's situated more securely, I place my hands on her shoulders and help her ease back until her body is diagonal to the floor.

"Now, point your toes and lean into it."

"But I'm scared." Her voice is but a whisper, and it moves me into action.

Protect.

Care.

Shelter.

These are the urges that slam over me. I can tell in the tremble of her fingertips, the firmness of her jaw, and the determination in her eyes, she hasn't had a man be those things for her in a long time. That's about to change.

"I've got you. Trust me."

She nods, firms her jaw, and lifts her arms up over her head. I steady my hands at her elbows and help her move back into the position. My eye catches the swirls running down her inner arms. As she stretches, I focus on the skin. After a couple seconds of inspection, I realize it's henna weaving in intricate swirls, petals, and dots up both of her arms. The designs are beautiful and seem to start at the crease of her elbow and feather out in both directions. Definitely not what I'd expect to see on the timid woman, but seeing them makes me eager to unfold the layers beneath her shy veneer and find out more.

I shift toward her ear. "Really good, Honor. You're doing perfectly. Hold the position for about thirty seconds. I'm going to move the rest of the class into the next position. You can catch up easy enough. Okay?"

"'K," she says but focuses on the ceiling. Her body laid out and stretched has me envisioning her form splayed out across my king-size bed. Once more, I clench my teeth and block out the stunning beauty.

Clearing my throat, I step toward my silks and get settled against them. "Now class, grip the silks above your head and sway from side to side. Let them slide under your arms and reposition yourself into a wide-legged squat, otherwise known as Goddess pose, or *Utkata Konasana* in Sanskrit."

Bad idea. Such a bad idea.

Directly in front of me, my frightened, wide-eyed dove spreads her long, lean legs out. She maneuvers the silks perfectly under her arms, keeping a hold above her head before she squats down, leveling her pelvis with her thighs. *Jesus, Mary, and Joseph.* I clench my jaw so hard I could break glass with my teeth. I can feel my nostrils flare at the magnificence in front of me. I have never, in all my years teaching yoga or otherwise, seen a woman so beautiful. The track lighting above shines down over her white hair, creating a halo. She's a true angel among us, and right then and there, I mentally promise myself and the universe that this woman will know her beauty, and in the end...it will be mine. All mine for the taking.

My voice is thick and raw when I address the class. "Now stretch out the left leg and lunge until you feel that sweet pull at the hamstring and groin, but don't go to the point where it hurts. It should hurt good, not be painful. We do not want anyone injuring themselves. I want you all to come back. Help me pay my bills." I crack the joke, and several of the students laugh.

Not my dove, though. She's focused a hundred percent on her position. Absolutely stunning. I could take a picture of her right now, and it could easily appear in a yoga journal with a caption highlighting aerial yoga. Men and women alike would flock to my class if they saw her light as I see it now.

Honor opens her eyes, and her lips puff open. What I wouldn't give to be standing directly in front of her. She'd be in the perfect position for me to take her plush mouth. It would be so easy to fold my shorts down, my dick hot and heavy in my hand, and touch her lips with just the tip. They'd be velvet soft but not nearly enough. I'd tap the side of her cheek with my fingertips, requesting entrance...

I shake my head, shoving the debauched thoughts aside. This innocent woman in front of me makes me want to do tawdry, dirty things to her, clean her back up, and start all over again. Christ, I'm in trouble with this one.

"The other side." I stretch out my left leg and repeat the first pose. "After you've gotten your groove, ease from side to side several times, then go back to center and allow your body to hang, giving the spine and hamstrings a nice, long stretch. And don't forget your breathing. Inhale fully and exhale completely."

For a few minutes, the class follows along with me, moving from side to side, finishing with the last pose.

"Go into a closed-leg squat, as if you're about to sit in a chair, then swing forward and move into airplane pose, which is a variation of Warrior Three. It's a newer pose recently added to the assemblage of yoga asanas also known as *Dekasana*. Allow your body to be supported by the silks under your arms as you open the heart and throat chakra, lifting your chin to the sky."

Honor shifts into the position perfectly, but once again, I'm reminded of the fatal error of putting her directly in front of me. As she stretches her body forward and lifts her pale, pretty neck to the sky, her large breasts press up and out, taunting me with their lusciousness. The view zips along my conscious mind, grinding against the part of me that's all carnal, filthy male. My cock reacts and rises to the occasion, wanting to spear between those large globes as she licks the fat head of my dick.

Christ on a cross, I'm fucked.

Moving a bit faster than I normally would, mostly because I don't want to embarrass myself by letting a class full of yogis see me fighting off an erection, I issue the next command. "Slowly straighten your legs, maneuver the silks to the hinge at your hips, and bring your hands to the floor to allow your feet to ease off the ground. It will seem as though you are in a variation of downward facing dog but with your feet just a foot or two off the ground. Keep your face level with your arms."

Please, God, keep their faces level with their arms.

I let go of the silks and look at the other patrons, needing to separate myself from the goddess in front of me. For the first time, I notice a familiar, bulky form in the back corner. I walk over to my buddy's side.

"Hey, man. Didn't see you there."

Clayton Hart lifts his head and grins. "I'm sure you didn't since your eyes have been on nothing but the slender blonde with the killer rack in the front row."

My mouth tightens on instinct, hearing Clayton's appraisal of Honor. I narrow my gaze. "Shouldn't you be at home with your gorgeous, pregnant *wife* and daughter?"

Clayton chuckles and stands. I glance around the rest of the class and watch them ease into their final squat.

"Needed a good stretch. Took on an NFL client today. Worked him and myself hard on the weights. My muscles are killing me. Your class helps put me back together." He grins before lifting his chin toward the front of the class. "What's the deal with the blonde? You haven't stopped looking at her."

I run my hand through my slicked-back hair and rub the back of my neck. "Not sure yet. Doin' a number on me, though."

Clayton frowns. "You don't usually tend to be sweet on clientele. You thinkin' about breaking your own rules?" Clayton pushes back into another stretch I wouldn't give in the introductory class. His body is jam-packed with muscles, and he could easily be a poster boy for *Men's Fitness*, but he's taken my class many times before and knows the movements and how to be safe. He's also a fitness trainer who knows his own body and what it needs.

"Man, I don't know. All I know is she's a game changer. There's something about her. I don't know what."

My buddy grins and lifts his body up into the silks like

a professional gymnast, all flexing muscles and heavy lifting made easy. "Wish you luck with that, man. Go get her." He winks.

I nod and head back to the front. For the rest of the class, I put them all through their paces, giving them just enough instruction to get comfortable in the silks and stretch out what the average person needs...back, neck, legs, getting out the usual stiffness a person feels when working a sedentary job or standing on their feet all day.

"Okay, last pose of the day. We're going to go into cocoon. Stretch out your hammock, slide it under your butt and along your back. Then shimmy your body into the fabric. It will stretch along with your form. You can either put your feet to your chest or just curve up. Bring your arms inside the swing, allowing the silks to cover you completely. Find a comfortable position that suits you because you're going to stay here for a solid five to seven minutes for *Savasana*."

Each participant gets into their swing, and I give them a minute to position themselves. Usually, I'd cocoon myself as well, but today I need to offer guided meditation for them and for myself. Walking around, I avoid Honor, needing to gather a little mental space as well as physical distance. Being close to her is like being in a vortex. All I want to do is get closer, plaster my body along hers, and breathe in her essence.

"Inhale, letting in peace and serenity, exhaling any remnants of frustration or irritation from your day. Allow yourself to float in your cocoon. This position mimics being back in the womb, where everything was safe and sound. Go to your safe place. Breathe into it. Remember here that you are protected, you are perfect, and you are loved."

Honor's hammock jiggles wildly before her small feet pop

out, and she sits up gasping for breath.

Shit. Sometimes this happens; people feel claustrophobic.

I rush over to her and curl my hands around her cheeks, tipping her chin up with my thumbs. Her eyes are wild and untamed, searching for an exit. "Breathe, Dove, in with me." I inhale long and slow. Her fingers wrap around my neck, and I place my forehead to hers. "Out slowly." Her fingers dig into my shoulders as she shudders out her breath. "In again..." For long moments, we breathe together until her body calms and the shivers wracking her frame abate. "You better?" I whisper, close enough she should be able to feel my breath against her lips.

"Yeah, I don't know what happened. I just..."

"It's okay. You probably felt a bit claustrophobic. We can work on that in future classes. We'll start by keeping your head out of the cocoon, and work toward full coverage."

She nods and licks her lips, letting me go. When her hands fall away, I force myself to take a step back. I hate it. Instantly, everything inside me calls to protect her. Wrap her up in my arms and never let her go.

Instead of going with my instinct, I go back to the front of the class and call out the commands to bring everyone back from their relaxation. When I've turned off the music and turned around to talk to my dove, she's gone.

CHAPTER FIVE

THROAT
CHAKRA

Those motivated by the throat chakra tend to focus more attention on using their five senses. It's important that they are able to touch, hear, see, know, and speak their intentions effectively.

HONOR

"Go to your safe spot. Breathe into it. Remember that here you are protected, you are perfect, and you are loved."

Nick's words roll around and around in my head as I toss and turn in bed.

You are protected.

I haven't been protected a day in my life. Not from my mother's wrath or my father's endless—and unmet—expectations. To both of them, I'm just the pathetic daughter they were stuck with. Hannon had been their pride and joy, until they found out he was gay and living with his boyfriend, Sean. Then they destroyed his life by threatening to ruin Sean's.

You are perfect.

Far from it, Nick. I groan and turn over onto my side, looking out the window. The moon is high and shining into my room, casting gray streaks of light onto my bed. I sit up and shove off the covers. My skin reacts with gooseflesh at the sudden chill, but I don't mind the cold. At least I can feel it. Tonight, I can feel everything—the sadness and grief, which swallows me whole, threatening to drown me. It anchors my heart with concrete cinderblocks while I attempt and fail at wading through this thing called life.

With heavy footsteps, I go to my special spot. Just like Nick suggested. Mine isn't all that special and comforting, but the window seat in my childhood room still beckons. Countless nights I've spent sitting here, knees to my chest, staring out at the world, imagining all I could be. Useless dreams of a child. Where would I go to school? Who would I marry? What friends would I make outside of these walls? When would I leave this life behind?

Twenty-six years old, and I'm still sitting in my window seat, wishing for a life I don't deserve. One I don't even know how to fight to have. Because my mother is right. I'm nothing. I'm certainly not perfect as Nick suggested we all are in class tonight.

Nick.

The unusually tall Italian yogi had every nerve in my body flaring white hot. I've never had such a visceral reaction to a man. Sure, I've been hit on, dated a few boys in college—one I even gave my virginity to—but nothing serious. Once a man finds out what kind of family I have, the fact that no one is good enough for a Carmichael, they leave. Unless, of course, he's part of the mighty one percent or the good ole boys club, where my father sits at the top of the heap. If a man is not one of *them*, he might as well move on. And they all do. Every last one of them has.

It's been years since I've had a man in my life in any capacity. My last year in college, I put pedal to the metal and blew my studies out of the water. I was Valedictorian, with the highest GPA in the class, and still my parents didn't flinch. Nothing made them proud. Maybe, if I become the prima donna charitable guru and socialite party planner like my mother, they might even hug me.

Do I want to be touched by them? Not anymore. I've long since lost any desire to make my mother and father happy. Only, somehow by not caring what they thought, I stopped caring about me and my goals and dreams. Now I don't have any.

You are loved.

Remembering the last line Nick said before I lost my cool in class tonight makes me cringe. I can just barely see the ugly scowl on my face through the reflection in the window. It's as unpleasant as my thoughts right now.

Loved is what I was when Hannon was alive. There's no one to love me now. No one who cares if I exist at all. I could take my life, and all that would happen is my mother would hold another charity event in my honor. Squawk to all her friends how, as twins, we couldn't be without one another and that I'd never been the same since Hannon passed. That part is true. I'm not the same. Though, even when my brother was alive, I wasn't anything special.

What does it take to become special?

I dig for the journal and pencil I've hidden under the plush cushion of the window seat and open it to the next available page.

Dear Hannon,

I tried something new tonight. Aerial yoga. I can imagine you laughing now, but honestly it was the most alive I've felt in years. Something about dangling in the air and letting your body fly free put some things into perspective. I haven't been living, Hannon. And I'm still not sure I want to, but I know I should want to, and that counts. Right?

Dr. Hart told me to try something new and physical to get my blood pumping and endorphins flowing. She suggested it as a substitute for, you know...the thing. And today it worked. Though, I had a weird episode in the class, kind of like a mini panic attack. Nick was right there to bring me out of my freak out.

Nick. That's my teacher's name, and Hannon, he's beautiful. Everything I'm never going to be. And I don't know for sure, but I think maybe he likes me a little bit. I don't want him to like me. Again, that's not exactly true. It feels good to have his interest, but I don't know how to be normal. Once he gets to know me, if I ever go back to his class again, he's going to see how strange I am. All men do eventually. And if they don't disappear before they see the real me, they will as soon as they meet our parents.

I'm not sure if I'm going to go to his class again, even though I enjoyed it. It was the first time I can recall that the weight I've been carrying around for the last two years lifted off my heart, giving me room to breathe.

Is it wrong to feel happy when you're not here to share it?

Hannon, I'm so screwed up. I wish I could be someone else. I wish you were here to tell me what to do, but you're not. You left.

Come back to me.

I miss you.

All my love,

Honor

★ ★ ★

This yoga room is different from the one I was in last week. It's smaller, more cozy, with candles and a beautiful mural of a forest along one wall. Since Nick's class, I've held up in my room, reading, journaling, and thinking about the sex-on-legs yoga instructor. I even Googled him and found out that he not only teaches yoga a handful of times per week, he owns and operates Sal's Gym & Fitness Center. I saved all of the pictures of him from his bio on the Lotus House website and the enticing photos of him boxing and teaching on the other website. Hands down, the man is fit, healthy, and makes my heart pound a million beats a minute. Because of said pounding, I decided to skip going to his class until I could get a handle on my inner freak. That didn't mean I didn't want to do yoga, so here I sit on my mat, waiting to start a class called

Vinyasa Flow with a woman named Grace.

Yesterday, I spent a long time refreshing the henna I'd placed over my scars. I even added it to the marks on my outer right thigh in case anyone sees me shower or change in the ladies locker room. For me, it's always been better to be prepared than to have to answer any questions. Besides, I think the ink looks pretty, and I've gotten really good at it.

Feeling a tad more confident when I see tatted-up patrons strutting around in just shorts and bralettes, I remove my bulky hoodie. I've chosen a brilliant green tank this time that seemed cheerier than the drab black and taupe colors I wear around Mother. Maybe I'll go online and pick up a few more outfits if yoga is going to become a regular thing.

No. Go out and shop for clothing. Get out of the house, Honor. That's what Dr. Hart would suggest.

I nod to myself and sit quietly in lotus pose while the people around me get situated. A bright-blue mat lands a couple feet to my right, jarring me out of my peaceful contemplation about where I could find yoga clothes like the ones I see on the ladies here.

"Hey, Dove," a deep, low voice calls out, sending a tremor of recognition through my veins.

To my right, I find Nick pulling off his shirt. He raises it slowly, allowing each brick of his abdominal muscles to make an appearance one toned slab at a time. I lick my lips, wondering what it would taste like to run my tongue through the lines of each indentation. My sex feels heavy as I imagine running my fingers along his square pecs before licking and sucking each of his nipples. I've never done that to a man. I'm ill-experienced in the bedroom. The dozen times I've had sex, I allowed the man to basically get me naked and do his thing.

I've never even achieved an orgasm that wasn't self-induced, and I rarely indulge in that pastime. I'm too lost in my own head and unhappiness. This man, though, brings all kinds of tawdry, sexual ideas to the surface.

Nick tosses his T-shirt on the floor near his mat. He thumbs the waistline of his track pants, and I swallow. As if putting on a show, he inches the loose pants over his hips, past his muscled thighs, and down to the floor, leaving him in a skin-tight pair of yoga shorts. They look more like boxer briefs, but I know they're not. These are lined and have a cool red stripe down the side, but good God in heaven above, his quads are cut. I want to lean forward and touch each hill and valley, memorize what the hair on his legs feels like fluttering across my palms.

"Keep up the eye-fucking, Dove, and you'll get a much more interesting view from the front."

A wave of heat flushes my cheeks as I snap my head down.

"Aw, you're really lovely when you blush. I like it. I'll have to make sure to flirt with you more often."

I bite down on my lips and turn forward. His magnetic energy pulls me to look over at him when he sits on his mat, only a foot or so away, but I fight it. He's so close, though, enough to touch without problem. I take a couple of slow breaths, trying to calm the fluttering sensation in my stomach from his sheer proximity.

I feel a heaviness enter my personal space when Nick leans close enough to whisper in my ear. The hair at the back of my neck stands on end as his lips brush the shell. I gasp and hold my breath.

"Why haven't you come back to class? Are you afraid of me?"

Afraid. Of him. Not even close. I whip my head to the side so fast we're nose-to-nose. His eyes widen, and then he grins like he planned on poking me to get a reaction.

"You don't scare me."

"Then what is it?" he taunts.

I narrow my eyes and focus on his. They're a blue, no, a grayish tone with hints of dark navy around the edges. Probably the prettiest eyes I've had the pleasure of looking into. "Maybe your class was too hard."

He chuckles but inches closer, our mouths only a couple inches apart and our noses even closer. "You were a natural once you got past your anxiety."

A natural. I've never been a natural at anything. The compliment throws me off guard.

"Really?" I'm scrambling for any nugget of positive reinforcement.

He nods. "Yep. You just need more practice. Come on Friday, and then I'll take you out to dinner after."

My mouth goes completely dry as the reality of what he just suggested resonates. "Did you just ask me out to dinner?"

"Smart *and* beautiful. I like that in a woman." His eyes blaze with desire as he smirks.

That smirk sears into my heart, making it beat fast, this time carrying with it anticipation and a note of excitement.

"Hello, class, and welcome to Vinyasa Flow. I'm Gracie Salerno, and I'll be your teacher today." A young woman's voice breaks through the staredown Nick and I are having. I glance to the front podium and see a startlingly attractive young woman who can't be more than a few years my junior.

Salerno. That's Nick's last name. I take in her more petite form, long black hair tied in a braid down her back, and gray-blue eyes. She smiles widely and tells us she'd like us to start in child's pose. I have no idea what that is and glance around, trying to figure it out.

"Sit back on your heels and then spread your knees apart, leaving room for your chest and belly to lie in between them. Then place your forehead on the ground and your arms either stretched out in front of you or behind you at your sides. Whatever's most comfortable," Nick instructs.

I watch Nick as he repeats what he's told me and gets into position. I do the same and lift my face just enough to make sure my body looks like his. When I do, he's looking at me too. I smile, unable to help the natural response he brings out of me.

"That's all I wanted. I hadn't seen you smile. Fucking beautiful." He winks. "Now pay attention or my baby sister is going to be mad at me for hitting on her clients," he whispers before placing his forehead back on the mat.

Not wanting to make his sister mad either, I place my forehead on the mat.

"We're going to breathe here for ten long breaths. During that time, think about what you want to get from today's practice. Focus on giving this time to yourself. It's for you. It's about you. Breathe it all in," Grace urges. I can hear her feet padding around each client doing something, but I'm not sure what until I feel her over me.

"Good." She places her hand on my sacrum, firmly pushing my hips deeper into the stretch. Then she runs her hand up my spine, which has the sensation of her taking the negative energy right out of my body and flinging it away. "Breathe in deeply, and exhaaaaaalllleeee." She drags out the word while pressing up my spine toward my neck. With each motion, I am lighter, more focused. She rubs at my neck, and I swear to God,

I could fall asleep. It's the most relaxed I've been in a long time. Before I get too comfortable, she moves on to the next person.

"Now I'm going to have you press up into table and go into your cat and cow transitions, pairing them with your breathing."

Surprisingly, she doesn't do the pose in front of the class, but everyone seems to know what to do. Everyone but me. How's that possible?

As if I said the question out loud, Nick speaks up. "Most people who take Vinyasa Flow have already taken the beginners' classes or other restorative type classes. You, on the other hand, just seem to jump right in."

I frown and watch as his body shifts up into a position that looks like a scared black cat on Halloween. Then he drops his belly down and arcs his spine, lifting his head up.

"Follow my movements, and I'll instruct you while you learn. Okay?"

I do as he says and pair my movements to his. He makes it look really easy, as though he's a born teacher or leader. As I get into sync with him, I realize I'm actually doing the class, and it's not easy, but it's not so hard I wouldn't come back. My muscles are straining while I hold a crazy position they call one-legged dog. Apparently, you start in a downward facing dog, which is essentially a triangle shape with your body, and then you pop one leg up to the sky. You then balance on your hands and one foot.

"Flex those feet, really press into the heel to get maximum length. You want to feel that energy pumping through your body and out that limb," Grace calls out. "Now flip your dog!" she says excitedly, and I about lose it, fumbling and swaying precariously close to eating my yoga mat.

Before I smash into said mat, Nick has jumped up and is holding me aloft, helping me twist my body the appropriate way. He grasps my hips, making sure I don't reach the ground or hurt myself.

"When you flip, you use the foot in the air as your momentum to turn over. Then both feet are on the ground, and the opposite arm goes up toward the sky."

He positions me the way he wants, putting his hands all over my body. It's the most I've been touched by another human in as long as I can remember. Everywhere he touches becomes hot, like he's branding me as his.

Grace takes us through so many positions I lose count and focus, only capable of moving alongside Nick, parroting each pose to the best of my ability.

Eventually, she brings us back down to the mat to lie flat on our backs for *Savasana*. I crinkle my nose and look around at the other students all happily lying down and closing their eyes.

"Pssstttt. Nick," I whisper, not wanting to bother the other patrons.

He opens his eyes, and I lose myself in them. They are so pretty, like the infinity pools at one of my parents' five-star resorts.

"What is it, Dove?"

"I don't know what this is?"

He grins. "Deep relaxation. We did it in aerial, but you had a...moment and didn't get into enough of it. This time, you lie flat on your back and allow yourself to drift off. It's awesome. I promise. Trust me."

"I trust you, Nick," I say, not believing I just admitted giving someone else my trust. But as Dr. Hart says, I have to let people in. I have to give of myself if I want to get in return.

"Then lie back and enjoy the ride."

Taking a deep breath, I close my eyes and let Grace's sweet voice lull me into a state of mental bliss. When she brings us back out of it, the rest of the class quickly wraps up their stuff, rolls their mats, and skedaddles. It's like ants scurrying away from a glob of candy melting on the ground. They've gotten their fill, and they need to take their piece back to the colony.

Me, I'm sluggish, the class having put me through my paces, proving I need far more exercise than once a week—more like three or four days. Mentally, it relaxed me. Put me in a state of ease and, dare I say, serenity.

Nick comes up behind me and places a hand on my shoulder. "You blissed out?"

I offer a small smile. His easygoing personality is infectious and his need to touch disarming.

"Yeah. Really good class."

He jerks his head back. "Better than mine?"

This time I give him a full grin. "Different."

"I like different," he quips.

"Do you really?" I ask, needing to hear from his lips that he's not like other men, although I don't think he could ever be. Nick seems to have such a sense of confidence and self-worth. It oozes from every pore in his beautiful body.

Nick tugs up his track pants. "Yeah, I do. You're different, Dove. And I like it."

"You don't know anything about me."

"Your body language speaks for itself. Besides, that's why we're going out on Friday after class," he declares as if I've already acquiesced.

Zipping up my hoodie, I look down at my pale-pink

painted toenails. "As in a date among friends?"

He comes closer, invading my space with his large frame and magnetic warmth. "Do I look like the type of man who takes a beautiful woman out on a date as a friend?"

I lick my lips and focus on his face. His jaw is firm and curved with a dark goatee and mustache, both perfectly matching the hair on his head. His facial hair is trimmed close and looks more like the heavy growth after a weeklong absence from shaving. On a scale of one to ten, his sexiness is a hundred and five. For a second, I lose my head and imagine what it might feel like to have that hair rubbing against softer and more sensitive places, like my neck, between my breasts... my thighs.

Nick offers the most sultry grin I've seen on him yet. "Where did you just go while staring at me and ignoring my question?"

Ignoring his question. What was it? Oh yeah, about dating a friend.

"Um...I don't know what you do with your friends."

"Doesn't matter, because you are not my friend. You are the beautiful woman I'm taking on a date Friday night. A date between a man and a woman. A man who's interested in talking, touching, and kissing the woman standing in front of him."

Sweet heavens! His words slam into me like a punch of lust to the chest. "My, you're forward." I gasp and widen my eyes, realizing what I just blurted.

He grins. "Get used to it, babe. There's a lot more where that came from. I say what's on my mind. I don't believe in lies or bullshitting. I like you. You're fucking beautiful. I want to take you out. Break bread. Nothing more to say to that other than yes."

"Yes?" I question, but he doesn't take it that way.

"Great. See you Friday for aerial. We can freshen up here and get ready. Bring a jacket. You'll need it."

"Uh, okay, but I didn't mean to say..."

He pulls on his tank, covering his succulent body. Shame.

"You didn't mean to say what? Yes? Too bad. I can see you're into me, Dove. Not gonna let you fly away this time."

"But..."

"Speaking of, give me your phone."

I blink a few times, having no idea where he's going with this.

"Your phone, babe." He opens his palm and wiggles his fingers in an impatient gimmie gesture.

I fumble through my bag for my phone. He grabs it right away and inputs a series of numbers. I hear a phone go off and see his phone's display light up on the floor near his sweatshirt, with my cell phone numbers glaring in white against the blue background. Goodness he's quick.

"Now I've got your number, and you've got mine. Let's touch base before class, yeah?"

"Um..." I don't know what to say, so I just nod.

He laughs, wraps his hand around my nape, and pulls me flat against his chest. The scents of citrus and leather curl around his sweaty form. He smells so good, I want to breathe him in all day. All too soon his lips go to my forehead, where he lays a long press before pulling back.

"I'd kiss those sexy-as-sin lips, but I fear you'd fly away." Nick smirks and pulls back. "Later, babe. Friday." He motions with a wave of his fingers while heading toward the door.

I'm left behind with my bare toes digging into the rubber

of the yoga mat, wondering what the heck just happened.

"Soooooo, you're going on a date with my brother!" The woman behind me squeals like a little girl and claps her hands. She has a bounce in her step when she embraces me into a God's honest hug.

I allow the girl to hug me and ease my arm around her to pat her on the back. Last hug I had from a woman was my nanny before I left for college eight years ago.

Grace bumbles around the riser with endless energy. "Do you have time for a coffee at Sunflower?"

"What's Sunflower?" I ask, trying to keep up with this ball of enthusiasm.

She stops where she stands, holding her hoodie. "Seriously? You've never been to Sunflower? Well, I'm going to change that right now! This is great. I get to introduce you to Sunflower and the gang that will be there. You're dating my brother. This is awesome. Wait until Mom finds out! She will just die. And you're so pretty! Do you happen to be Italian? Even one percent counts with Ma." Grace explodes with her battery of questions.

"Oh my, what have I gotten myself into?" I sigh as Grace loops her arm through mine.

"We're going to be the best of friends. I can just feel it already!"

CHAPTER SIX

Tree Pose (Sanskrit: Vrksasana)

Tree pose is a beginning yoga pose in all classes including aerial yoga. It may seem a bit harder when you are several feet off the floor, but the positioning of the body is still the same. One foot is balancing flat against the silks. One knee is bent with the sole of the foot pressed into the opposite leg (not the knee). As you can see in the picture, one arm wraps around the silks and the other stays behind the silks, for additional balance. The hands rest at heart center keeping the energy flowing through the body.

HONOR

"I can't believe you've never been to Sunflower. It's right next to the yoga studio, and they have the best...the *best* lattes and treats. You're going to just *die* they're so good!" Grace smiles widely as she pulls open the door of the bakery.

The scents of fresh baked bread and cinnamon rolls billow in the air. My mouth waters, and I'm reminded I haven't eaten anything since the granola bar I had before class. "Smells divine."

Grace nods excitedly, her eyes bright and shining. "Hi, guys!" She gets into the long line while waving over to a table where two older women sit alongside a handsome man with dirty-blond hair as well as a lovely brunette wearing a pair of medical scrubs. The male is holding the brunette's hand on his thigh.

I wonder how nice it would be to have someone's affection like that. A man who wanted to hold my hand while having an outing with friends. I try not to stare and instead concentrate on the displays of sinful delights to choose from.

Grace nudges my shoulder and lowers her voice. "The redhead is Jewel Marigold, and the blonde with big blue eyes is Crystal Nightingale. The two of them are the yoga gurus of Lotus House and the co-owners. The blond hottie is Dash Alexander. He teaches tantric yoga and all the couples yoga classes, often with his wife, Dr. Amber Alexander. She's a resident at UCSF Medical Center. Word is they are going to try to get pregnant soon! Eeek!" She squeals into my ear at a lower decibel than her normal high volume but enough to have me veering away to protect my eardrum.

I shake my head. The level of excitement in this young woman is incredible. Her love of life in general is commendable. I'm not sure a person could be around Grace for long and not be filled with glee and jubilation. It surrounds her like a golden bubble of light.

"Are you excited about going on a date with my brother?"

She blinks sweetly, changing the subject so fast I get whiplash.

"I guess so."

A little scowl forms on her face, and it's basically the equivalent of smacking a puppy. Not a pretty sight, but again, it changes within a second as we make our way to the front of the line and are greeted by the same woman who signed me up as a member at Lotus House.

I blink a couple times and stare at her name card. Dara. Yes, that's the same name.

"Hi, Gracie. What's shakin' baby?" She nods my way. "Made a new friend, I see."

Grace puts her arm around my shoulders and tucks me close, as if we are long-lost sisters separated at birth. "Totally! She's Nick's new squeeze." She uses some jive talk I understand but would never utter myself.

"Really?" Dara's Caribbean-blue eyes widen nearly to the size of the stunning cupcakes sitting on the lower level of the display.

Hadn't seen those when I walked in. Maybe I want one of those instead of the cinnamon roll. *Hmmm.*

"Uh-huh. He's taking her out on a date on Friday."

Note to self: do not say anything to Grace you don't want repeated and printed in the *San Francisco Chronicle*.

"You're taming the wild man, eh?" Dara says to me.

I shrug, not really knowing how to respond, so I settle on redirection and obfuscation. "Not really. It's not a big deal. He just asked me out."

Dara puts a hand to her hip and cocks one side out, showing some serious cool-girl attitude. I don't know what to make of it. "Did you not know that Nick doesn't date clients at Lotus House?"

I pucker my lips and shrug again. It really isn't my business whom he dates.

"Did you take one of his classes?" she asks.

"Yes, I took his aerial yoga class last Friday." Shoot! That reminds me that this Friday, I technically have a blind date my mother set up. Now I also have one with Nick. How in the world did I go from having no dating life to having two in one day?

"Oh, so you're not just Grace's client. You're Nick's too? Mmm-hmm, I see what's happening here," Dara says with a pout and a chin bob like she's got it all figured out, while I have no clue what's happening between Nick and myself.

"Which would be what?" I inquire, genuinely wanting to know her take. If the laundry is out drying, might as well let it fly in the breeze.

"The Italian Stallion took one look at you and saw nothing but light. Same as I see. Only you're drenched in purple goodness, honey."

"Purple what?" I've gotten lost somewhere.

"Your aura, sweet girl. It's purple with a tinge of light brown. I don't like seeing the brown there."

"Ooookkkaaay. I'm sorry," I offer, not really knowing what else to say, but I make a mental note to go online and purchase a book on auras from Amazon.

Dara tips her head back and laughs. Grace does as well.

"You can't be sorry for your aura. It is what it is. Just means we've got some work to do. You're not very confident right now in the situation or in where you are in your life. It's okay. We all have times in our lives where we're in a state of flux. You'll find your way." Dara leans forward conspiratorially. "And if that happens to be in the bed of an Italian man, more power to ya, sista!"

Pinpricks spark all over my nerve endings with her suggestion. "All righty, then. I'll have the cinnamon roll and a very strong latte, as well as whatever she's having." I point to Grace and pull out a couple of twenties and drop them on the counter.

"Mmm-hmm. I get you, girl. You're nervous about the Stallion. I would be, too. He's a definite catch." She nods and finally carries on with her work.

Grace beams. "Thank you, bestie," she says, breaking up the tension and gesturing to the money on the counter.

"Least I can do. You taught a great class."

Dara gets our items, and I take the tray while Grace bounces over to the table with the foursome she knows. They each give her hugs, smiles, and all of their attention. What I wouldn't give to be able to feel free and safe in my own skin.

Grace pops back over and sits in the chair opposite me, her braid swinging along with her enthusiasm.

"You know, I admire you." I surprise myself when I admit my thoughts out loud. Then I mentally give myself a pat on the back because Dr. Hart would be proud of that. I may even tell her about it.

My new friend's eyebrows furrow. "Why? You're the one with the perfect hair, skin, eyes, and body. I mean, your boobs are sooooo awesome!"

I burst out with laughter. An absolute first for me, especially in a packed dining space.

"Not gonna lie." She lifts a finger and points to my left and then right breast. "My brother is going to love those. He's a boob man. You should totally wear a shirt that shows off the ta-tas on Friday! He'll lose his dago mind! Oh, I know! We should go shopping this week! Find you something awesome. What do you say? Say yes!" Now I see this is a familial trait with the Salernos: well-meaning but pushy.

Then again, I haven't gone shopping with a female since my college roommate. We didn't even like each other but had been stuck in the same space for four years and attempted to be friendly. Turns out our problem was me being too prissy and she too gothic. Needless to say, we didn't share the same tastes in clothes, let alone stores to shop at. With that—retail therapy—having been my one and only foray into female bonding, I figure it couldn't hurt to go with Grace. It's definitely getting out of the house and following the new list of things Dr. Hart suggested I do. Venturing out was a big one.

"Sure," I agree once more, breaking out of my hidey-hole.

On that note, Grace pokes her finger into her cinnamon roll, scoops up some frosting, and then plops her finger into her mouth. Absolutely abhorrent manners. There is never a reason one should place their finger into their mouth. Ever. So because she did it, I do it too. A little thrill of excitement at breaking good-girl societal rules ripples up my spine.

I let out an unladylike moan once the frosting touches my taste buds. "It's so good."

"Told you!" Grace shimmies in her chair, dancing to a beat only she can hear.

"Grace, where would one purchase good-quality yoga attire like what you're wearing?"

She lifts her head, and I swear the smile she gives is one of the cat having eaten a canary variety. "What's your budget?" Her honest question comes out around a mouth full of roll. Gross and yet still endearing. I'm beginning to think this woman could be covered in excrement, and the world would still find her adorable.

"Budget? I have no budget. Ever." I say it before I can filter out my mother's ingrained words, realizing too late how hoity toity and stuck up it sounds.

Grace pleases me again by not flinching or showing the slightest unease. "Sweet! Guess we're going to get the best and hit lululemon in Frisco!"

"And for helping me, I'll purchase you an outfit of your choice as well."

Her eyes get huge. "For real! No way. You are crazy, girl. One top costs like two hundred dollars!"

"Then we must get you a few of them!" I half joke and wink. If the girl takes me shopping, I'm giving something to her in return. "Wish not, want not, Gracie," I say, using the nickname I heard her brother use.

She takes another bite of her roll and dances in her chair once more. I follow along, eating my roll with a fork, sans the dancing, but I definitely do it smiling.

★ ★ ★

"And you'll never believe what I did!" I pace behind the couch in Dr. Hart's office.

She leans back and places a hand over her baby bump. Today she's wearing a silk T-shirt dress that perfectly accentuates her protruding belly. I wonder if one day that life is in the cards for me. Before this week, I wouldn't have even dared give it a thought. Now, I don't know.

"What did you do?" Monet smiles, her lips painted a pale, glossy pink that goes well with her outfit. She looks like the goddess of Mother Nature. Fertile, with long flowing curls, pink lips, and a caring smile.

I shake off the random thoughts and go back to my pacing. "I accepted a date," I offer proudly. "With a man."

She chuckles. "That's great. Where did you meet?"

"At the place where I'm taking yoga."

"And how is that going for you, the yoga?" She alters my train of thought, breaking my desire to talk about Nick. It's all about Nick lately. Every waking thought is about him or his sister.

I frown. "Fine. No, better than fine. Great. I'm working my body and muscles in ways I never dreamed, and I even made a friend." I straighten my spine and lift my head.

"A friend?"

"Yes! We're going shopping this week. And she's the sister of the man who asked me on a date. She also teaches at the yoga studio."

Dr. Hart leans forward placing her elbow on her knee. "I'm... I must say I'm really pleased with this progress. A new physical activity, a new friend, and a date. You've had quite the week, haven't you?"

I come around the couch and plop down. Dr. Hart smiles instead of calling me out on my lack of poise.

"I'm sorry. That was rude and inappropriate," I chastise myself.

She frowns. "No, it was a woman excited about her week, eager to tell me about it. Not rude. Not inappropriate. Now, continue. Let's start with the yoga. How do you feel it's helping you?"

I run my hand through my hair and think about how I lose myself, moving into each position. How everything around me just seems to slip away. There's no anger, no grief, no fear. Just my body being pushed in healthy ways. "I think mentally and physically it's helping me to balance some of the scrambled thoughts in my mind. It's making me let go of the negative feelings that I have when I walk into the class. I leave feeling more refreshed. Does that make sense?"

She nods. "Very much so. I find yoga gives me a place of peace. Somewhere I can let my mind wander and just focus on my body and the movements."

"Yes, exactly."

"Now, the friend."

"She's younger than me," I point out right away, though I'm not sure why. There's nothing wrong with having a younger friend. "And she teaches Vinyasa Flow. She's a very excitable and happy person. Nothing seems to bring her down."

"And what do you think makes you connect with her?"

That's the real question. "I don't know. It's more that she knows I'm going to go on a date with her brother, and for some reason, she clung on to me."

"Not some reason. Perhaps she sees a nice girl who's new to the yoga scene, and she wants to extend a friendly hand. Lots of people out in the world become friends and are often opposites of one another. Maybe she sees poise and class in you that she doesn't have and would like to learn. Maybe she just thinks you're new and cool. Or maybe she wants to impress her brother's date. Whatever the reason, it doesn't matter; she chose to be your friend. You have to choose to be hers in return."

"I gave her my phone number, and she's texted me a dozen times already." I twirl my onyx ring around my finger.

Dr. Hart chuckles. "Eager, that one."

"Yeah, I'll say." I smile, thinking about the variety of things she's texted. Some were links to tops at the yoga store. Others were yoga poses. One was a selfie of her and Nick. I secretly made that my background on my phone.

"But isn't it nice to receive those texts from someone who genuinely wants to talk to you or get your feedback?"

I nod. And she's right. It really does feel good to have a friend. Picking up my phone and seeing texts from Grace gives me a sense of importance. Usually the only texts I get are from Sean checking in with me. Now I've got Sean and Grace texting to me. And supposedly Nick is going to check in with me this week too, prior to our date. I'm very eager to see if that happens.

Which reminds me that I've got to figure out a way to break off the date with my mom's suitor, but honestly, I can hardly be bothered. I think I'm just going to ignore Mother and leave before the man is supposed to arrive. I've got yoga that night before I'm supposed to meet him anyway.

"Grace is going to take me shopping this week before my date with her brother. We're going to get yoga clothes for classes and something that shows off my boobs. Her words not mine."

Dr. Hart chuckles. "That sounds like fun. Are you looking forward to it?"

Am I? Yes and no. I glance off toward the window, thinking about the best way to answer her question.

"This isn't a ball in Washington DC where you'll be meeting the President of the United States," Dr. Hart states.

I shake my head. "No, that was a couple months ago. I don't care for the man. Too pompous for my liking, and his wife reminded me of an alien. So much Botox and lip fillers she didn't seem human anymore."

Dr. Hart blinks a few times and presses her lips together. "Okay, that analogy didn't have the desired effect. What I meant to say, Honor, is a shopping date shouldn't be scary. It's meant to be fun."

"But what if she figures out she doesn't like me or realizes how strange I am?"

Dr. Hart sits back in her chair and rests her fingertips against her lips. "Honor, you might be shy and a little introverted, but you are not strange or weird. I'd like you to get that out of your head. Find a way to abolish that nonsense, because I've spent the better part of three months getting to know you, and I like you very much. You're sweet. Kind. Intelligent. Reserved. And perhaps a bit socially awkward, but that doesn't make you a person people wouldn't want to spend time with."

"It doesn't?"

"No. It doesn't. And the sooner you realize it, the more fun you will start to have. I promise. Will you work on giving yourself a break? Try not to think too harshly of your personality. Go into this shopping day with your new friend with an open mind and, better yet, an open heart."

I nod, tears welling up behind my eyes. I clear my throat and breathe through the meaning behind her words. Still, I'm not sure she's right. I've spent many years being the odd duck. Just because one overly nice girl has latched on to me doesn't mean I'm no longer the weird, bizarre girl I'd always been in high school and college.

"I'll try." It's all I can promise her.

"Good. Tell me about the man you met."

Instantly a sense of anticipation and excitement rushes through me. "His name is Nick." On hearing his name, Monet frowns. Maybe she knows a Nick who does yoga. Nonplussed, I carry on. "He teaches yoga at the studio I go to. He's Italian and definitely the sexiest man I've ever met."

Dr. Hart's frown deepens, but she doesn't say anything.

"I took his class last week. Then I had some type of weird episode in his class..."

"Wait a minute. Episode. Explain this to me." Her eyes flash with concern as she picks up her legal pad of notes.

"We were doing this position where you're in a cocoon..."

"Aerial yoga? The Italian man named Nick teaches aerial yoga?" she asks, her voice tight and restrained. I wonder if she knows my Nick.

My Nick. He's not exactly mine. "Yes."

Dr. Hart purses her lips. "Continue."

"Well, I was hanging in this hammock, and he told the class to curl up inside of it and find a resting spot. Then he started talking about feeling safe and protected and loved. My heart started to pound; my skin got ultra-hot, and I couldn't breathe."

"Sounds like you had a bit of a panic attack. Those can be very scary and serious. How did you come out of it?" she asks with her doctor first, friendly therapist second tone of voice.

I clear my throat and think back to when it happened. "I popped my feet out of the hammock and scrambled to the surface for air. Nick was right there, holding on to me. He told me to breathe with him, and I did for long enough to get my heartbeat back to normal. He placed his forehead against mine and forced me to focus on him alone. It worked. Once I could breathe more normally, he eased back and finished up the class. I, however, bolted immediately!"

Dr. Hart nodded and scribbled something on her pad.

"Why did you leave so quickly?"

I bite down on my bottom lip.

"He seemed like he liked me."

"Okay, and why does that make you uncomfortable?"

"He doesn't know me. I'm not that likeable."

Dr. Hart leans back, crosses her legs, and rests a hand on the roundness of her belly. She moves her hand around the fabric in lazy circles. I've never felt a pregnant woman's baby. Come to think of it, I've never even held a baby.

"You are... We just went over this, Honor."

I frown, cross my arms over my chest, and press against the back of the couch. Skipping the "I'm likeable" conversation, I go right to what's on my mind. "You know, I've never held a baby."

My doctor stops rubbing her stomach. "I'm going to go out on a limb and say you're bringing this up because of my pregnancy?"

"Maybe." I tilt my head.

"Have you ever thought of being a mother?"

I half snort and choke on the gag that tightens my throat. "And end up like my mother? An abuser?" I scoff and turn toward the doctor, missing the importance of what I just revealed.

Dr. Hart's lips turn into a flat, white line, and her eyes flash with anger. "Honor, may I?" She gestures toward the couch.

At the firmness of her tone, I respond immediately, shifting to the other seat to make room. I sit ramrod straight, my hands in my lap.

The doctor rises and comes to sit next to me. When her hand touches mine, I flinch. She pulls back, eases sideways, and tips her head toward me. "Remember that honesty we talked about? The trust we must have with one another in order for you to get healthy mentally?"

I nod slowly as a sense of dread throbs at the base of my spine, crawling up each vertebra until a heavy sensation makes my limbs feel weighted and unmovable.

"Honor, has your mother physically harmed you?"

I focus on her gaze as my mouth goes completely dry. Fear. Bone-chilling fright coats my tongue, making it impossible to swallow. Not being able to speak, I jerk my head once.

Dr. Hart inhales slowly, her nostrils widening enough for me to know she's reining in her response, and I think it's one of anger. "Did this start when you were a child?"

I grip my inner thighs, wishing I had a blade. Instead, I dig my nails into the skin a couple inches above the hem of my skirt. The shock of pain soothes the fear swirling inside, allowing me to speak, but just barely. "Yes," I mutter and dig my nails deeper.

"When was the last time she hit you? How long ago?"

I shake my head and keep digging into my flesh. I'm certain there will be crescent-shaped indentions in my thighs when I leave today. I hold back the urge to scratch along the tender skin, wanting the pain but fighting the desire because I know it's not right. I glance at the doctor, and her focus is on my face. She hasn't moved a muscle, and I don't think she sees how much I'm struggling with this discussion.

"Honor, you said you trust me. I'm here only for you. To protect *you*. To help you. Not your mother. Now can you please tell me, when was the last time you remember your mother hitting you? Were you ten, twelve, a teenager?"

She assumes I was young, which makes the truth that much harder to admit. Tears form and fall down my cheeks.

Instead of wiping them away, she bends forward and grabs the tissue box on the table in front of me. I don't want to grab for it, because that would mean I'd have to stop digging my fingers into my thighs. The pain would stop, and I *need* the pain to get through this.

"No, no, no. I can't." I shake my head.

Dr. Hart goes for my hands. Her eyes narrow as she looks down. "Let go, Honor. Stop hurting yourself!" Her words are forceful and direct.

I swallow around the lump in my throat, the tears continuing to fall as I lessen my grip. She eases my skirt up to midthigh, finding the indentations from my fingernails. Thankfully, she doesn't touch me.

What I didn't plan for was her also seeing the scars from my high school and college years. "You have much older scars on your inner thighs." She states this matter-of-factly.

I nod.

"Honor, when was the last time your mother hurt you physically?" This time, she holds my hands, and I clutch at them like a lifeline.

I admit the filthy truth. "Last week."

Dr. Hart purses her lips and gives a pensive jerk of her head. "Okay. We're going to fix this together. You hear me?"

I nod and then do something so out of character, I'm shocked I even do it. I pull her into a hug. She holds me close and pets my hair. The instant relief of having someone care rolls through my body in waves. I let it all go, sobbing against the crook of her neck.

"I'm going to help you, Honor. You're not alone. But the first thing you need to do is leave that house. Immediately." She eases me back so she can look at my face. "Can you do that? Stay in a hotel until you find a place of your own?"

"A place of my own?" I mumble, my voice small and childlike.

She nods. "It's time for you to take the next step. Not only for your mental health but your physical health and safety. For now, get into a hotel. Tell your parents whatever you need to in order to leave. Preferably do it when they are not home. You're twenty-six years old with a hefty inheritance. It's time to put your wealth to use to protect you."

"Okay, Dr. Hart."

"I want you to email me daily with a list of things that you've done for yourself that day. It can be as simple as you slept in when you wouldn't normally. Or you went to yoga. You took a walk. You met up with Grace. I'd like regular communication via email," she says while writing something down on her yellow pad. "Here's my email address. Can you do this?"

"Yes." I start to feel a bit of confidence in the decision to leave. It seems so simple. Move away from my parents and get out from under their reign. "I'll do it." I grab the piece of paper with her email on it like it's a lifeline. Now all I have to do is go home, pack up the things I want to take with me, which isn't much, and leave. Just leave it all behind.

Freedom is on the horizon. My freedom.

For the first time in a long time, I am genuinely excited. I have a small plan in my head. Get my stuff and move into one of my hotels. Start shopping for a home. Maybe Grace would want to do that too. She seems to like the idea of any type of shopping. Email Dr. Hart my progress. I can do this.

I *will* do this. For me.

CHAPTER SEVEN

THROAT
CHAKRA

Individuals ruled by the throat chakra are humble people. They are very good at controlling their ego and their emotions, which can also come off as blasé or lacking compassion when in reality, they don't tend to engage in self-fluttery.

NICHOLAS

I'm jittery as fuck when I pull out my phone three days after I scheduled a date with Honor. I can't seem to control my knees from bouncing all over the place as I sit on the bench in the locker room at my gym. I'm raring for some action of the physical kind. I need the release that comes with sparring in the ring or fucking the hell out of a beautiful woman.

Ever since my time in the army, I've needed regular exercise. Man-to-man, hand-to-hand, or hitting the sheets are the only things that work the nagging tension out of me. The shit I saw out in the deserts of Afghanistan taught me to stay up on my toes, hit a full run in a second flat, watch my six at all times, and learn how to pack a mighty punch. Those skills have not left me in the three years I've been home.

My time in the service was exactly what I needed just out of high school. I was a loose cannon, not knowing what to do with myself or my life. My grades were average—Cs, straight across the board in school. Nothing to warrant anything but a hard seat at a local junior college. Of course, my father wanted me to go into the winemaking business, and I could have. I know enough about making wine, what with all the shit my father drilled into my head over the years. Except something inside me just couldn't do it. I needed to find my own way, be my own man, and the service was a stellar option.

I've always been a patriot. Proud American through and through. And when our country lost so many innocents on 9/11, that knife cut deep into our collective soul, the blood of the victims turning our soil red. I knew that I too had to throw my hat in the ring. Put up or shut up. Once I finished school, I went straight into an eight-year commitment with the US Army.

Those eight years were some of the best and hardest I've ever had. Each day I served taught me more about mankind and its ability to bounce back after repeated horrors and setbacks. It also taught me more about myself, the kind of man I want to be. I've killed terrorists and lost brothers on the battlefield. Every single last one of those wounds sits under the surface of my skin at all times. Unlike some of my brothers in arms, I've found a way to keep the nightmares at bay. Opening up a boxing gym, being able to let out my aggression, has been a natural way for me to heal some of the past hurts.

Yoga is how I deal with the mental side. Finding strength physically and mentally has been my way to cope, deal with the stress received in the desert. Still, I don't regret going. I know in my heart, I fought for my country and did the best I could to help make the world a better place for me, my family, and my future family. I'm proud of the sacrifice I made and hold that time close to my chest.

One would think after serving two consecutive enlistments, having stared down the enemy and risked my life repeatedly, I wouldn't be nervous as shit to text a willowy blonde about a date she's already agreed to. And yet, here I am, running my hand through my hair, gritting my teeth.

Maybe I should wait until after the smackdown with Trent?

Immediately I toss that idea out the door. I want to let her know I'm thinking about her. Get her thinking about me and our date. I jab at the buttons on my phone and pull her up. Seeing the name I programmed for her makes me grin. *Dove*.

Looking forward to our date. Are you?

I read and reread the text several times, like a lovesick buffoon, before I decide "fuck it" and just send the damn thing. Why the hell I'm so worried about what this woman is thinking is beyond me. I haven't been hung up on a broad in...hell, ever. Usually women are either one of my sisters, my buddies' women, or the yogis at work. I spend an evening with women outside of my everyday sphere and move on about my business, no harm no foul. Those gals I see for a night of fun know the score. They're not in it to win it or have me put a ring on it. I certainly don't take them on dates.

Sure enough, a blonde with gray eyes, one helluva rack,

and a penchant for not making eye contact, and I've lost my mind.

My phone dings in my hand. A buzz of excitement surges through my arms and legs.

Yes, me too.

I scowl at the three words. That's it? No "Can't wait to see you, Nick" or "I'm imagining you naked, Nick." Nothing. This woman is harder to crack than a hundred-year-old safe. I rub my fingers through my hair and rest my palms against my temples. What do I say to encourage more communication? I thought maybe she'd give me something to go on, maybe flirt a little. Not this woman. Then again, I shouldn't have expected her to be like anyone else. I've seen her all of two times, and she's got my balls in a vise and my mind on overdrive, imaging all the ways I want to touch her.

Grinding my teeth, I crack my neck and then type out my response.

What are you doing right now?

I read the message again. Yep. Okay, you have to use more than three words to reply to something like that. I click *send* and pick up the tape to wrap my fingers.

The phone goes off on the bench besides me.

House hunting.

When I read the two words on the screen, I about toss my phone against the cluster of metal lockers in front of me. Realizing my temperature is rising, I start my yoga breathing to calm down. It's just a coincidence, not a big deal.

Nick, you already know she's not a talker.

It's going to be my job to bring her out of her shell, get her comfortable enough with me to say more than a handful of words. She'll have to on Friday. I grin, thinking about where we're going. I know it's kind of cheesy to do Italian food and putt-putt golf, but I want something easy, and everyone loves Italian food. If she doesn't, she'll never fit into my family. My mother would have a hernia. And putt-putt will give us time to talk, get to know one another. If I take her to a movie, we'd spend two hours not saying anything to one another. Sure, it's dark, and I can hold her close, but I'd end up spending the time with a semi from the smell of her hair alone and would not get anywhere near learning about her.

Honor makes me want to *know* her, inside and out, not just fuck her. Correction. I want to sink my cock so deep inside her slender body she never forgets me, but I'm okay with getting there slower. Taking my time. I haven't been in this type of situation since high school, and I find I'm a bit rusty. The challenge, however, is rather exciting. This girl is different, and I wasn't lying to her when I said I enjoy different. I don't need another bimbo bouncing on my cock. I'm turning thirty years old in a month. I've got a gym that's on the rise and solid clientele at the studio. I've got my own pad above the gym I'm happy in—for now—but one day in the not-too-distant future, I'd like to take a wife. Share my world with someone. Buy a home, fill it with children.

I can already see bringing Honor to Sunday night dinner with my family. My sisters would fall all over themselves in love with her. She's the exact opposite of them. Blonde to their brunette. Willowy and tall to their petite stature and overabundant hourglass figures. Pearly pale skin to their darker-toned Mediterranean. She's the opposite of every woman I love, and I can't help but notice the beauty in that. She's special. Honor Carmichael is one of a kind, and I intend to make her mine.

Wanting to keep her chatting, I text her back.

Why? Off to box. Will check back with you later, Dove.

I type out the quick question and let her know I won't be responding right away, but I do want to hear what has her house hunting. The fact that she needs a new place doesn't sit right in my gut. A million questions enter my mind, none of which I can answer with so little information.

The need to get in the ring is electrifying my skin, zinging each nerve with static electricity. I'm pumped and ready for action.

Right on time, Trent enters the locker room. The professional baseball player is not a small guy. Our friend Clayton has kept Trent trim and in top form, holding his position on the Oakland Ports for a long time. From what I understand, he's closing in on needing to renew his contract once again. Rumors are he's thinking of retiring at thirty-two. Then again, if I had a sweet woman like Genevieve warming my bed every night, making my brood meals three times a day, and basically spreading love and light all over the place, I'd consider hanging up the towel too. Not that I'm ever going to be able to do that with what I make. I'll have to work until I die.

"Hey, man." He tosses his bag on the bench, already dressed in his workout gear.

"You ready to become minced meat?" I goad.

Trent's eyebrow rises, and he punches his hand. The loud

smack echoes off the metal lockers in the otherwise empty room. "You think you can take me, son? I'm about to serve you up a can of whoop ass!"

I grin and take Trent's hand in a firm, friendly handshake. "Good to see you, brother."

"Likewise. Now, I've only got an hour. The Alexanders have Will and Mary tonight; Row is hanging at a buddy's pad, and Viv's got some type of surprise for me waiting at home. Usually that means fuck-hot lingerie and a night I won't soon forget." He grabs the tape and starts wrapping his fingers.

"Looks like we need to get you in the ring, then. Soon as you're done taping, let's hit it." I hook a thumb over my shoulder. "Meet ya there with the headgear and gloves."

"Cool. No pot shots to the dick. I'm going to need that fella later." He smiles widely, and I shake my head, grinning.

This is exactly what I need. Male bonding time in the ring to get my mind off a hot, timid blonde.

★ ★ ★

Sweat pours down my face, coating my chest and abs. Trent is no better when we make our way back to the locker rooms.

"Shit, man, you were a beast out there," he grumbles. "Got some shit on your mind or what?" He wipes his face with a hand towel.

I grab my own towel and pat my cheeks. "Let me ask you this. You've got a smokin'-hot blonde..."

"Watch it..." Trent growls. The man is beyond overprotective toward his wife, Genevieve. With good reason. The woman is a sprite but with a bangin' body and a beautiful personality. She's a dead ringer for Gwen Stefani in her early years.

I chuckle and ignore the warning. "What I mean to say is, you had to chase Viv a little, right?"

Trent runs the towel over his hair and then drops it around his thick neck. "Yeah, a little. Why? You found a woman who's got your dick kinked?"

"Not exactly. Met her at yoga a week or so ago, then saw her again in Gracie's class. Asked her out. We're doing that on Friday."

Trent sits down on the bench, legs open wide as he removes his shoes and socks. "Thought you didn't mix business with pleasure."

I roll my eyes and clench my teeth. My own rule is haunting me with everyone I know. It is true. I don't date the clientele. That shit can get messy quick.

"Honor's different."

Trent grins. "If she's got you breaking your own rules and taking her out on a bona fide date...I'll say. When was the last time you dated a woman? Picking them up at a bar, taking them home, and feeding them breakfast the next morning doesn't count."

I frown. *Shit.* I'm predictable as hell. Have I really been that shallow since I returned from Afghanistan? I rub at the old bullet wound in my thigh. I've got another to match it on the back of my shoulder, as well as some ugly shrapnel scars running down my right hip to upper thigh. The bullet wound in my leg aches after a solid sparring session, but nothing ibuprofen, a hot shower, and a glass of wine won't fix.

"Your silence answers that question. What's the deal with this woman?" Trent asks, stripping off his sweaty shorts, leaving him in boxer briefs.

I stand up and focus on his face because no man wants another man looking at his junk. Period.

"Not sure. She's beautiful. Blonde with these sad eyes. Makes me want to put some light in 'em, you know? But she's timid, shy. Doesn't say much. It's *effort* getting her to share."

Trent crosses his arms over his massive chest and rubs a hand through his facial scruff. "You're gonna have to break her of that. One thing I know about women is communication is key. I have no fucking idea what Viv is thinking ninety percent of the time. And usually, whatever it is, is fucked-up shit she doesn't need to be worrying over." He frowns. "Like how she looks after having a baby. If I think she's fat. Do I like her meals? Is she a good mother? Fuck! The crap woman put on themselves..." He shakes his head. "Dude, it's whacked. My system for keeping Viv in check is to keep her talking. And most women *love* to talk about their feelings and shit. You pick up the important bits and take care of your woman, and you're solid."

I nod, but fuck all if I know how to do that. "I'll take any suggestions you've got."

Trent clasps my shoulder and squeezes. "Easy. Get her talking on the phone. She can't go quiet the whole time." He laughs, grabs a fresh bath towel from his bag, pushes down his underwear, and heads toward the showers.

Get her talking. Genius. Why the hell didn't I think of that? I pull out my phone and grin, seeing a new message from her.

It was time for a big change. Be safe.
Don't hurt yourself.

She's worried about me getting hurt. A wave of happiness

blankets the initial frustration I had about getting her talking. Trent's right. I just need to force her out of her shell. Make her talk to me. Decision made, I remove my clothes and hit the showers. I want to be clean and settled in my home when I call her back.

Forty-five minutes later, I relax into my plush leather couch. It was a hand-me-down from Dawn and her husband, Lorenzo. When they bought their first home, Dawn wanted to redo it all. Since Lo's goal in life is to make my sister smile, he agreed. The timing for me was perfect. I'd just gotten home from serving my country and needed everything. A lot of what I own now was hers, but I've added to it over the years. Put my own bachelor spin on it. The couch is the softest, smoothest leather, and the cool chill I feel when I first sit on it is unparalleled, as if it's welcoming my heated skin.

Grabbing my phone, I press *call* on Honor's number and wait.

It rings four times before I get a breathy, "Hello?"

I chuckle. "Hey, Dove."

"Nick, um, hi," she offers meekly.

I grin, lift my legs along the length of my couch, and cross my ankles, settling in. "Thought I'd give you a call, find out more about this house-hunting business. You moving out of your current place for a particular reason?"

She clears her throat. "Well, yes."

"And that reason would be..." I prompt, determined to get my girl talking to me. If anything, I need to break up her shyness toward me. Make her comfortable.

"Um, I was still living at home."

That's it, no other response.

"Dove, you're going to have to give me more than that.

Here's the thing: I talk, you answer. Feel free to ask a question of your own. Then we'll go back and forth. I want to get to know you better." I lower my voice to what I hope is a seductive timbre.

"Why?" The one-word question strikes like a sucker punch to the gut.

The fact that this woman doesn't see her worth, her beauty, and why a man would want to spend time with her, talk to her, has me grinding my teeth.

"I believe I told you that I found you attractive and sweet. You've got these big eyes I could stare into for days."

"You think so?" Again her voice is breathy, uncertain.

Still the sound goes straight to my dick, making him perk up. I grip my erection between my thighs and readjust to a more amiable position for us both.

"Dove, I know so. Now why is it time to leave your parents? How old are you, by the way?" I realize I don't even know.

"I'm twenty-six. And I, uh, know it's odd to still be at home, but I was away at school for a long time and didn't see the need to leave again. Until now."

Good, this is good. She's said more in that one response than I think she has in the entire time I've known her. "What's your degree in?"

"I have a Master's Degree in Business Administration from Stanford."

"Master's! Damn, baby, that's amazing. What do you do for a living?" I ask, imagining Honor as a college student wearing a plaid skirt and a button-up sweater I could peel off her.

"Uh, not much."

I frown. "You currently unemployed?"

"You could say that, technically...yes, I'm unemployed."

"Aw, it's okay. I'm sure you'll find the right job for you. With a business degree from a school like that...I'm sure the bigwigs downtown will be fighting to hire you."

She sighs, and the sound goes straight to my dick, making him even harder. Fuck, I need to get laid, preferably by this tight little blonde who is making me crazy.

"I'm not exactly sure what I want to do."

"But you gotta make money, right?" I joke flippantly, wanting to make her laugh. She doesn't.

"Hmm, I...I have an inheritance that's allowing me to take my time."

She probably lost a grandparent or some shit. Sucks, but not what I want her thinking about right now. Time for a subject change. "That's good. If you can swing it, don't settle. When I got out of the service, I roamed around for several months, a bit lifeless, not sure what to do with myself after being a soldier for eight years. And then one day, I walked by this rundown gym. There was a For Sale sign on the window, so I walked in and bought it."

"Just like that?" She has awe in her tone. Now that's what I want to hear. A bit of surprise and happiness.

"Just like that. I'd saved all my money from the service since I had room and board and food in my belly. I used most of it to buy the gym with cash. Came with an attached apartment, so now I'm a home and business owner."

"Smart."

I grin stupidly at her compliment. "Well, I won't say it's the best investment I've ever made, but it's made me happy. I've got a home and a job doing what I love. Though it still needs a lot of work."

"A lot of work?"

"Yeah, there's only so far my money could go since I paid cash. Didn't want to owe any bank. Now I'm working hard and fixing it up as funds become available. One day, though, it's going to be the top boxing gym in the city."

"Wow. I'm impressed."

I smile into the phone. "You're easy to impress. I like that. Means you're not stuck up."

"Oh, I don't know. I've been called prissy." She laughs lightly.

Her laughter makes me beam with delight. "Like hearing your laughter. Makes other parts of me happy too," I admit, wanting her to know what she does to me. Though, I should ease her into my devious ways with her being so skittish.

"Mmm." She hums into the line, and I swear my dick jumps at the sexy sound.

"You excited about our date?" I remind her of what's happening on Friday.

"Yes. I am. What should I wear?"

Now that's a normal girl response I can relate to, having grown up with five sisters. "Something casual—jeans would be fine—but like I said, you'll need a jacket."

"I can do that."

"I'm glad, babe. You get some rest. We'll talk more, yeah?"

"I'd like that, Nick. Good night."

"Night, Dove."

Hanging up the phone, I can't help my insta-grin. She didn't tell me her life story, but I got my girl talking. I've learned that she's highly educated, really smart if she has a degree from Stanford, but also unemployed. Which is rather strange. Even if she graduated after six years, that means she's been without a job for two full years. Inheritance or not, that's a long time. More for me to dig into on our date.

As far as first calls go, I'd consider that one a win. Bit by bit, I'm going to break down the shy walls Honor Carmichael has built until she lets me in completely. I'll never understand my overarching need for her until she's bared it all.

CHAPTER EIGHT

Wheel Pose (Sanskrit: Chakrasana)

Wheel Pose in most yoga classes would be considered an intermediate to advanced level asana. There are many ways you can hurt the back and body by doing this pose incorrectly. Start by sitting in the hammock with most of the silk crawling up your lower back so you have a large base holding your form. Allow the legs to fall naturally down toward the floor. Use your hands to slowly inch down the silks, going into a back bend. The head and neck should fall naturally. Do not strain. If you are flexible enough, arc back so the hands can take hold of the ankles or feet. This position should only be done in the presence of a certified aerial yoga teacher or after many successful attempts.

HONOR

"This would look incredible on you! You have to try it on!" Gracie exclaims, holding up a fitted, black, *sleeveless* dress.

The thought of a sleeveless dress practically gives me hives where I stand. An itch to pull down the arms of my sweater prickles at the back of my neck. "I prefer longer sleeves." I bite my lip and try to hold eye contact with Grace.

She worries her lip and then taps it with her index finger while evaluating the dress. "Okay. The length and low neck work for you?"

I offer my new friend a small smile in return. She doesn't know how much her go-with-the-flow attitude and no-questions-asked personality eases me. While Grace is exuberant, fun, and one hundred percent an extrovert, she doesn't attempt to force her choices or personal style on anyone else.

On the other hand, the women my mother coerces to hang out with me do. I loathe having to sit through lunches where brainless, rich women talk about the newest fashions or gossip about who is getting work done and why. I know the second I leave them alone they are all talking badly about me. Poor Honor Carmichael, daughter of Judi Gannon-Carmichael, the one who will never live up to her family's expectations. The woman her own mother is trying to marry off for business gain.

I let out a long breath and focus on the new top Gracie is holding up. It's beautiful, flowy, and nothing like what I normally wear. I love it instantly. It's a deep emerald green with cutouts along the outside of the sleeve. So, it shows the outside of the arm in peek-a-boo holes but not the inside. My henna and what's hidden beneath it stay a secret. And the top is so funky and fun.

Grace's eyebrows go toward her hairline as she holds it up for my assessment.

"I'll give it a try." I grin and glance back down to the rack of clothes in front of me.

"Yes!" Gracie hisses excitedly. "I knew I could find you the perfect things."

"Well, I need a whole lot more. As in, an entire wardrobe full of new clothes." I make the split-second decision. If I'm going to work on finding myself, I should probably purchase my own clothes, not just wear the things mother has placed in my closet on a regular basis.

Her mouth drops open before curling into an evil grin. "I'm going to load you up, sister! You just wait. You need a new look, I'm the girl for you. Budget?"

I shake my head.

"Righteous! I'm going to go get one of those bags to hold all the stuff you're going to try on!" She dances her way toward one of the checkers.

A red jersey dress with three-quarter sleeves and a deep V in the front catches my eye. I pick it up and evaluate it in my size. It's sexy but understated, and the fabric would feel luxurious against my bare skin. It's a deep crimson that's way outside of my comfort zone when it comes to color palettes. My mother would hate it. I start to put it back on the rack on autopilot.

"You have *got* to try that on. Girl, you'd look so sexy in it, and my brother's eyes would bug out of his head! His favorite colors are black and red." She winks saucily.

Black I figured out on my own. The two times I saw him he was wearing all black. Plus, the pictures of him online all had him wearing black as well. "Maybe I should get something black, then?" I can feel my cheeks heat at the bold suggestion.

Gracie waggles her eyebrows. "Yes, you definitely should. And it wouldn't hurt to get some red and black lingerie to boot!" She knocks her hip into mine exaggeratedly.

I cough into my hand. "You're getting a little ahead of yourself, don't you think?"

She adds another blouse to the bag she's now holding. This one a soft yellow. Again, not something I'd pick for myself, which makes me eager to try it.

"You're deluded if you think my brother doesn't want to get into your panties." She blinks a few times and lets that sink in before continuing. "I mean yeah, he's my brother, but I'm not blind. He's a hunk. All of the women at Lotus House are hot for him."

Her comment makes my heart sink. I've seen the women at Lotus House. They are all attractive beauties. Not to mention, many of the clientele are young, svelte college girls. "Really?"

"Oh, don't worry. You're the only one he's ever asked out from work. He has a really strict policy about it too. Then you come along and—whammo!—rule is shot to shit."

"Shot to...what?" I'm confused.

"Meaning, he must really like you to break his own rule against not dating clients from the studio."

"Oh." Huh. Why would he do that?

"Yeah, oooohhhhh..." She drags out the word. "Told you. Now let's make sure you look fantastic and make my bro want to weep at how pretty you look for your date on Friday!"

I'm not sure anything could make a macho man like Nick Salerno want to weep, but I have nothing to lose. Doing my best to follow my friend's lead and go with the flow, I grab another cleavage-popping blouse, this one black with a sassy long tie at the waist that wraps around the body twice before tying in a bow. I hand it over to Grace, and she plops it in the bag.

"Atta girl. We've got some serious shopping to do if we're going to get you set up in a new wardrobe."

"How about we do what we can today and plan another date for next week?" I dig my thumbnail into my palm, wishing I hadn't jumped the gun or been too eager.

Stupid, Honor. Stupid.

Grace, oblivious to my inner turmoil, just bobs her head. "Sounds like a plan, Stan." She moves over to another rack of clothes, lifts a top, scrunches up her nose, and puts the top back before moving to the next.

I let out a relieved sigh. I glance down at my hand and see the thumbnail imprint dug deep into my palm. I use my thumb to rub out the spot of pain. Thank goodness I didn't dig deep enough to cut the skin. That would be hard to explain. Ringing out my hand, though, I congratulate myself on putting myself out there, even though it was hard to do.

Breathe, Honor. You're doing great.

Hannon's voice comes to me, soothing the notes of tension spiraling down my spine as I rub the center of my palm.

Slowly but surely, brother. I'm finding it.

★ ★ ★

Monet,

See, I'm learning. :)

Today was a good day. Two notable things happened. First, Nick called me last night. We texted a few times, and then he actually called me by phone. I didn't think he would really check in with me, but he did. We talked about him having served time in the army and my graduating from school. I didn't know what to tell him about living at home with my parents. I'm nervous he's going to find out about how horrible my family is. I'm not sure what to do.

What I realized while talking to him is that I have no idea what I want out of my life. Is that normal for a twenty-six-year-old person with a college degree? I should want to be something big, run a company, or serve on one of the countless boards of directors for one of my family's holdings, but the idea does nothing but bore me. It would make my father happy. Maybe. Not a lot makes him genuinely happy. I'd like to talk about this at our next session.

The second new thing I did was go on my shopping date with Grace. It was nerve-wracking at first, but I got the hang of it. She made me try on more clothes than I currently own. I ended up bringing home tons of bags of clothes I wouldn't normally try on, let alone purchase. And you know what? I'm looking forward to wearing them. Kind of like putting on the new clothes makes me feel like I'm a different person. Like I can be anyone I want to be. Does that make sense?

Best,

Honor

I finish typing up my daily email to Dr. Hart. Just the act

of doing this task has me thinking about what has changed in my life over the past two weeks. I've moved into a hotel and soon will find my own place. I also have a girlfriend whom I genuinely like spending time with. Grace makes me want to be something I'm not. Try new things I wouldn't try. Live a little. I'm taking yoga classes four times a week, which is physically pushing my body in a healthy way. And I'm going on a date with a man. A devastatingly good-looking man. I've lived more in the past two weeks than I have in the last two years. Hannon would be so proud. I wish he was here to share it with.

The sadness that comes with thinking about Hannon wafts around me, but it doesn't pull me down to that ugly place where I need to do terrible things just to *feel* something. I'm already feeling something, and it's good and positive. It's excitement about what's ahead, not dread and fear or anger. I'm looking forward to what this next week will bring. I just have to get through my second aerial yoga class and my date with the Italian Stallion.

Now the fear of not being enough for a man like Nick prods my psyche, but I push it back like Dr. Hart taught me. Redirect. I pull out my phone and bring up Sean's name.

I've made a new friend. Her name is Grace, and she's lovely. She teaches yoga. You should try yoga with me sometime.

Once I finish typing the message, I set about hanging my new clothes in the walk-in closet. The nice thing about having an endless bank account is you can stay in a fully furnished penthouse in a five-star hotel without batting an eye. It has all the luxuries of living on my own: great furniture, a pool, gym, a walk-in closet, and a tub that's big enough to bathe a small whale. Plus, I technically own it, so I can take my time finding the right place for me.

My phone buzzes in my robe pocket.

Bunny, that's awesome. So happy for you.
I want to meet her...soon?

He wants to meet Grace. Only Grace doesn't know about Sean or Hannon, and I'm not sure when or if I'll ever go there with her. Is that something a person needs to share with friends? I'll have to ask Dr. Hart. Sharing is a new thing for me and one I'm not exactly eager to get into. I prefer to have my relationship with Grace be light, not covered in my darkness.

Maybe at yoga sometime? I go four times
a week now.

Instead of my phone buzzing his response, it rings in my hand. Sean Tillman flashes on the display.

"Hello."

"Honor...baby girl, I'm so happy you made a new friend. And yoga four times a week! Tell me everything!" he insists, a hint of pride in his voice, sounding like the old Sean of years past.

At hearing his jovial tone and letting his excitement coat my nerves, I settle into the huge bed and curl my knees up against my chest, covering my toes with the comforter.

"She teaches yoga at the place I go. Sean, she's crazy, and fun, but mostly, she's really nice and sweet."

He laughs. "Sounds like a good friend to have. You met her when taking her yoga class, you said in the text? And who knew! Honor taking yoga. Hannon would love it." He laughs.

Hannon would love it.

My heart sinks as I remember that my brother is not here to share in this new development in my world. Worse, the man he was going to spend his life with is moving on and dating another man.

I sigh, the sound weighing down the conversation. "Yes, she's the exact opposite of me. Smiles a lot. Happy all the time. And she's a great yoga teacher."

"I'd like to take her class with you sometime. You know I want to spend time with you. Just us, doing something productive." His tone is somber, coated with the emotions he's not saying. It's not lost on me that I remind him of what he no longer has. He does the same to me. Together we're definitely a sad pair, but we're also the only two people who loved Hannon and will remember him forever.

"It's okay if it's too hard still," I whisper, wanting him to have an out. "I just wanted you to know that I took your advice. I'm seeing Dr. Hart regularly, and she's helping me, Sean. I've moved out of my parents' house, and I'm... Well, I'm doing a lot better right now. I don't have it all figured out, but I'm getting there."

A heavy breath precedes Sean's response. "Bunny, I'm relieved to hear that. I worry about you. You're family. Part of the only family I have left."

I clear my throat as my eyes water. I press my fingers into my temples. "I know you do. And I love you for it. And we'll always be family."

"You promise?" His voice cracks.

"Yeah, I promise."

"I'm glad I called. Let me check my schedule, and I'll text you when I'm off next. You can take me to one of your classes. Maybe the one with your new friend Grace."

Closing my eyes, I smile, imagining him meeting my new friend. "I'd like that, Sean. I love you."

"I love you too, Bunny. Get some rest and take care of yourself."

"I will," I say instead of lying and placating him with an "I am" that is empty.

★ ★ ★

Lotus House is teeming with energy when I arrive, date-night bag slung over my shoulder. Dara is at the counter, and she waves me over.

"Hey, girl... I hear tonight is the night." She grabs my hand and squeezes.

"Grace?" I offer, knowing this is where she's getting her information.

She nods. "Um-huh. She's so excited, that one is bouncing off the walls telling everyone that her brother is dating her new best friend."

I laugh and shake my head. Though, the idea that I'm anyone's "best" anything makes my heart beat double time with a sensation I don't recognize.

"You know she means well, right?" Dara's gaze is direct and unwavering.

"Yes, I do. And I appreciate her high spirits as it pertains to her brother and me having a date, but it's not really a big deal."

Dara jerks her head back. "Not a big deal?" She makes a noise with her lips that's a cross between a shush and a psst. "Every girl in here besides the teachers would die to be in your shoes. You've basically caught yourself a unicorn, honey. That man does not *date*. What I hear, you're the first in years."

I frown. "I'm sure he's seen women besides me," I whisper, not wanting others to hear our conversation.

She snort-laughs in a way that has me grinning. "Oh, I don't doubt that Nick has *seen women*. A lot of women. On their backs. Naked." She snaps her fingers. "Dated, wooed, taken home to his mama Josephine? Nuh-uh." She waves her index finger back and forth with a sassy edge.

"Well, he hasn't offered to take me home to his mother either."

She leans against the counters. "My bet, next Sunday you'll be ass in the chair at the Salerno family table."

"Sunday? I'm not sure I understand." I frown, wondering what's so important about Sundays.

Dara grins and winks. "You'll see. Hey, Nick!" She calls out to the man in question, who must have entered behind me.

I don't turn around, still nervous to see him. The air electrifies as warmth closes in on the back of my body. A featherlight touch caresses the side of my cheek from behind, pushing my hair to the side. Nick's citrus and leather scent invades my senses, and I grip the counter in front of me until my knuckles turn white against the pressure.

"Dove..." he whispers against my ear.

I let out the breath I was holding as chills ripple up and down my back. His nearness is intoxicating, making me light-headed.

"Christ. You smell amazing." He nuzzles against my neck, and I close my eyes and lean back into him without realizing I'm doing it. My body seems to react on its own, wanting to be closer to him. "Like roses in the spring." He inhales and exhales, his breath falling warmly against the shell of my ear.

SILENT SINS

I tremble against his bulk. He lays one hand on my hip and squeezes. "You look beautiful."

"But you can only see me from behind," I manage through a suddenly dry throat.

"I know. And it's a great fucking view." His hand moves from my hip and boldly cups my right ass cheek, making me squeak. "Been dreaming about this ass for a week. Now get it moving to class. I want you right up front where I can see you." He firms his hold on my ass, and I have to bite back a moan.

It's been so long since a man has touched me in a sexual way, I'm not sure how to handle it, other than to take what he's offering and be grateful.

"Got it?" His breath teases the hairs on my nape.

I nod.

"Words, Dove. I want your words." He growls against my neck. The vibration rolls through me like sap dripping down a tree. Slow, fluid, and mesmerizing.

"Yes, Nick. I'll be there in a few minutes," I mumble through the arousal seeping into my bones.

He hums against my skin, inhales deeply, and squeezes my ass once more before he's gone.

"Catch you later, Dara," he says over my shoulder as if he wasn't just twirling me into a heady sexual haze, making my mind complete and utter mush.

Dara bends forward toward the counter, smirks, and places her chin in her open palm. "You are *so* gone for that boy."

She is not wrong. There is absolutely no denying the power Nick's voice alone holds over me. It hits me like a two-ton truck slamming into a concrete wall.

I want him.

For the first time in as long as I can remember, I've found

something I *want* with reckless abandon, and his name is Nick Salerno.

"Yeah," I mumble and shakily push away from the counter, my legs weak at the knees.

Dara chuckles. "Go get him, girl. Make that boy your man!" she urges.

"I don't... I don't know how to do that."

She cants her head to one side. "From the way I just saw it, you're already doing it. That man's aura glows a fiery red the second he lays eyes on you. That's *passion* and *desire* burning bright as the sun, sweet thang. Not a whole lot you need to do." She shrugs, her blue eyes gleaming a crystal ocean blue. "My suggestion...just keep being you."

I take a deep breath and nod, not making eye contact. She doesn't need to know that I don't even know what being me looks like. Instead, I head to the door, use my lotus-shaped key card, and enter the hallway heading toward the girls' locker room. I put away all my stuff and pause at the mirror nearest my locker. My own image greets me.

Tall, thin frame, long blonde hair curled in the beachy look I learned from watching videos online. I've got minimal makeup on, and my gray eyes still look a bit sunken in for my liking. Attempting to be bold, I unzip my hoodie and leave it open. Underneath is a black, cropped, yoga bra-type contraption that has several crisscrossing sections along my back and shoulders. Its halter style gives my larger bust enough support, but it's long enough that it reaches my last rib, leaving my abdomen completely bare. The pants I'm wearing fit close to the body and have this fold-over, whimsical, multicolor flap that looks like it's splotched with paint. According to Grace, this is "the shit" and her brother will swallow his tongue when he sees me in it. I took that to mean it looked good on me and promptly bought it. And it's black.

I hope he likes black on me as much as he likes it on himself. Feeling stupid, I let out a long breath, zip the hoodie back up, and head to class.

When I arrive, it's completely full except for the single hanging yoga hammock in the front. Nick is holding the silks, eyes to the door.

Breathe. He's just a man.

Who am I kidding? Nick is not just a man. He's an insanely sexy one. A man I've not stopped thinking about since I met him. A man I'm going on a date with after class tonight. What have I gotten myself into? He is far out of my league, yet he wants to take me out. I don't get it.

Nick holds out the hammock for me as I make my way to the front.

"Thought you might bail." He smiles rather shyly.

I firm my chin and force myself to hold his gaze. "No. I want this." *Correction. I want you,* but I keep that bit to myself.

"Me too. You ready to be taken on an aerial journey?" He rubs his hands together.

"Yeah."

"Good. Let me take you there." Innuendo is thick in his choice of words as he turns and addresses the entire class. "We're starting standing tonight. I want you to get settled with the silks low at your back, your legs stretched out in front of you. I'm feeling good tonight..." His gaze catches mine, and he winks.

My heart pounds out of my chest, and my temperature rises. Before I get situated, I unzip my hoodie and let it fall to the floor near my mat. I turn around, press the silks into my lower back, and stretch out as the rest of the class has.

When I look back at the front, Nick is staring at me. His eyes bounce from my face to my chest, to my bare abdomen, and down to my painted toes and back up. His jaw firms, and a muscle in his cheek ticks while his eyes run over me like a brand. Nick ups the ante when he yanks up his black T-shirt and tugs it over his head, giving me a front-row seat to the hot male yogi show.

Again, my temperature spikes, heat nipping at my flesh in places I'd rather not think about for fear I might spontaneously combust. I lick my lips and run my hands up and down the silks above my head, imagining they are Nick's muscled arms.

One of his eyebrows rises, and he grins. The bastard knows what he's doing to me. It's probably why he chose to put me up front. So he could watch my every reaction to him and his ridiculously beautiful body.

What Nick doesn't know is that I'm a professional at not displaying my feelings. I'll just blank out my emotions and focus on the yoga movements, not on the insanely attractive man on display.

The only way to play his game is to ignore him.

"Never let them see you sweat, Honor."

It's what Hannon used to say, and I call up on that sage advice now.

It works through most of the class...until it doesn't for Nick.

CHAPTER NINE

THROAT
CHAKRA

*Beyond all other chakras, Throat Chakra couples are most
likely to experience love at first sight. It's not uncommon for
this chakra couple to know within moments of meeting that
they are meant to be together.*

NICHOLAS

The second Honor's zip-up sweatshirt comes off and I see
her large breasts encased in black, stringy spandex, my dick
punches at the front of my loose pants. I have to bite the inside
of my cheek—hard—in order to hold back the wood that's dying
to spring to attention.

Shit. Fuck. Damn.

Nothing but pearly white skin and a flawless form greet
my vision. Everything around her disappears, fades out, until
I see nothing but her beautiful body. Honor's white-blond hair

curls enticingly around her face, making me wish I was closer and could push it behind her ear and kiss her silly. Her lips are a glossy pink that I want so badly to taste, I can feel the ache deep in my chest.

This damn woman.

Everything about her sets my soul aflame, and I've barely scratched the surface of getting to know her. One thing I do know is tonight, it's going to be hard as hell for me to finish up the evening with just a kiss and a request for a second date. I'm going to have to put myself in serious check or somehow take the edge off first.

Gritting my teeth, I watch her shimmy her delectable body into the hammock and lean back, matching the class. This position is no better on my little—quickly becoming *big*— problem. Her chest lifts up toward the ceiling, and she runs her arms up and down the silks. This move has the adverse effect of me envisioning her running those same small hands up and down the length of my cock. Preferably not now but when we were alone. The location be damned. If it were just the two of us in this room, I'd sit her ass in the silks and take her hard and long until she begged for me to stop or roared in pleasure. Whichever happened first.

I cross my arms low, holding my wrist with one hand, ensuring the rest of the class doesn't see my desire for the blond goddess before me. What I need is to get a handle on my body's reaction to her, but so far, that has not been easy. Just her breathing is enough to get me hard as a rock.

Needing to cool off, I walk the room, readjusting people where necessary until I'm distracted by the sound of giggling behind me. I turn around to find Grace, her head upside down as she arcs into position.

"What are you doing here, troublemaker?" I whisper and pretend to be affronted, but I can't ever be mad at Gracie. Her happiness and good nature are infectious.

"Wanted a front-row seat for the show." She chuckles and sits up, smiling, and then nods her chin in Honor's direction.

"Class, sit up, close your eyes, and take five full breaths in, allowing the air to completely fill your lungs, and then exhale until there is no air left." I glare at my sister while the class follows through on my command. She stares me down, not backing off. I roll my eyes and address the class in a huff. "Once completed, turn to your side and go into half-moon, allowing the silks to hold your ribcage while you ease into it. Gracie here will show you how it's done. Won't you, Grace?"

Grace sticks her tongue out and goes right into the pose, her body alignment perfect. I've taught her well. A bushel of pride fills my heart as I watch the class mimic her position.

"This pose is also known as *Ardha Candrasana* in Sanskrit. It's an excellent hip and chest opener. If turning to the side is too much for you at this phase in your practice, shift the silks to your abdomen and stretch your arms out in front of you, going into Warrior Three. The impact is less, but you will still get a good lengthening throughout the sides of the body."

I make sure everyone in class has the position before I head back to the front. Bad idea. Honor is facing my hammock, arms stretched out forward as if she's reaching for me. It takes everything I have not to touch her fingertips, making even the smallest physical contact. I know myself too well. Once I touch her, it will be over. Instead, I hold back, wondering why I asked her to come to class in the first place. Probably because I wanted to spend as much time with her as possible, but having her here, close enough to touch and not being able to, irks me to no end.

For the rest of the hour, I put the class through their paces and finish with *Savasana* or deep relaxation, this time with them lying on the floor instead of in the hammock. It's not my usual modus operandi, but change is necessary. At least that's what I've been taught over the past decade.

I left everything I knew when I entered the army. Change.

Exiting the army, I came home not knowing what was up or down. Change.

Wandering endlessly around a Berkeley neighborhood and coming across a gym for sale. Change.

A beautiful woman with sad eyes enters my life. Change.

Life is full of changes. It's what we do with those changes that makes all the difference.

When I bring everyone back from their relaxation, my entire focus is on Honor. Her movements are sluggish, relaxed, more so than I've seen before. As if the stars and the moon and the universe itself have smiled down on me, everyone leaves before my dove is finished with settling her belongings. Easing the door shut, I pad across the wood floors and capture her from behind, bringing her back flush against my front.

Her lovely gasp sounds throaty and loud in the otherwise empty room. All that's left is us and a Chopin piece playing over the studio speakers. I turn my goddess around, grab her waist, and lift her back into the silks hanging behind her. Her butt hits the hammock, and before she can protest, I've got the silk protecting her back. She opens those long legs of hers wide so I can fit my body between them. In a second flat, I've got my mouth on hers.

She moans into our first kiss, sending jolts of pleasure down my spine to lie heavily at the base. She tastes better than I imagined. Like vanilla and mint mixed together. Her tongue is tentative as I explore her, but her arms and legs are not, wrapping around my form like a lust-drunk teen. I love every second of her eager need to be closer. I wrap my hands around her body, lean her back into the silks, and drink from her mouth like I've been dying of thirst. Her lower half rubs against my iron-like erection, and I growl my pleasure into her mouth. I suck her bottom lip and then her top. She mimics each move with one of her own. A nibble here, more suction there, until I'm completely lost in her. I could spend the rest of my days with only these lips to kiss, and I'd be a happy man. I pull away far enough so we both can catch our breath.

In that moment, her eyes blaze a silvery gray I'll never forget for as long as I live. My heart pounds, and my skin sizzles with heat as I stare at the stunning woman before me. Energy flickers and pops off my form like sparks from a welding iron as my fate becomes sealed.

One kiss was all it took.

One kiss and I'll give her everything.

One kiss and I'll lay down my life.

One kiss and I know she is meant to be mine.

One kiss and I have seen my forever in her eyes.

My voice is scratchy and rough when I speak. I need to know. Need to hear that I'm not the only one.

"Tell me you feel this? It's crazy. Wild. Untamed. I can't begin to understand it or explain it. All I know is, I don't ever want to let it go. Let *you* go."

"Then don't," she whispers, her eyes glued to mine, timid and afraid yet hungry and dark with arousal.

"Oh, Dove, nothing could keep me away from you now that I've had a taste."

★ ★ ★

I can't stop grinning. I've got Honor's slim, small hand in mine as I lead her down the hallway. Thirty minutes ago, I was kissing this beautiful woman—*my woman*, if I have anything to say about it. I surprised myself when I shared what I was feeling, but it felt right. At the time, I was scared she'd run, being so skittish. Instead, she leaned in and kissed me again... harder. I know she's worried about what's burning between us, but I don't know why. All I care about is that she's giving me a shot. Giving this amazing thing between us a real go.

When we exit Lotus House, I let go of her hand and walk over to my Chevy, and she heads toward a flashy-as-hell black Mercedes coupe.

She stops when I don't follow her and then turns on her heels. "Oh, did you want to drive me?"

I grin and walk over to her. "Yeah, Dove. That's kind of what happens on a date. The man drives the woman. Or at least, I drive *my woman*."

Her eyes widen at my rather blatant statement, but the sooner she gets used to my possessive ways, the better, because I will make her mine. That kiss sealed it for me. There's no going back after that. I will do whatever it takes, work my ass off if I have to, in order to make her see she's for me and I'm for her. Period.

"Um, okay. Will you bring me back to my car?"

I grin, looping my arms around her waist. "Tonight or tomorrow morning?" The sexual innuendo rolls off my tongue so fast, I grit my teeth, wishing with my whole heart I could take it back. "I'm sorry. I didn't mean that."

She frowns. "You don't want to be with me...um tonight?"

Honor bites her lip, swallows, and then glances to the side.

Damn it, I'm screwing this up. I cup her face with both hands and brush my thumbs along her cheeks. They're warm, and I can sense the pulse underneath her skin, pounding out a nervous rhythm. "I do. More than anything. But you're worth more than one night's roll in the hay."

She blinks sweetly before lifting her gaze to mine. "I am?"

"Yeah, babe. You are, and I'm going to make you see that. Now, come on. Ride with me so we can talk. I'll bring you back to your car later."

"Okay," she says as I loop my fingers with hers.

I get her settled into my Camaro and run around the front before getting into the driver's side.

"This is a very cool car. Like in those fast car movies." She runs a pale hand along the dash stitching.

I chuckle. "*The Fast and the Furious*? I don't know about that. Though your car... How does a girl just out of college afford something like that?" I glance to the side and catch her frown in the passing streetlights. "Not that it's any of my business," I add rather lamely, already having overstepped my boundaries.

She's quiet for several minutes before she looks out the window. "That inheritance I told you about... It's um, rather large. The uh, well, the Carmichaels own..."

She's about to lay it all out, and it dawns on me that it's really making her uncomfortable, so I shut it down. "Honor. It's cool. But instead of buying a flashy car—" I waggle my eyebrows to get her laughing again. It works; she loses the tension in her face and turns toward me. "You should consider your options. Maybe invest in something that's going to secure your future. Cars come and go. When I had a good-sized chunk of change...well, I told you what I did with it."

"You bought a business," she reiterates directly, showing she's been paying attention.

"Yeah. I set myself up with my dream job, babe. I love to box, work out, coach others. I'll never be a millionaire doing what I do, but I'm happy. And as it grows and I make it bigger, it will provide for me and my future family."

"Is that what you want?" Her voice is timid and unsure.

"Is what what I want?"

"A family," she asks in a tone I can't define.

"Yeah, someday in the not-too-distant future. I'm going to be thirty in a month. One of my sisters is married with a baby on the way, another about to get engaged, and heck, all of my friends are settling down. Just seems like it's nearing the time to go that route. How about you?"

Honor shrugs noncommittally. "I don't know what I want."

"What did you want to do with your degree?"

Another shrug.

I'm beginning to loathe the shrug. It prevents her from speaking to me, and I prefer her talking. "Words, Dove."

Honor lifts her arm and places an elbow on the side of the door, her fingers resting against her scalp. "Honestly, I didn't have a plan. My father chose it because that's what his degree is in, my brother's, and all the rest of the Carmichaels before him."

The dry, almost sad tone with which she responds has me scratching my head. "Did you like your coursework?"

"Not particularly."

Alarm bells start clanging in my head. Why would she spend six years going to school to obtain a degree she didn't want? "And now that you have this degree, you don't know what to do with it?"

"You could say that."

"I did say that. I'm just wondering, babe, what your plan is?" I grab for her hand, lift it, and kiss the back, letting her know I'm here for her and interested.

She sighs so heavily, I can sense the weight of it like a physical anchor landing in my own lap. "I'm working on that now, Nick."

Her words are soft and laced with a brokenness I can't quite understand, but I plan to get to the bottom of it very soon. Every question I ask her seems to bring on more questions about my shy girl. I wonder if I'll ever get to the heart of her; I sure as hell hope so.

"I like the idea you had of investing my inheritance, though." She offers a small smile.

I grin and kiss the back of her hand, feeling good that I may have helped her with something I can see she's been struggling with.

"Now you just need to figure out what you want to do with the rest of your life. Or, at the very least, the next five to ten years."

She nods and focuses her gaze front and center. Even though I think I may have helped her work out an issue she's been having, our line of discussion also seems to have an adverse effect, making her overly quiet. Thankfully, we reach the restaurant, which I anticipate will break up some of the unusual anxiety surrounding her.

Like the gentleman my mama taught me to be, I open her door and help her out of the car. She smiles shyly and looks up at me. I was taken aback when she came out of the locker room after our kiss fest wearing a pair of skinny jeans, low, brown suede ankle boots, and a matching leather blazer with a colorful scarf around her neck. Simple but elegant at the same time. Perfect in every way. So much so, I can't keep my hands and eyes off her. Since our kiss, I've had an overwhelming urge to hold her hand, touch her hair, keep her close.

Women don't normally affect me this way. At least, none before her. Then again, I've come to realize, since the first minute I laid eyes Honor Carmichael, there is something unique about her. I can't put her in the same round hole as other women because she's more of a square peg. Hell, she's a freakin' trapezoid.

The hostess leads us to a small curved booth in the corner of the restaurant. The lighting is low but not so dark you can't see well. Just enough to give the place a warm ambiance. There's a white linen cloth on the table and a single candle. Next to it, a magnificent red rose has bloomed to full capacity, standing tall in a translucent vase.

Honor slides into one side of the booth and I into the other until we come around and our thighs touch. Honor immediately lifts her delectable ass, leans over, and sniffs the rose on the table, humming low in the back of her throat. That sound calls out like a siren to my dick, giving me a semi. I grit my teeth and breathe slowly through my nose, calming the urge to take, rut, and claim this woman beside me.

Once she settles back down, I place my hand high on her thigh and give it a squeeze. She doesn't say anything or attempt to move it, thank God. I *have* to touch her. The urge is overwhelming.

Efficiently, she removes her scarf and slides off her blazer, setting it over the hook next to the booth. The top she's wearing underneath catches my eye. It has cutouts running from the shoulder down to her wrist. It's whimsical, pretty, and looks great on her. Especially the deep, plunging scoop neck that gives me a healthy eyeful of her sinful tits. *Hot damn, they look good enough to eat.* My mouth waters at the sight of the pillowed globes, and I know I'd give my eyeteeth if I could take a single bite...or ten. Instead, I lift up my hand and bite down on my knuckle.

Fuck, this woman is going to kill me with blue balls, and we haven't even made it through our first date. More reason to never date and just get to the filthy parts. The part where I slam her up against my bedroom wall and put my hands all over her while my mouth is busy with her sizeable rack.

I grip my hand into a fist and clear my throat, once more trying my damnedest to calm the lustful beast inside, the one dying to get out and play.

"Did I tell you how gorgeous you look this evening? That color looks amazing on you." I dip my gaze down to her chest again. It's like I can't stop. They're calling out my name, begging for attention. Inherently, I know it's a douche move, but it's like she's put them on display for my eyes only. Bravely, I force my gaze to hers.

Her entire face lights up at my compliment. "Thank you. I got this while shopping with Grace."

I chuckle and place my elbow on the table to lean more fully into her space. I want her feeling, smelling, and seeing as much of me as she'll allow. "Gracie is good at many things; shopping is high on the list. I usually employ her help with buying birthday and Christmas presents for the family."

Her eyes sparkle when I speak. "You mentioned you have another sister who's having a baby?"

I grin and rub the pad of my thumb along my bottom lip. Her gaze goes there, watching every movement. Mission accomplished. I close my eyes and sigh, reminding myself to be good.

"Yeah, Dawn. She just announced it last weekend at family dinner night."

"Are you excited?" She fiddles with the menu.

"We all are. It's the first in our family, so it's a big deal."

"How many are in your family?"

Oh boy, now there's a loaded question. "My mother, Josephine, and my father, Sal, had six of us. I'm the only boy."

Her doe eyes widen so large, they remind me of one of those squeeze dolls where you squash the body and the eyes poke out of the head.

"You have five sisters!"

"Yes, ma'am. All younger."

"Wow. That must be something."

"Something else!" I quip, and she giggles. Her laughter is music to my ears.

The waiter comes over and asks what we'd like to order.

"Do you mind if I order for us?" I ask, knowing what are absolutely the best, most authentic Italian dishes on the menu.

"Sure."

"Anything you don't like or have an allergy to?"

She shakes her head.

"We'll take a bottle of my family's Cabernet, the manicotti with Bolognese, the bleu cheese chicken gnocchi, and the house salads. Family style, please."

"What does family style mean?" she asks when he leaves.

"They bring enough food for the entire table to share. Italians are fond of food, and we like having options. Except, of course, when it comes to our women." I curl my hand around her nape and bring her close, tipping her chin up with my thumb. "No sharing there."

She swallows, and I watch as her delicate neck moves. "That's, uh, good. I think."

"Oh, it is. Means once you're mine, you're mine. Do you want to be mine, Dove?"

She licks her lips, and my dick throbs. I lean into her, our lips a scant inch from one another.

"Yes," she says breathily, her eyes a dark, gunmetal gray.

"Good answer," I whisper against her lips before kissing her.

With this kiss, I explore her lush taste, licking inside and enjoying the sweetness her mouth has to offer. The little nymph sucks my tongue and swirls her own in tantalizing figure eights across my bottom lip. Just when I'm about to plunge my tongue into heaven more fully, the waiter clears his throat.

I reluctantly pull back from that tasty appetizer to find her eyes are still closed. A rosy hue covers her otherwise pale cheeks. She opens her eyes slowly, looking a bit dazed and thoroughly kissed. Smugness creeps into my chest while I chuckle and hold out my glass for the steward to fill it.

"As requested, your family's wine. Is it to your liking?"

I take a sip. "Always, my man. Always. You can't go wrong with Salerno Hills, can you?"

He nods. "Not in my time here serving it."

Honor glances at the wine and then at me. "Your family owns a winery?"

I smile with pride. "Yep. Best damn red in the Bay."

"That's fantastic!" She picks up her glass, takes a healthy swig, and rolls it around her mouth before swallowing. Looks like she knows a thing or two about wine as well. "And it's really good!"

"You act surprised. Of course it's good. We're Italian. My family has been making wine for decades. Centuries, really, if you go back to our family tree in Italy."

"My family owns things too. This is so wonderful." Her voice is a higher volume than normal, showing her excitement.

For the life of me I can't figure out why she's so happy my family owns Salerno Hills winery, but I don't question it, wanting her to offer information instead of me having to drag it out of her.

Her smile is so bright, I fall in love with it instantly, wanting to see it on her face all the time. My new goal will be to put that smile on her face as much as possible.

"Really glad you think so. What does your family own?" I swirl the red in my glass, allowing it a little time to breathe.

She raises her glass and waves her other hand in the air nonchalantly. "Oh, a third of the real estate in San Francisco, another quarter in Los Angeles, and an entire five-square city block in New York. Bunch of other stuff too, businesses overseas, some sports teams, I think. Not really sure anymore."

I set down my glass of wine and stare at her for so long, all the light leaves her eyes. *Holy fuck.* She doesn't just have an inheritance. Honor Carmichael is *wealthy*. Insanely wealthy.

Shit. Fuck. Damn.

CHAPTER TEN

Plow Pose (Sanskrit: Halasana)

An inverted pose that lengthens the spine and stretches the shoulders while rejuvenating the nervous system. It's considered an intermediate pose. Beginners should start with an assisted shoulder stand by placing a chair in front of your head. Placing your feet on the seat of the chair and stretching the body up high while supporting the lower back with your hands. Once you are comfortable, ease the legs over the head, starting with knees first and then full legs. The head and neck should be completely relaxed to allow for the throat chakra to open.

HONOR

The darkness swirling in Nick's eyes after I blurted out some of my family's holdings makes my stomach clench and twist.

Dread prickles along my spine like tiny demons marching up and down, stabbing me with their pitchforks.

Why did I admit that?

He told me his family owns a winery. They sell the wine at this restaurant, which doesn't look too shabby, even though it has a more casual appeal. I guess I assumed that meant he came from a financially stable background. From the hard look in his eyes, the firm set of his jaw, I'm not so sure.

"Does, um, my family's wealth shock you?" I ask, eyes on my red wine.

Nick lifts his hand and rubs at his scruffy chin. It reminds me of how good that hair felt against my mouth when he kissed me earlier. Makes me dream of it brushing against other places. I swallow around the lump in my throat and bring the wine to my lips.

He pauses my hand at the wrist, and I place the glass back down, wrapping my fingers around the thin stem.

"Shock? No. Not a lot shocks me. Surprise? *Damn straight*. You just don't seem like that type of woman."

In a normal situation, this kind of statement would make me unerringly happy. Right now, it's confusing, and his tone borders on condescending.

"And what type of woman would that be, Nick?" I raise my chin and focus on his hard jaw and chiseled cheek bones. The Italian Stallion nickname is accurate on so many accounts. He's hard, dark, and beautiful at the same time.

He lifts his gaze and smirks. "Hey, hey, now. Don't get your panties in a bunch. It's just I've been around a lot of women in the past who wanted a guy with a heavy bankroll. Those are *not* circles I play in."

No, no, no. He's misinterpreting and turning things

around.

He continues before I can stop his line of thinking. "I'm ex-military. I own a boxing gym. My office is a run by *me*, not a board of directors wearing five-thousand-dollar suits." His gaze is sincere and sad at the same time.

I have to fix this. The last thing I want is for him to see me as a type of girl who thinks money matters more than happiness. Money has practically *ruined* my life. It did ruin Hannon's. I grip his hand between both of mine.

"I'm not that girl, but I can't change where I came from."

He swallows and purses his lips. "Neither can I."

The waiter chooses this moment to bring our food. He sets down the manicotti and gnocchi at the top of the table and then places our salads in front of us.

I let go of his hand, putting both of mine into my lap.

Nick curls his hand around my nape. "How's about we eat, continue our date, and let the chips fall where they may, huh?"

Hope rings eternal in my chest. I nod and offer a small smile.

"Okay, now let me get you plated up." He lifts the manicotti and places a rolled-up stuffed noodle thing smothered in meat sauce onto my plate. Steam billows around the top, sending mouthwatering scents into the air. "Manigot." He says the word with an Italian flare, pulling me out of the weird funk we'd entered minutes ago with our heavy discussion. "Have you ever had gnocchi?" He lifts the bowl and scoops some of the potato pasta and chicken onto the side of my plate.

"I think so, but it was square and pillowed looking." I frown and use my fork to turn over the rolled potato.

He grins. "This place is the second-best place to eat Italian food in town."

"Second-best? What's the first?" I ask while he plates his own food. As much as I want to dig into the succulent-smelling food, my manners override my senses, and I wait for him to serve himself.

He flashes a sexy grin my way. "My mother's kitchen, of course!"

We both laugh, and I poke a piece of gnocchi, blow on it, and put it into my mouth. A taste sensation explodes across my taste buds. The mixture of alfredo, blue cheese, and the potato pasta is utter perfection. "I don't know about your mother's cooking, but this is incredible."

He takes a bite of his own and smiles around it. When he finishes, he nudges my shoulder. "This is *good*. Ma's is unparalleled. Swear." He crosses his heart with an index finger.

"Maybe one day I'll be lucky enough to taste it. Then I'll be able to compare." I cut into the manicotti, and the ricotta oozes out of the shell, tantalizing my eyes as well as my taste buds.

Nick doesn't take another bite, just watches me eat. "Oh, I think you might be able to compare the food sooner rather than later." He issues the statement almost like a warning. One that heightens my nerves and sends a little thrill shooting down my spine.

"Should I be scared?" I ask, actually thinking I might be scared already. I've never been taken home to meet the parents. The men I dated were in college. We'd have a couple dates, a handful of intimate times, and they'd move on.

What would Nick's mother think of me? A dowdy, shy, woman with no job and no talent. I frown and prod my food, trying not to let my fear override the discussion. It's not like it's happening today.

Nick takes a large bite, chews, and ends with a smirk. "Absolutely. Ma's a handful." He answers my question about being scared. His response does not make me feel any calmer.

"Is she like Grace?" I smile, thinking of my new best friend. Her words, but I'm starting to wish they were true.

He chuckles. "Gracie is a ball of energy for sure. My mother is that, times a thousand, but armed with a wooden spoon or a spatula. She's always cooking." He shakes his head and spins his wineglass.

"Is that her favorite thing to do?" I want to know more about his family. They sound so down-to-earth and real. The exact opposite of mine.

Nick sips his wine and leans back. "Yeah, I'd say cooking is way up there, along with being judgy." He chuckles, but I am not laughing in return.

"Why, um, is she judgy?"

"Because she's a Catholic, guilt-driven, Italian mother of six. She's got nuthin' better to do than get all up into her children's lives." He chuckles.

I frown. "Why does she care?" My mother hasn't even realized I've moved out, and it's going on a week.

Apparently that question rattles Nick, because he turns in the booth and focuses on me and not our dinner. "She's a mom. She cares *too* much. From whether or not we're sleeping well, to having a good job, to food in our bellies, to time spent on things we love. Then there's the hugs and kisses." He shrugs. "All good moms worry, poke, and prod their children, wanting the best for them. I'm sure your mother does too."

Hugs and kisses. Um, no.

Cares too much? Not a chance.

Making sure I'm doing something I love? Ha! That's a

good joke.

Wanting the best for me? Only if it suits her purpose or my father's business deals.

All of this reminds me I never canceled on the date mother had planned. I haven't been home all week, and I don't plan on ever going back. She never even bothered to call and find out where I went, when I'd be home, or why I'd taken most of my possessions. The date, though, that's going to make her angry. A little snarky side to me I haven't been acquainted with before grins evilly.

"Why are you smiling?" Nick brushes my bottom lip with his thumb. Just that little touch sends warmth and arousal spiraling through my belly. It distracts me so much, I answer honestly.

"I was supposed to go on a date tonight with a man my mother chose for me. She's going to be mad when she realizes I ditched him."

Nick squints. His voice is rugged and sharp when he responds. "You're dating someone else?"

Wait, what? I shake my head. "No. Goodness, no." I'm still shocked Nick asked me out and wants to see me. I'd never date two men at once.

Nick's jaw tightens, and he sits up straighter. "Then explain."

An uncomfortable feeling settles heavily in my stomach, making the food I've eaten rather nauseating. I curl my hand into a fist, pressing my thumb into my palm, searching for the jolt of pain I need to push through. I scratch at the spot with my nail, trying to pierce the skin.

"Well, my mother wants me to see a man she thinks is good for the family business. I don't want to see that man. I want to see you." My entire body is tight, tremors of unease sliding along my skin as I wait for him to speak.

Instead of getting mad or being the growly Nick I've seen a few times already, he tips his head back and laughs heartily. So much so, he tucks an arm around his waist and holds his ribcage with the effort.

Um, not the response I expected, but I guess it beats anger. Slowly, that knot inside me untwists just a sliver, and a glimmer of hope eases along my psyche. "Uh, Nick? What is so funny?"

He laughs a bit more, and I watch as his skin turns a rusty gold and his cheeks pinken attractively. He's so masculine. From his muscled forearms, up his large biceps to his corded neck, every flash of tanned skin I see makes me want to lick and bite it. A shiver skips its way through my limbs, making the space between my thighs heavy and needy.

Nick presses his thumb and forefinger of one hand into his eyes and then rubs his face. "That's a classic Mom maneuver! She trying to set you up." He smacks at the table. "My ma's tried that with every Italian woman's daughter from her bunco group. Nice to see that your mother is no different."

I blink and try to understand what he means. My mother wants me to marry for business, and Nick's mother wants him to marry an Italian woman.

"I'm not Italian." I toss this out because nothing else he says makes any sense.

He grins widely. "It's okay. We'll tell her you're five percent. It's enough. Trust me. A white lie goes a long way with my ma. She may not believe it once she meets you, but she'll go with it to make herself feel better."

"Are you saying, if I'm not Italian, your mother isn't going to like me?"

Oh my, that's almost as bad as the idea of me bringing Nick to meet my parents. Which incidentally will never happen. They would absolutely *not* approve. If he's not worth seven figures or more, he's unworthy of sharing space with a Carmichael. At least according to Judi and Timothy Carmichael.

Nick wraps an arm around my shoulder and tucks me in close. "She's going to love you. Don't worry. You'll come to dinner next Sunday. Do you know how to cook?"

I've never cooked anything in my life. We had servants for that. And in college, I ate in the cafeteria or went out. Now all of my meals are made and delivered by the hotel. Not wanting to dig a deeper hole with Nick, I give a little shake of my head and bury my face into the front of his shirt. He smells so good. The leather scent reminds me of the plush leather seats in his muscle car. The hint of citrus is lighter tonight but still there, hiding in the background. I breathe him in, wondering if it's the last time I'll get this close. There's nothing smart about attempting to be with Nick, regardless of the way he makes me feel. He's everything good, strong, and right in the world. He deserves a woman who's worthy of his attention. I am not that girl, but I'm too selfish to not let this play out a little longer. The memories of this time with him will be such a beautiful spot to revisit when I'm lonely.

"Eh, it's okay. If she asks you Sunday night, just dodge the question and ask to help. She loves a woman eager to assist."

"Why?"

He rubs his lips against my temple and kisses me there. I close my eyes and soak up what could be the last time I experience this.

"Because she's the boss."

"Not your father?" I question.

My father is king and my mother is his willing, evil queen. She does his bidding and is the perfectly put-together socialite. Everyone in my mother and father's circle wants to be like her. It's impossible to live up to her standards when the bar is set so high.

Nick chuckles, and the movement has me sinking deeper against his side. I set my hand along his hard chest, appreciating the thump of his heart against my palm.

"Not a chance. My mother rules the roost, and my father brings home the bacon."

I hum against his chest, taking it all in. His family sounds colorful and, if Nick and Grace are anything to go by, rather lovely. Except meeting the rest of them seems daunting. I'll need to discuss it with Dr. Hart before I can commit to it, if we're still seeing one another by the end of next week. The more he gets to know the real me and sees there's nothing much there, he'll lose interest like every other man I dated back in college.

"Are you done eating?" He kisses my forehead when the waiter leaves the check.

I nod, realizing he's cleaned his plate, but I didn't eat very much. He brought up so many things I want to think about, most of which make me nervous and twitchy. I'm not quite sure what to do with myself now that the date is ending. The easy answer is to slip into oblivion the only way I know how. I hate the thought the second it flashes across my mind. Worse, I despise myself for thinking it. More reason to open my flesh and let the ugly out. I dig my thumbnail into my palm much harder than before. A sharp pinch of pain courses through my hand and up my arm, bringing with it waves of blessed relief. Thank God. I sigh against his side and let it wash over me.

Nick eases away, and the warmth from his body leaves me feeling cold and detached. He pulls out his wallet and sets a few twenties into the black bill holder.

"Come on, Dove. It's time for the second half of our date."

His comment spins around my mind, drawing me back to the here and now. "There's more?" A flicker of renewed excitement comes to life inside my chest.

He smirks, and that sexy tilt of his lips makes me want to drown myself in all that is Nick Salerno.

"Of course! Come on." He holds his hand out, and I take it, knowing if Nick holds out a hand to lead me somewhere, I'll follow blindly. No questions asked.

★ ★ ★

Nick opens the passenger door and helps me out of the Camaro like a true gentleman. I stand outside the car and look up at the brightly lit sign. "Hole in One Mini Golf."

I smile widely and bite my lip. Before I can speak, Nick has me pressed up against the car. He lowers his face and leans his entire body against mine, which forces a small whimper to escape my lips due to the sheer ecstasy of his nearness.

"Mmm, I like how you respond to me, Dove. Means you're going to be dynamite in the sack."

I lick my lips and close my eyes, imagining our bodies naked, all over one another. Nick doesn't make me wait long. He presses his lips against mine so softly, I have to lean forward to get more. He grins against my mouth as I take the hint. He wants me to lead the kiss this time. Lifting up onto my toes has our pelvises aligning more directly. I can feel Nick's hardening length through his jeans. He groans, tips his head, and runs his lips along the column of my neck. A river of pleasure skitters along every one of my pores until I swear I can feel him... everywhere.

"You're so soft and sexy, Honor." He pushes his nose into the space where my neck and shoulder meet, nuzzling me there.

A ribbon of pleasure skims through my form, making me squirm and thrust against his hard body. I want more. I need more.

A subtle breeze chills the spots where Nick has kissed. I shiver, wrap both arms around his body, and run my fingers through his thick, dark hair. Each strand is like satin, flowing through my fingers.

"Fuck! Can't get enough of being close to you." Nick's tongue comes out, and he licks the length of my neck and across my clavicle. I can't recall a man licking along my skin with such dedicated purpose.

My skin feels electrified, hot, and arousal wets my panties. I groan, unable to take it anymore. I want this man more than my next breath. Grabbing a fistful of his hair, I wrap my other hand around his chin and force his face up to mine. I smash my lips over his. Within a nanosecond, he opens his mouth on a moan, and I take full advantage, licking him, sucking my fill. I plant the flat of my tongue against his and *taste* him, opening as wide as I can, starved for this man who's been driving me to distraction these past couple weeks.

The eager way I take his mouth, suck on his tongue, and bite at his lips has him reacting like a man ready to throw his woman over his shoulder. He runs his hands up and down the

AUDREY CARLAN

length of my back until one comes down over my ass and along the length of my denim-clad thigh, where he hikes my knee up to his waist. He curves his hips toward my center, rubbing his erection over the place I need him most.

I rip my mouth away from his, taking in as much air as possible. He doesn't stop, pressing me hard against the car, rubbing his length against me while his mouth nips and bites at the top of my breasts.

All I can think about is the two of us, no clothes, and a bed. "Want you..." I whisper into his ear and bite down on the sensitive cartilage.

He squeezes my ass in a bruising hold, grinding me on his cock. "Fuck yeah." He groans, runs his other hand up my shirt to my breast. He plumps the flesh, molding it in his hand. "Love your tits. Can't wait to get my mouth on them." He kisses the plush tops and licks along the edge of my bra line.

"Get a room!" comes a random voice, followed by a bunch of male chuckles.

Over Nick's shoulder, I can see a group of three teenaged boys, gesturing and laughing at us.

"Fuck her against the car, man!" one says and whistles.

"Hell yeah!" another boy calls out with a fist pump to the air.

I flush all over, my skin feeling even hotter than it was with Nick pushing against me. My brute allows me to drop the leg he had pinned while his body starts to shake. I hide my face against his neck, panting, attempting to calm the raging arousal consuming me.

Nick's laughter fills the air, and he places a sweet kiss along my neck before curling both his hands around my nape so he can lift my chin with his thumbs. He moves in and kisses me once, twice, three times sweetly before curving an arm around my shoulder and tugging me to his side and around toward the park.

"Guess we got carried away there." He squeezes the ball of my shoulder.

I wrap an arm around his waist because it feels like the thing to do, and anything that keeps me close to Nick makes me happy.

"Yeah," I offer shyly, watching our feet move toward the entrance.

"Are you embarrassed?" He nuzzles against my neck but keeps us moving forward.

I shrug and nod at the same time.

He laughs. "Nuthin' to be embarrassed about. We're two consenting adults who can't keep our hands off one another. Frankly, this is a new experience for me. I rather like it. Not in any hurry to take the edge off either."

I stop walking and turn in his arms until he stops and focuses on me.

"This is new for you?" I ask, wonder and awe in my tone.

He puts one hand on my shoulder and pushes a stand of hair behind my ear with the other. "Yeah, babe. I don't get all hot and bothered up against my car all the time. I don't get hard in restaurants just from being close to a woman, and I certainly don't get wood while teaching yoga."

That bit surprises me. I hadn't noticed him getting hard in any of those places, except at the car when I clung to his body like a leech.

"Dove, it's all you. *You* do that to me." He head-butts my forehead and smiles. "You make me lose my mind. I'm crazy about you."

"I don't... Why?" I have to know. None of it makes a lick of sense to me. I mean, I know I feel that way about *him*, but I'd never assume in a million years that Nick would have even a scant inch of the same desire for *me*. Of course, he's told me I'm pretty, and he likes my body. He's made that clear, but what he's saying goes far beyond that.

"Honor..." He looks deeply into my eyes. "Babe, who hurt you? What man made you doubt your effect on the opposite sex?" It's practically a whisper in the wind because I ignore it the second it comes out.

I shake my head and try to move out of his arms so I can get away and find the space I need. Nick doesn't allow it.

His voice alters, becoming softer when he continues. "Ah, don't worry, Dove. I'm going to erase everything that came before me. Starting tonight. It's me and you. In this together. Wading through the landmines of relationship stuff and enjoying the hell out of one another. How does that sound?"

I lick my lips and glance up. His eyes are honest, dark, and filled with courage. He could get me to agree to anything with just one look.

"Okay." I say it, but I'm not confident I mean it. I don't know what being in a relationship means. I'm not sure how to react, what to say and do. "This is new for me," I admit and drop my head, looking down at my feet. There's dust around the toes of my suede boots from the rock-and-gravel lot surface, but I can easily wipe them down. Wipe away the grime. I wish my internal filth was so easy to remove. My scars included.

Nick chuckles, causing me to lift my head and meet his gaze. "Honor, I'm so far outside of my comfort zone with you, I don't know where the hell this is going or how to get there. All I know is that I want to go there with you. Is that cool? Can we just do our own thing? No preconceived notions about what should and shouldn't be?"

The question wars in my head and twists around into him wanting to be causal. I understand casual. That's all I've ever had. "Are you talking friends with benefits? Did you want to see other people too?"

His head jerks back, his jaw getting tight right in front of me. *Uh-oh.* Not the right question. I step back, and he follows.

"No one but *me* is touching *you*. Got it?"

I swallow and nod quickly.

"And all this"—he gestures from his chest and down his ripped body—"is all yours, if you want it. We're exclusive. So fucking *exclusive*, you tell your mother you are off the market. Got me?" His words are as harsh as sandpaper over metal.

I nod, but his words ripple through my mind on repeat.

Exclusive.

All yours.

Off the market.

Little flickers of excitement pound a heavy beat in my heart. I'm going to need to spend some serious time dealing with this in therapy. Thank God my appointment is in a couple days.

"I want words, Honor. Give 'em to me. Say, *I'm yours, Nick. You are mine. For as long as we both want this.*" His tone is deathly serious. "Words, Dove."

I clear my throat. "I'm yours, Nick. You're mine. For as long as we both want it."

"Good girl. Now hold on to your man. Let's play some golf. Have you ever played mini golf?"

I shake my head. "No."

"Wonderful. Then I'll teach you. Would you like that?"

"Yes, Nick. I'd like you to teach me everything." I smile and glance up at his profile, bowled over by how masculine and graceful his genetics made him. I'll bet his mother and father are stunning too.

He looks down at me and grins. He's so beautiful, I want to kiss him again. He shifts his head down and steals my idea, planting a quick, hard kiss. "That's good, Dove. I'm an excellent teacher."

"I'll bet you are."

CHAPTER ELEVEN

THROAT
CHAKRA

The throat chakra couple will understand one another deeply. They can always relate to the other's needs and feel a great empathy toward one another. They often communicate with their thoughts and feelings rather than words.

NICHOLAS

The gym is full and pumping with patrons a few days later when I summon Honor via text to come visit me. We haven't seen each other since our date, but I've had her talking on the phone and texting regularly. There's something comforting about having a woman I can text and call at my leisure. She's the first person I text in the morning and the last one I talk to before I go to bed. Hearing her sultry, timid voice through the line eases my soul and calms the demons I work daily to keep at bay. Her voice gives me peace, allowing me to rest after a long work day. I can only imagine what it will be like when I have her in my bed. Sex is absolutely on the menu this week because I can't hold back any longer. I've known her three weeks. Twenty-one days and some change. It's the longest I've ever given a woman before getting inside her. Still, I'm not going to wait until Friday's aerial class when I have the time to take her out again and woo her properly. I need to *see* her. Put my mouth on hers and sip from her goodness.

She's light and sweet. Exactly what I need after a few days of working my ass off, growing my business, and teaching nonstop at Lotus House.

I *feel* her enter the gym before I see her. The air charges, sizzles at my back. Currently, I'm sparring with Trent in the ring. Bad idea to be distracted when a man like Trent Fox is in the vicinity. The second I'm off my game, he smashes a gloved fist into my ribcage.

"Ugh." I bowl over, take a breath, and lift my gaze to his, clutching at my sore side. *Damn it!*

He's grinning, white teeth looking blue around the mouth guard, sweat pouring down the side of his face. "Come at me." He waves a glove toward his body. "Don't tell me you're tired already. I've barely broken a sweat," the fucker goads me, but a flicker of white shimmers at my right, distracting me once more.

I turn my head and see my feisty best friend Mila Powers approaching Honor, Atlas hot on her heels. Shit, this is bad. Another punch hits my chest. "Fuck!" I roar and get my head back in the game before Trent makes hamburger out of me. He'd love it too. Dude's been readying for battle with me for months. Finally on break from pro ball, it's obvious he's been putting in the practice time in the ring.

Once I get into it, I bum rush Trent and nab a one-two punch. One fist crashes against his abdomen, the other to his chin.

His head flies back, neck veins popping with the effort as he stumbles. "Shit!" He bounces against the ropes where I let him have a second to catch his breath. The hairs on the back of my neck stand up again as I feel eyes on me from my side. I bounce from foot to foot, backing up. I can just see Honor on the side of the ring, Mila chatting away.

I groan. "You done?" I ask Trent, hope filling my tone.

Trent grins again and glances to the side. "Why? You got a hot date with a leggy blonde?"

"Man, don't you even think of looking at her." I growl possessively. He loses his mind if anyone so much as makes a face toward Genevieve, and he thinks he can prod my beast? Hell no.

Trent shifts fully, places his gloved hands on his hips, and holds my gaze but calls out to our friend. "Hey, Mila, who you got with you?" He winks, and I grind my teeth into the guard, digging in with all my worth.

"Oh, you mean this tall drink of water, Fox? This lovely lady is Honor Carmichael. She's here for Nick."

"Really?" Trent pulls out his guard, lifts his gloved hand, and tugs at the ties with his teeth, loosening them. Good thing he has his own.

"Dude..." I warn as he removes both gloves.

"What? Chill. I just want to meet your girl." He smiles an I'm-so-going-to-embarrass-you smile before heading to the opposite side of the ring.

I tug at my gloves, remove them, and then pull out my own mouth guard. "Hey, Dove. Glad you found the place okay." I rip off my head gear and lean against the ropes, my body wanting instantly to get closer to her.

She nods shyly, her eyes looking exceptionally blue. She's wearing a white sundress that is molded to her body perfectly and a light-blue cardigan. Half of her hair is up, parted down the center. If I didn't know any better, I'd swear she had been skipping through a field of daisies. Probably smells like it too.

I hold down the ropes, kick a leg over, and hop down next to her. Without saying anything, I slip my hand around her waist and tug her to my side. Her face tips up invitingly. I lean down and kiss her, long enough to get a tiny taste but not too long to embarrass her in front of my friends.

"Hi," she offers with a small smile when I pull back.

"Hi yourself." I curve her closer to me so I can nuzzle into her neck where her wildflower scent is strongest. I inhale deeply, letting her essence wrap around all of my senses. "Want to introduce you to some of my friends, although it looks like Mila's already skipped ahead."

Honor giggles, and it's the sexiest sound, all sugar-coated and sweet. I'd like to bite it off her lips back in my private office, but a humor-filled male voice intrudes. "You gonna make out all day or introduce your friends, bro?"

I roll my eyes and find Atlas with his arm looped around Mila's shoulders, his curly hair a mop-like mess falling into his eyes.

"Where'd you come from?" I lift my chin in his direction.

"Just picking up my wildcat." He grins. "So glad I have killer timing." Atlas reaches out a hand toward Honor. "I'm Atlas Powers, by the way."

Honor shakes his hand. "Honor Carmichael."

He knocks his head to the side. "And this spicy Latina is

my wife, Mila."

"We kind of already met." Honor smiles.

"I'm Trent Fox..." Trent offers a meaty hand.

Her eyes widen. "Oh, the professional baseball player?" Her pink lips open on a little gasp.

He glances at me and grins evilly. "That's right, sweetness."

I grind my teeth at his choice of endearment. He knows it pisses me off, too, the smug bastard.

"I've, um, seen you play. You're very good. My father considers you one of his best assets," she adds rather strangely.

Assets?

"Babe, what are you talking about?" I ask her.

She lifts a hand to her mouth and clears her throat before looking down and away. "Um..."

"Oh shit!" Trent curses. "You're Honor *Carmichael*, Timothy Carmichael's daughter." He rubs a hand through his hair and then laughs. "Feel like I'm speaking to royalty. Shoot, your father's the reason I'm considering another three-year contract."

He was considering leaving pro ball? What?

"You quitting ball, man?" Atlas jumps in on that last admission, the same way I do, but for me it's more internalized.

Honor's father is Trent Fox's boss? *What the everloving fuck?*

"I'm not exactly following. How is he responsible, and why didn't you mention the fact that you're considering leaving baseball to your best friends?"

Trent groans, lifts his soaked tank, and wipes his face with it. "Yeah, her dad owns the Ports and a couple other teams, but in the NFL, if I remember correctly?" He leaves the question open for Honor, but she just shrugs and twists her fingers around one another.

Shit, she's shutting down.

I wave my hands between the crew. "How's about you go back to the part about you quitting?"

"Ugh, I don't know, guys. Viv and I are talking about it. She wants another baby; I'm not getting any younger, and the game is tough on the body. I miss my wife and kid when I'm gone. Not to mention, my leg has been acting up again, and I don't know..." He lets out a frustrated breath. "Just getting old. But Tim, your dad, really wants me in for another three years. And he's offering me a truckload of dough, making it hard to turn down." He winks.

"Yeah, my father is good at throwing money at the things he wants. He never loses." Her voice is flat, devoid of emotion. Suddenly, she turns to me and runs her hands down my chest. A zap of electricity rips through my overtaxed muscles.

"Um, I'm glad I got to meet your friends, but I think I'm going to go." She hooks a thumb over her shoulder toward the door. Her entire body is ramrod straight and strung so tight, I feel her muscles bunch and jerk at her back.

I hook my arm around her waist and bring her up against my sweaty shirt. "Dove, you just got here. I want to show you around my place." I look up at my friends but keep her next to me. "Guys, we'll catch up later, and Trent, let us know what you end up deciding. Yeah?"

"Yeah, cool. I will. Honor, tell your dad I said hi, and I'm thinking about it. Okay?"

She gives a noncommittal "Mmm-hmm," which is more of a mumble.

The rest of the crew disperses while I lead Honor by the hand back to my private office. When I close the door, the sounds of the clanking weights, the men pounding the punch bags, and the normal hubbub fades away. Everything narrows down to one thing... Honor.

"Nick, I..." Honor starts, probably planning to give me some spiel about needing to flee, but I'll have none of it.

"Get your ass on my desk. Now," I growl, my need for her ramping up to a thousand degrees.

She widens her eyes, swallows, and then runs her fingertip along the black, beat-up desk, littered with paperwork.

"On top of it?" She leans both hands on the desk behind her while I hold my position.

I cross my arms over my chest so she can see them flex. Her eyes go right to the movement, and she licks her lips.

"Ass to the desk. I won't repeat myself." My words brook no argument.

She trembles but, shockingly, leans back, curls her hands around the edge, and shifts her weight on top. "Then what?" Her voice is breathy, sultry, and I can tell from here she's turned on, practically panting for it.

Commanding her was something I'd been toying around with. From our calls, her timid ways, and shy demeanor, I've figured out she needs a little push toward moving outside of her clearly defined box. It's part of why I don't think she knows what she wants to do with her inheritance or her life in general. I get the feeling my girl is floating in a place of uncertainty and unease. I want to be the one who breaks her of that. If me taking control, ordering her to get out of her head a bit, will ease the tension I see in her face and body, then, by God, I'm going to give it to her. With pleasure. Hers and mine.

Of course, it doesn't hurt that the idea of me telling her what to do and her doing it makes me hard as granite.

"Slip off your sweater."

She lifts her pale, shaking hands, unbuttons the single button, and shrugs her shoulders until it falls to the desk behind her. "And?" Her voice is rougher than normal, almost gritty.

I smile. "Lift up your skirt and open your legs so I can see your panties."

Her doe eyes seem to get bigger as her hands move down her thighs in a slow caress that spears me straight in the balls.

"Do it," I goad as my nuts swell and then tighten.

She's not unaffected either. Her chest is moving more rapidly with her increased breathing, making her tits stretch against the cotton of her simple girly dress, showing me a nice pair of erect nipples pushing against the fabric.

"You like me watching you do what I say, don't you? Teasing me with your gorgeous body in that flimsy dress?"

She bites her lip and lifts her chin as her fingers curve around the hem of her dress and drag it up her creamy thighs. A triangle of white lace is all I can see, but damn if I'm not going to touch.

"What do you want, Dove?" And right now, that endearment has never been so accurate. All in white, her wings spread out, leaving her center open and vulnerable just like the snow-white bird.

One of her eyebrows rises up on her forehead as she firms her jaw. A sense of pride fills my chest as I watch her find the courage to ask for what she wants. I get the feeling she's not often asked for something she needs. The people pleaser in her is probably used to it being the other way around. A giver, not a taker.

"I want you to touch me, Nick." Her words are small and

insecure. I plan to break her of that.

"Touch you? Is that all?"

She shakes her head almost imperceptibly. "No."

I drop my arms and get closer, though not close enough to touch. It kills me not to push her back on my desk, cover her body with mine, and pound into her wet heat. Because I know it's wet. The room fills with the scent of our combined arousal, making my dick harder by the second.

"You want me to touch you, and what else?" I step in between her legs and run my nose close enough to her skin that she should be able to feel my heat along her neck without the physical contact.

"Kiss me." She leans her neck to the side, and I move forward, laying a series of small kisses against her slender neck. The sigh she gives makes me want to dirty her up even more, but there's time for that.

"Where do you want me to touch you?" I press both hands to her knees. "Here?"

She nods, and I smile against her skin.

I ease my hands up to the middle of her thighs. "Here, Dove?"

"Yeah..." She breathes out the word and rolls her head back.

The temptation of her smooth, succulent skin is too much, and I give in just a little, kissing and licking along her neck and the upper parts of her breasts.

"So good." She hums, her eyes still closed.

"Where else do you need me?"

Her hands fall over mine on her thighs. She pushes my hands up toward her center. When I get to her pussy, I run both thumbs along the damp fabric I find waiting for me. I groan and press my thumbs into the lace. She tips her pelvis back against the desk, gifting me access to the heaven between her thighs.

"Do you want me to touch you here? Fuck you here?" I growl against her neck and bite down.

"Oh my, yes." She rolls her hips in offering.

I ease my fingers into the top of her tiny lacy panties and shred the skimpy sides until the fabric falls away from her. She gasps, and that sound is all I need to lose control.

Enough of this game. "Once I take it, Dove, it's mine. You want to be mine?" I grit my teeth, offering her one last out. There is no going back for me. We've been playing with something serious for the past three weeks, easing into it, but I'm not fucking around. I know this woman is what I want, but I want to know that every inch of her is mine to take, to fuck, to one day possibly even love.

"Please, Nick."

"Tell me you want this. To be mine?" I pet the lips of her sex, exhilarated by the wetness I find there. All for me.

Her eyes open, and they are dark, endless pools of lust. "I want you more than anything."

"Fuck yeah," I growl before taking her mouth in a punishing kiss.

She gives as good as she gets, her tongue warring with mine. She tastes of vanilla and mint, unique to her. I love every swipe of her flavor, but I need to *really* taste what's mine.

"Lean back. Offer your pussy to me, Dove."

Her body trembles as she nods. She places her elbows behind her and leans all the way back onto my desk. Her blond hair falls over the other side of my desk, along with papers, pens, pencils, and folders. I don't give a flying fuck.

"Christ, you're the most beautiful thing I've ever seen. Put your legs on the desk and open wide."

Her flat shoes fall to the floor with a loud *thunk* as her bare feet come up to the desk, momentarily hiding her nakedness. I'll have none of that.

"Open for me." I hold my hands in fists as she eases both legs open on the desk, baring it all.

I run both of my hands from her spread knees to the inside of her sex, where I pet the puffy pink lips that greet me. "You're so soft, pink, and mine." I open both lips with my thumbs, revealing *all*, before I hit my knees in front of the desk and lay my mouth over her wetness.

Her hands fly into my hair when I drive my tongue deep inside.

"Nick!" she cries out, but like everything I've come to know about Honor, even her sexy sounds are whisper soft. She moans, and her body tightens when I suck on her little clit and do a round of figure eights over the fat bundle of nerves. I want more of those sounds. She squirms and rocks her hips into my face, losing herself and getting into it. Just when I think she might be used to my ministrations, I lap at each lip and insert two fingers knuckle deep.

She's tight as fuck and just as sweet. Her taste is thick and honeyed, like a bee's nectar sipped right from the hive.

"Oh!" she calls and moans when I hook those two digits I planted, finding the spot that will make her cream all over my fingers. I rub and tickle that patch mercilessly. Her body rocks and rolls as she loses it to me.

"Nick, Nick, Nick," she says as she locks her thighs around my head and arcs her body, orgasming all over my tongue. I lap her up, tasting, loving, drinking deeply from her body.

"I can't fucking get enough," I growl around her pussy. My

face is dripping with her essence, and I lick my lips and pull away to take a breath. I'm dizzy with lust when I stand, stare at her open, throbbing cunt, knowing I'm never going to be done with this woman.

"You're going to have to sit on my face, day and night, Dove. New fucking job for you." I run my fingers through her pretty pussy and twirl around the reddened knot mindlessly with my thumb, deciding what I want to do next.

She jerks and sits up. "No, no, no. My turn."

Before I can figure out what she's got on her mind, Honor pushes my body back until I stumble a few paces, standing right in front of the leather couch I have on the opposite side of the room.

She hops off the desk, stands in front of me, and loops both hands around my gym shorts. Quick as shit, she tugs them down to my ankles. My erection pops up, happy to be free and pointed at the woman he wants to penetrate. I grip my dick and run my hand up the length until a drop of pre-cum exits the slit.

"Mine," Honor growls low in her throat. Then she lifts both her hands to my chest and pushes until I fall into a seated position on my couch. Once my ass lands on the leather seat, her knees slam to the rug. She places a small hand around the base of my cock and licks the pearl at the tip.

"Shit, Honor. I didn't expect you to return anyth..."

She cuts me off by swallowing me down her warm mouth.

"Shit. Fuck. Damn. Babe..." I get out and thrust my hips deeper. She takes it. Fuck, she takes it all. Every goddamned inch, way down her throat. I curl my hand into the hair at her nape and grip it hard. She moans, proving that she likes a little roughness. Hell, the perfect goddamned woman, and she's all for me.

Honor pulls back and then laps at every inch, as if she's getting to know my cock better. With one hand wrapped around my length, she rubs in her saliva, stroking up and down, tighter at the base, a thumb swirl at the top.

"Suck me, Dove. All way the back. Want your lips on me." I grip her hair tightly and tip her head back, touching her cheek with the head of my cock. "You gonna do what I say? Suck me the way I want you to?"

She nods, mewling with her desire.

"Words, baby. I want your words," I remind her.

Her eyes are half-hooded and filled with desire. "I want to suck you the way you want it," she whispers.

"Does it make you wet, sucking on me, knowing that beyond that door is a room filled with men and women who could come knock on the door at any time?"

She nods, even though I told her not to. I tighten my grip on her hair, pulling at the roots. "Words," I grate between my teeth.

"God yes, Nick. Please, let me make you feel good."

I ease her head back toward my cock so her mouth is hovering over the tip. The entire thing is bulging and ready to blow. It's been too long since I've had a woman's mouth on me.

She flicks at what she can reach with her tongue, sliding the tip into the slit at the top. I groan and let go of her hair, allowing her free rein to just get me off. "Just do me, babe. Do me how you want to. I'm so fucking gone for your mouth, your lips, your goddamned perfect pussy." I thrust up into her mouth as she goes down, giving me the best blow job of my life. Poems and romance novels are dedicated to this kind of stellar head. I think Shakespeare probably wrote about it too.

"Fuck!" My balls draw up tightly. The edgy prick of

pleasure and pain splits across my lower spine and flows through my groin. I curl my hand behind her neck. "Gonna come, Dove. You taking me down your throat?"

She hums and sucks harder, longer, with a wicked swirl at the tip before she takes me to the root, her nose against the close-cropped hairs at the base of my penis.

"Shit." I cry out as the orgasm roars through my body.

"Fuck." I thrust up into her mouth again, and she takes all of me.

"Damn." The expletive leaves when the last of my release slides out of me and into her waiting mouth.

She swallows it all, lapping at me until every last shudder has left. I come to with her head resting on my lap, my softening dick a few inches from her face, and my fingers easing along the length of her hair.

Content.

Honor seems content, sitting on her knees, while I come down off my high. She's giving me what I need in more ways than I could have ever possibly imagined. Submission and beauty.

I tap her cheek with my free hand. "You okay down there?"

She smiles, blinks prettily, and then nods.

"Dove, do I have to fuck your mouth again to get you talking to me?"

On that question, I'm gifted with her beautiful laughter.

"Crawl up here. I want your mouth on mine."

"'K," she says sleepily and stands as I pull up my pants and reach for her. She settles easily into my lap and against my chest.

I kiss her deeply and for a long, long time, wanting her to know that this was more than just a hook-up in my office.

When I'm sure she's been thoroughly thanked, I ease her back so I can look into her eyes.

"You know I didn't intend this. I wanted to court you properly before we fucked."

She smiles, and it lights up my heart. "I'm happy, Nick. Happy for the first time in a long time."

I mull that over. "I have to get back to work. I've got clients to train and a gym full of people to keep safe, but I want to talk more about this. We good for now? We'll talk more later after we've had some time to mull it over?"

"Yes. I'm so good."

"Yeah you are." I head-butt her forehead gently and kiss her lips again. She tastes a little like me and a lot like us. Basically, tasty as fuck. I want so much more, but instead, I stand and let her glide down my form to her bare feet.

I look around and notice the papers that were all over my desk are on the floor. Her panties are a shred of lace dangling off my ruler sitting in a cup. Everything's a bit of a mess, but I'll have to deal with it later. I sigh heavily, knowing it will be a late night, when all I really want to do is spend time with a goddess.

"Mind if I use your computer?" she asks randomly. "I want to look at a couple possible places for purchase. I'll pick up the papers too." She grins, and her cheeks pink up. *So freakin' pretty.*

"Course you can. *Mi casa es su casa.*" I kiss her once more, turn her around, and smack her ass. "Go ahead before I bend you over and fuck you against my desk this time."

Before I can hear a response, I turn on a heel and leave her behind. Looking at this woman in her sated glory would have me making good on that promise. Instead, I go back to the gym and dive into work. A smile on my face and a beautiful woman in my heart.

CHAPTER TWELVE

Knees Chest Chin Pose (Sanskrit: Ashtanga Namaskar)
This position is excellent for opening the throat chakra.
Starting in table position, you anchor your hands and ease
your chest to the mat first, leaving your tailbone pointing
to the sky. Flatten your forehead against the mat and
stretch out your arms, getting as flat along the mat with your
upper body as possible. Releases tension in the neck, arms,
and lower back.

HONOR

Nick's office is a complete and utter disaster. Not only is his computer archaic, it's slow as molasses.

When I first sat down, I turned on the computer and realized it was going to take a while to use his internet. Made me wonder what type of service he had, which led me to poking around the overflowing file cabinets.

Turns out, Nick may be an excellent yoga teacher, boxer, and lover, as I'm slowly finding out, but he's terrible at administrative business functions. His filing system is atrocious. Not to mention he has an entire file full of invoices that need to be mailed out, all of which are well over a week old. How can he bring in any money if he's not sending out the bills?

First things first. I pick up the papers and toss my panties into his top drawer, feeling bold and brazen in that decision. Of course, it took me a full ten minutes to decide to tease him with those. After the sex we had on his desk—and couch—I can only imagine how explosive it will be when he puts his huge penis inside me. The stretch alone will be insane. I cross my legs over one another and clench down, imagining his thick length.

That line of thinking leads me to other, racier thoughts about bending me over his desk as he mentioned. I think I'd like that. I've never been taken in such a primal way. I've seen it on TV or in movies a hundred times, but it's not something I've had the pleasure of experiencing with my past lovers. And none of them went down on me the way Nick did. I'm pretty sure college boys learn the art of cunnilingus through trial and error. Sadly, I must have been on the low end of the learning curve during that timeframe. In one go, Nick ruined me for all other men. I'm forever going to compare any future lovers with this man.

Future lovers.

If Nick heard me say that or even knew I was thinking it, he'd probably spank me. Imagining that spike of pain against my bare ass... That would be far more pleasurable than a razor blade to my arm or thigh.

Shaking off the sex thoughts, I evaluate each and every piece of paper in his office and then put each one into an appropriate pile. On top of his file cabinet, I find a big package of new manila folders, so I make good use of those to organize all of his files. I fold up the invoices, address the envelopes, locate a roll of stamps, and get those ready for mailing. After that, I set them on top of my purse, figuring I could drop them off at the mailbox for him.

Once I've got his desk organized, I tackle the rest of the file cabinet. Hours slide by as I work. I finish labeling and filing all the remaining paperwork before I approach the computer. His system for filing here is nonexistent too. There are at least fifty files on the desktop. Documents that need to be in an electronic folder, new folders that needed to be created. Then I found a file with his financials and dig in. I love a good budget and expense sheet. Not that he has one of those. I find a single spreadsheet an accountant drew up for him three years ago when he started his business. He hasn't kept good records this entire time. How the heck has he gotten past the IRS and state tax board?

I start detailing his expenses based on the credit card and bank statements I find. Apparently, he did do his taxes but didn't claim nearly enough, just the basics of the building and equipment. He didn't claim his own pay, or the utilities, the towels he uses to wipe down machines, or the cleaning products. I find so many potential deductions, I'm scowling while I'm setting him up with a new foolproof system.

"What are you doing?" I hear over my shoulder as I type in his electric bill from the last six months into a separate tab on my spreadsheet. How can he not know his normal utilities are a deduction?

I don't look at him, needing to finish the line item I was almost done with. "Categorizing your expenses. You're not writing off nearly enough on your taxes. You should be getting a load of money back this year. I'll make sure of it." I firm my jaw and click to the gas bills section.

Before I can continue, Nick turns me around in his rolling chair. "Babe, it's nine o'clock. I didn't even know you were still back here. I just locked up for the night and saw your car. I figured you'd left after our fun time earlier." He grins.

I shrug. "Your office was atrocious."

He laughs and taps my chin so I focus on his pretty green eyes. "This is true. But that didn't mean you had to clean it. Though, I'm not gonna lie and say I'm not thankful. I am. Thank you."

The simple thank you digs deep into my chest, making me feel light and warm.

"What else did you do?" He looks around, obviously noticing all of the files are put away. He walks over to the four-drawer, standing cabinet and pulls open the top one.

I jump up and to his side, rather excited to show him everything I've accomplished. "I've made files and alphabetized all of your members. Each person has their own file along with copies of their invoices that have been paid, due, or overdue. Then here, I've got this month's invoices and next month's along with a prewritten envelope and stamp so you're ahead of the game."

He grins and thumbs through the files, shuts the drawer, and pulls out the next. "Holy shit, Dove, this is incredible. You did all this for me?"

Heat suffuses my cheeks, and I bite my lip and shrug.

Nick grabs me around the waist, plastering me against his

chest. "You're too good to be true. The best head I've ever had, the tastiest pussy, and you're smart as hell. What am I going to do with all this goodness?" He curls his hands around my neck and then lays his lips on mine.

His arm slings across my back, bringing me as close as possible. I love that he does that. Makes me think he never wants me to get away. I melt into his arms and kiss him back until I've lost my breath.

He rips his mouth away with a voluptuous, "Ahh."

I chuckle and rub the scruff on his chin. I press my thighs together, still feeling the heated burn from earlier. Yep, it was delicious having his scruff against my skin.

"I also got your expense documents together and up-to-date. I still need to enter the rest of the year's credit card purchases and set up a solid quarterly plan for paying your taxes."

"Why?"

"So you don't get penalized by Uncle Sam, and it's easier to pay quarterly payments. Not such a large sum at the end of the year."

"Want a job?" He's joking, but it smacks me like a blow to the face.

What I did today... I enjoyed it. Got swept away in the administrative aspect of Nick's business. Maybe it was using the knowledge I'd been taught in school and being able to put the skills into practice, or maybe it was because I was helping the guy I'm seeing. Whatever the reason, I genuinely felt good doing it. Accomplished.

"I'd like to help out with your office needs if you don't mind."

"Ah, Dove..." Nick frowns and sighs. "I can't afford to pay

you."

Now that I know. I've just organized his finances. He needs to get his billing up-to-date and his finances totally in the black before he can ever consider taking on staff.

"No, I know. But I had...um...fun doing this for you. And I don't, well you know, have a job or technically need one." I run my finger up and down his black, ribbed tank, not sure how to best word what I want.

"You telling me you want to help out your man for nuthin'?" His jaw is hard, but his eyes are soft.

I purse my lips. "Kind of. It will allow me to get back into the business side of my degree. Kind of like being back in the ring again." I attempt to put it into terms that relate to his business.

He chuckles. "Babe, you don't know anything about boxing."

I shake my head. "No, you're right. I don't. But I do know how to run a business. If you'll let me help, I'd be so grateful."

His head jerks back, and he cups my cheeks. "You're offering to help me, out of the goodness of your heart; no one's offered that. I'm not stupid. Of course I'm going to take you up on it. But don't feel like you have to. You can do what you want when you want. Come and go as you please."

My eyes light up. "Can I have a key to the gym?"

He chuckles. "Yeah, babe, I'll have a key made for you. Now since we've both worked a long, hard day, how's about we go up to my pad and order some pizza?"

"Pizza?" I scrunch up my nose. That is not something I've had in over two years.

"Yeah, Dove, pizza. You know...cheese, pepperoni, olives, sausage, the good stuff. Do you like pizza?"

"Not sure. I haven't had any since college. I've kind of forgotten what my favorite is, but I like all the ingredients you've mentioned."

Nick shakes his head and grabs my hand, leading me out of his office and down the hall. "Hasn't had pizza in years. What am I ever going to do with you?"

"I can think of a thing or two," I offer in the sexiest voice I can muster, surprising myself that I'm being so forward.

He stops at the base of a staircase near the back entrance. "You want my mouth on you again, Dove?" Nick's tone is growly and suggestive.

"Um..." I sway my hips from side to side.

"That's a yes." He leans forward and puts a shoulder to my abdomen, where he lifts me into a fireman's hold.

I kick my legs. "Oh my goodness. Nick, put me down!"

"Not a chance. I'm taking you to my place, I'm eating you, and then we're ordering pizza and eating that. Then maybe I'll eat you again. You got a problem with my plan?"

I shake my head.

He growls in warning. Words. He always wants my words.

"No, Nick. No problem. All yours."

"Damn straight." He smacks my ass hard and takes the stairs two at a time.

★ ★ ★

My brute of a man did not lie about going down on me or eating the pizza last night. Though, at midnight he led me down to my car before moving things to the next step, claiming he wants to take me out again before we spend the night. Which I thought was sweet and yet oddly strange since we'd already had our mouths and hands all over one another's naked bodies.

I wiggle my toes and evaluate my pedicure, when Dr. Hart enters her outer office.

"Come on in, Honor."

"Hello, Dr. Hart!" I practically skip into her office.

"It's Monet, again, Honor. And you seem..." Her eyes narrow, and she taps at her bottom lip with her pencil. "Happy."

I sit on her couch and spread out my flowery new dress Grace helped me pick out. "Oh, I am."

She smiles softly. "Would you care to tell me about this sudden change in your demeanor?"

Playing with my skirt, I trace a bold red flower that twines into an orange one. "It's Nick."

"The new yoga-teaching beau?"

I smile. "Yes, he's a boxer too. Owns a gym. And guess what!"

Dr. Hart frowns, which is weird for her—she doesn't usually—but I continue on anyway.

"He's letting me organize his office. I'm going to help run his gym. He's absolutely the worst at keeping files, and managing his money, and well, anything that involves the side that's not physical or related to the gym's equipment or how to deliver a punch correctly." I say all of that in a flurry of excitement, not wanting to forget a moment of such a great, new experience.

Another frown.

Again, I carry on. "And he's going to take me to meet his family on Sunday. He has a big family." I smile in front of Dr. Hart for the first time in what feels like forever.

"Five sisters?" She tosses out the exact number of Nick's siblings.

I gasp in awe. "Why yes. And they make wine. Well not all of them, but most of them. Nick wanted to be his own man after he..."

"Left the army." She finishes my sentence.

This time I narrow my gaze and frown. "Dr. Hart, I'm getting the feeling that you know my Nick."

She nods but issues her own question. "Before we get to that part, how about you start from the beginning and tell me how you two met and when he asked you out?"

"Actually, that was a strange accident." I beam, feeling the flutter of the memory when I was afraid to take his class after meeting him. "Well, three or so weeks ago, I wasn't going to go to his class again because I was embarrassed, and frankly, the man makes me nervous. Maybe not so much anymore, but being in his presence is like having a horde of bees buzzing all around me. I'm twitchy, itchy, and uncertain but exhilarated and excited at the same time. You know?"

With that question, Dr. Hart smiles. "I understand that feeling perfectly. I get it every time I see my husband, Clay."

"Yeah, I can imagine. Your husband is a hunk." I glance at the picture on her desk. Though, I still prefer the Italian Stallion. Nick is beyond my fantasy man.

"That he is. Now how did you meet up the second time?"

"Oh. Sorry. I ended up taking his sister Grace's class, and he had decided to take her class that day too. After the class, he asked me out."

"And you said yes."

"Um, kind of. More like he made me say yes." I chuckle. "I'm not sure Nick is the type of guy women say no to. Nor do I think he'd allow that of any female he was courting." Not that he's courting me anymore since he said we're *exclusive*. And after yesterday on his desk, and last night at his house, there isn't anyone I'd rather spend my time with.

"No, on that I would say you are right," she responds, making it clear she does in fact know my Nick.

"Dr. Hart, I'm sensing there's something you're not saying."

She nods. "Usually that's my line." Dr. Hart's shoulders slump, and she rubs at her belly as if it's a nervous gesture. Definitely not the response I was expecting with my great news.

"Let me ask you this. Is this Nick the same Nick that teaches at Lotus House in Berkeley? Nick Salerno?"

"Yes! You do know him." I smile widely, but she doesn't return the gesture, which makes me instantly uncomfortable.

Dr. Hart sighs, and it sounds heavy and fraught with unease. "I know him very well, I'm afraid."

"Afraid? Are you trying to tell me he's not a good man, that I shouldn't date him?" Then it slams into me like a baseball ball bat to the back of the head. "Oh, my God! Have you dated him?" I cover my mouth with my own hand as the image of Dr. Hart and Nick kissing enters my mind. A sourness floods my gut and swirls, dangerously mixing up the cappuccino I had before attending my session.

My doctor shakes her head. "No, I haven't dated him. He's a friend, a brother type. I spend a lot of time with many of the same people."

"Okay. Thank goodness. So you know he's a good guy, and you're not warning me off him?"

She lifts her hands and waves them in front her. "No, no, not at all. Nick Salerno is an amazing man, and if you've caught his eye, and he wants to be with you, that says something about you. It just also means I have intimate knowledge of the man you're very likely going to want to talk about more often in therapy."

"Which means what?" I twist my fingers together, sensing the unease filling the air in the room.

Dr. Hart lets out a long breath. "Honor, what it means is that it may not be ethical for me to continue being your doctor." Her eyes are somber and filled to the brim with what I can only guess is sadness.

No. Oh no. I shake my head. Shivers of fear and dread ripple up my spine and out my arms. I clench my hands into fists, digging my nails into my palms fiercely with no concern whatsoever if I wound them.

"No. I'm finally doing good with someone. *With you.* I need you, Dr. Hart. You can't turn me away." Anxiety and alarm prickle at my skin as if hundreds of ants were crawling all over my body. I start to scratch at the length of my forearm, digging into the skin to ease the tension. It doesn't work.

Monet gets up, her burgeoning belly seeming to lead the way before she sits and grabs my hands so I can't move them along my tingling nerves.

"Honor, I don't want to lose you as a client. I'm just worried about being able to give you a blind perspective on your relationship and the inner workings of it when I know both parties. Do you understand my position? What I'm saying?"

I lick my lips and grit my teeth.

She doesn't want to see you anymore.
She's probably been looking for a reason to get rid of you.
Poor, stupid Honor.

"Let's talk about this. Figure out a plan. I can recommend

an associate if that's what we need to do. But there are options we can discuss first..."

Her words are a jumble in my mind. Just another person who wants to get away from me.

Honor the cutter.

The loser.

The rich little brat whose brother killed himself and left her behind, alone.

"Honor, what's going on in your mind? What are you thinking right now?" Her words seem genuine, but how do I know that for fact anymore? She wants to get rid of me. Pawn me off on someone else.

"What do you care?" Tears prick the back of my eyes as the anger and distrust seep into my mind.

Her head jerks back, and a hand goes over her heart. "I care very much. We've been in a professional relationship for months now. Of course I care about your well-being. But I need to do what's best for you as well. And that may be finding you another therapist who doesn't know you or Nicholas personally."

I huff. My well-being. All she cares about his getting rid of me.

She's lying. Just like everyone else. My mother, my brother, Sean. For all I know, Nick is lying to me too.

I stand up, ripping my hands away from hers and pushing them through my hair, tugging at the roots. The prick of pain at the top of my scalp flares with a brilliant flicker of ease. Just one blessed speck of freedom in that split second of pain firing through my system.

"Fine. Whatever you want, Dr. Hart. I'll save you the trouble of letting me go as a client and just leave now. You no longer need to worry about poor Honor Carmichael."

I rush out of her office, feet moving faster than my mind can keep up. Her voice is calling for me to stop, to stay, as I step onto the elevator.

"Honor, please..." She makes it to the metal doors where I stand. She's holding her pregnant belly and breathing heavily. I almost feel sorry for her, but I don't allow the part of me that cares to the surface. Only the dark, numb side of me is present.

She takes a deep breath. "I'm not trying to hurt you. I'm trying to help you the best way I know how."

"By pushing me away." I shake my head. "You're just like everyone else."

This time she shakes her head and reaches for me, but the doors on the elevator start to close. I hold out my hand. "It's fine, Dr. Hart. I'm nobody. You don't need to worry about me anymore. I'm sorry I took up so much of your time. Have a nice life." I finish as the doors close, leaving me in the steel metal box alone.

Alone is where I'm supposed to be. I'm not good enough for anyone. Especially Nick. I'm not sure what I was thinking. Living a lie these past several weeks.

He asked me to go to his mother's. I'm not good enough to meet anyone's mother, let alone Nick's and all his sisters. Even Grace. She's everything I'm not. Love and light and pure beauty. She's untainted by the world and doesn't need a toxic friend bringing her down.

Absolutely not. There's no way I can show my hideous face in front of people who are worthy of so much more.

The elevator whooshes me down to the lobby level. Tears streak my face as I dash out of the building and hail a cab.

Just as I get into the cab, my heart cold and dark, my cell

phone rings. I don't even have the state of mind to view the display before hitting the "answer" key.

"Honor Carmichael, you ungrateful little heathen. You better answer your mother when she speaks to you." Her words are acid, pouring over my soul, making gaping holes I'll never be able to fill.

"I'm here." Physically.

"The staff have informed me that you apparently moved out without giving word."

"Yes."

"And you're living in a hotel..." she starts.

"It's my hotel, Mother." I answer on autopilot because it's true. My grandparents left me several, but when Hannon passed, I got all of his money and inheritance too. The hotel I'm in is one I own outright.

"How dare you disgrace our family name. Living in a hotel like a gypsy." She tsks, and I can imagine her waving her finger at me like she's done more times than I can count over the years when I've disappointed her.

"Pack your things, and come back home. If anyone has found out about your little stunt, I'll tell them you were enjoying the spa services and checking in on your property."

"I'm not coming home." Where the gumption to make that statement came, I'll never know. Maybe some latent juju from Nick popping to the surface. My stomach twists and rolls with every breath I take.

She skips over my comment and continues her rant. "And how dare you miss a date I scheduled for you. Do you have any idea what position you put me and your father in? This is the son of one of his top business partners. It's a coup that he's even willing to consider merging our families with a little piece of nothing like you. Thank God you have a pretty face, because the good Lord knows what you're doing to the rest of your hideous body. Marking yourself like a common criminal."

"Mother, stop..."

"You are so beneath your genetics it's despicable. Every day I wonder why it wasn't you instead of your brother. At least he could have been cured of his disease."

Rage unlike anything I've ever experienced pours through my system like red-hot lava.

"He was gay! Hannon was gay, not sick! He didn't have a disease. You and Father threatened the only good thing he had in his life. So he took that option away. It's all *your* fault he's dead!" I screech into the phone.

The cab driver ignores me completely. I don't care what he thinks. I don't care what anyone thinks anymore.

"Don't be so melodramatic. Hannon was weak. I'm training you to be strong. Don't you see that?" Her voice is ugly and laced with hatred. "One day you will thank me for setting you straight. Now I expect you to be back in your room and dressed to entertain. We're having a ladies luncheon tomorrow with all of your friends."

"They are not my friends." Each word she spits out makes the holes inside of me larger, to the point where I don't know where I am or who I am anymore. "I'm not coming home." It's the last thing I say before I power off my phone.

I have one destination in mind. One place to go, to take myself where the hurt subsides and the ugly bleeds out. I need it badly.

The remaining minutes fly by in a haze of self-doubt and loathing as we roll up to my hotel. I pay the cab and rush to the private penthouse elevator. I don't look up from the floor because I don't want anyone to stop me from where I need to be. What I need to do.

The guilt and the hate war inside me.

Dr. Hart doesn't want to treat me anymore. She doesn't care about me.

My mother hates me.

I hate me.

Go to Nick's. He'll be there for you. Hannon's voice slips into my subconscious, but I press against my temples. Not now.

I need this.

My keycard opens the door, and I rush into the bedroom and then the en suite bathroom, where I pull out the drawer. Everything inside falls to the floor in a clatter of makeup products, brushes, combs, and the small zip-up kit I've hidden in the very back. The one I haven't used since I met Nick.

I open the two-inch by four-inch case that used to hold nail clippers and pull out a shiny, new double-sided razor. I push up the sleeves on my forearms, point the tip of the blade to my skin and press in. A bright crimson drop of blood appears and with it...my salvation.

Digging in, I swipe down in a three-inch line. Blood pools and drips down my arm, but it's not enough. The pain is never enough. My tears are scalding hot as they run down my cheeks. More. I need more. I stick a new bare expanse of skin, lower than I've gone before. The henna is nowhere near this this area. I don't care. I flick my wrist fast this time. Opening a larger wound, digging deeper. Farther than I've gone before.

Pain, nothing but blessed pain fills the empty void surrounding my heart and mind.

I blink around the tears and let the instant bliss kick in. It's heady, reminding me of when Nick is kissing me. Gripping the blade tightly in my palm, I feel the double-sided razor slice my skin. I close my eyes and slump to the side along the floor.

It's okay now. I'm better here, I tell myself as my vision fades in and out. Red pools around my arm and wrist, making a small puddle on the tile floor. So much blood. But it doesn't matter.

Nothing matters.

I'm nobody.

Not worthy.

Even Nick will forget about me soon enough.

Nick, the sweet, brute of a man, is the last thing I envision when the world around me goes blessedly black.

CHAPTER THIRTEEN

THROAT
C H A K R A

It is important for a throat centered individual to nurture honesty and self-control. If the chakra is blocked, lies and untruths come to the surface more easily.

HONOR

I dip in and out of consciousness seeing nothing but white.

White walls.

White blankets.

White coat.

I blink a few times and feel my hand being lifted, held by the warmth of another. I turn my face to the side and find Sean in his white lab coat. Standing next to him is a brunette woman I've seen before but can't place.

"Bunny? Wake up, honey." He pats my hand and kisses the top as the brunette walks to the other side of the bed.

She opens my eyelids with thumb and forefinger and then flicks on a light, blinding me. "Dr. Tillman, her pupils are equal, round, and reactive to light."

"It's okay, Dr. Alexander. I'll take care of her stats. She's family."

Family. The word makes me grimace. Our family unit died along with my brother. It's me who's been holding on to Sean, not letting him go be happy and free with his new partner.

I turn my head to the other side, not wanting to look at his kind face and the memories that go with it.

"No way, Honor," he snaps, and I glance back to him. "No way in hell you're avoiding me. You scared the bejesus out of me. When they brought you into emergency, honey, I lost it." His voice cracks, and he swallows. "I couldn't even tend to you. I watched them pump blood into you and save your life."

I swallow around the cotton coating my throat. Save my life. "What? What am I doing here?" I don't remember what happened. The last thing I can recall is being hurt and angry with Dr. Hart, and ugh, my mother. She called, but it's all a blur.

Sean's jaw tightens, and his lips go white and flat. "The maid at your hotel found you earlier this morning, lying unconscious in a pool of your own blood on the bathroom floor, with barely a pulse. A razor blade clutched in the palm of your hand."

I groan and attempt to lift my arm to my face to wipe along my eyes. The brunette holds my arm down and shakes her head. The other has an IV sticking out of it and attached to tubes going to a monitor and bags of fluids. This is a nightmare.

"Honor, you took a razor to your arm and wrist and cut up the palm of your hand pretty severely. Not exactly the first time if what's hidden under the henna is any indication." His eyes soften and flash with concern. "Bunny..." He uses the nickname he and my brother always used. An old joke from the past. "You tried to take your life last night?" His voice cracks, wracked with unspoken emotion.

Again, I turn my head and try to remove my hand from his. He doesn't let go. Thoughts of what I must have looked like when they found me, what he must have seen when I arrived by ambulance... Shame coats every pore, and I close my eyes. Hot tears leak down my cheeks as his words delve into my psyche.

Did I mean to go that far?

When I lost Hannon, I wanted to. Thought about it so many times, but I was always a coward. I could never take it that far. Something always stopped me.

Sean curls a hand at the back of my neck and turns my face to look into his eyes. "I didn't know how deep your grief went. I'm sorry, Honor. I should have been there for you. Watched out for you. Hannon would have..."

"Hannon's dead," I say flatly. "He's gone, and he's never coming back." The words on my tongue sting like acid, each one hurting more than the next, but it's the honest truth. I need to truly accept that fact and stop living my life based on the loss of him.

"Honor..."

Tears pour from my eyes. "Just go. Leave me alone. That's all I'm ever going to be is alone." The dread in my voice is undeniable.

"The fuck you are!" A deep growl I recognize instantly flares against my senses like a wall of flames.

My eyes immediately go to the open hospital door.

"You better get your hands off my woman, Doc, or you and me are going to have some serious problems." Nick's tone is rife with danger and fierce possessiveness. No one's ever claimed me the way he did in that moment.

Sean removes his hand from around my neck and my upper thigh.

Oh, this is bad. So, so, bad.

"Excuse me. Who the hell do you think you are? This is my sister," Sean says loudly, and for a second it makes my heart swell with love for him, remembering a time when hearing him say that would have been old hat. Not so much anymore. Hannon's gone, and Sean is moving on with his life. I'm not his responsibility. I'm not anybody's responsibility.

"You're her brother?" Nick looks at Sean's much darker features, the exact opposite of me, confusion rife within his features.

"Her brother's dead," Sean states, devoid of emotion, and that sends an arrow straight through my heart because I know how very true it is.

"What the fuck?" Nick shakes his head. "Get out of my way." He pushes past Sean and comes to my side. He gets low, his eyes assessing me from head to toe and zeroing in on my bandaged arm, wrist, and palm. His jaw gets tight as his dark gaze flashes with anger. "Who hurt you?" Both of his hands go into fists. "Give me a name. A single name and I'll take care of him."

Tears fall down my cheeks again. I'm not worthy of this man. "Go home, Nick. You don't know what you've stepped into."

It's as if I verbally punched him in the nose with how he jerks his head back. Slowly he inhales, nostrils flaring as he clenches his teeth before leaning his forehead against mine. His breath is minty fresh when it floats over my skin. "Dove...

my woman's hurt. I'm *here*. Right *here* until you're better. That's how this is going to go down."

"Your woman? Nick!" The brunette who had tended to me smiles. I think Sean called her Dr. Alexander. She enters the room this time with a new set of bandages. Mine are soaked through.

"Amber? You taking care of my woman?" He doesn't miss a beat and apparently knows my female physician.

The pretty doctor grins, lifts her head to the sky, and places both of her hands in a prayer pose. "Thank the good Lord above for this blessing." She breathes in obvious gratitude and then lifts my arm. "And yes, I'm taking good care of her."

Amber is Dr. Alexander, which reminds me of how I know her. It's from that one time when I'd been at Sunflower Bakery with Grace. The doctor was holding hands with her husband, having coffee with the yogis. Great. Now everyone's going to know what I've done.

A sense of dread mixes with the filth of why I'm lying in this hospital bed. A sour taste blooms on my tongue as it dawns on me that everyone is going to find out my secret. I reach for the pink cup of water near my side, but Nick gets to it first. Johnny-on-the-spot that one, titling the straw to my eager mouth.

"I'm sorry, Honor. Who's this man that's claiming to be your mate?" Sean asks, nonplussed. He's been in my life for many years, and this is the first he's hearing of him. I should have told him about Nick sooner, but I didn't know where it was going. I had no idea he'd want to be with me. As in, the relationship type. And now here he is, holding my hand, petting my cheek, taking up every ounce of personal space I have.

"Um...he's Nicholas Salerno. My uh..." I let the sentence

fall off because we haven't exactly had that discussion.

"Like I said, I'm her man. Now can you update me on her prognosis?" he demands flippantly, his eyes never leaving mine for a second.

Sean narrows his gaze and then looks to me. His shoulder falls, and he frowns. "I'm afraid I can't do that. Honor will have to discuss with you what happened on her own terms. Dr. Alexander? Are you done?"

While the men were verbally battling, the good doctor promptly and rather efficiently changed my soiled bandages.

"Thank you," I murmur, wishing she'd just leave. Wishing they'd all leave so I could wallow in peace.

Sean and Amber exit the room and close the door.

"Fuck, babe." Nick sits in the chair by my side and brings his face close, kissing me. The gentle press of his lips is worshiping, reaffirming. His kiss speaks of intense relief and concern. When he pulls away, he doesn't go far, only a few inches from my face. "How did this happen?"

I swallow, firm my resolve, and decide if he knows the truth, maybe he'll be so disgusted he won't bother with me anymore. It's as good a plan as any. He deserves to know what kind of woman he's committing to.

Using up every ounce of courage I have, I say the words I'm sure he wouldn't ever expect to hear.

"I cut myself. I've been hurting myself for years. This is just the first time it went too far. Apparently, I passed out last night on the floor in my hotel. The maid found me in a pool of my own blood. She must have called an ambulance."

Nick clenches his teeth, his jaw firming into what looks like chiseled granite. I continue undaunted. If it gets him to leave me alone, free himself of the nonsense that he should be with me, then all the better.

"Sean Tillman, the doctor who was here, is my dead brother's ex-boyfriend. He used to be family. Now I don't know what he is. So that's it. You can leave now." I inhale slowly. "Nick, you don't need or deserve any of this."

He scowls before responding. "How's about you shut it and let me decide what I need!" His voice is hard, firm, and without a hint of where he's headed with his thoughts on what I've just said.

To say I'm frightened to hear his reaction is an understatement. I'd rather have holes drilled in my teeth than listen to him tell me how horrible I am or see the pity in his eyes. It's a look I'd recognize anywhere because my mother gives me the same one anytime I'm within touching distance. Whatever he has to say and throw my way, I'll take. I deserve whatever disgust and disappointment he's going to spew anyway. I'll store it all inside. I'll need it in order to let him go.

"What led to what took place last night?" His question is calm and direct. Not a lot of emotion, which I appreciate.

I lick my lips and focus on his gaze, trying to make sense of his question. "Each time is different. Last night went too far."

"That's not what I asked, Dove, now is it?" His words this time come in a bear-like growl. "I asked what happened yesterday to spur this action? The night before you were fine. We talked on the phone. You said you had an appointment in the morning and would come to the gym to start work. You didn't show. I worried. You didn't answer your phone. I had no way to contact you. I was out of my mind, Honor. I knew with my entire being something was wrong and had no fucking way to fix it. Do you know what that's like?"

If the bed wasn't holding me up, I'd have fallen through the ground. "Nick...I'm sorry. I wasn't in the right frame of mind."

He curls his hand around my neck and swipes at a tear falling from my cheek. "I get that. But the only way I found you was by calling every hospital until one of them had a patient with your name. Do you have any idea how fucking scared I was? Do you, Honor?" This time his voice is full of emotion. Fear, anger, concern, and a little of something I can't begin to define.

"Nick..."

He cuts me off before I can genuinely apologize.

"No, Honor. I want to know what happened before you hurt yourself. The straight-up truth."

Tears cloud my vision as I think back to yesterday. I started the day out happy. Excited, even. "I, uh, went to see my psychologist. Dr. Hart."

He tips his chin up and sets a heavy hand to my thigh and the other to my shoulder. It's as if he can't stop touching me. "Monet Hart?"

I close my eyes and take a breath, trying not to revisit the emotions that came with yesterday's episode. "Yes. She figured out that the two of you are friends."

"Yeah, and? She's a great doctor, good at what she does, I hear. Amazing woman too. Her and her husband, Clay, are some of my best buddies."

Him touting her praise rankles my nerves, but I shouldn't care. He'll leave me soon enough, so it doesn't matter what he thinks of other women. "Yes, well be that as it may, she said she couldn't be my doctor because the two of you were friends."

Nick scrubs at the scruff on his chin; the sound of his whiskers scraping along his palm is like a balm to my battered soul. It would be so easy to drown in his nearness and the peace he brings with him, to wrap my arms around him and never let go...but it's wrong. Bringing Nick down to lift myself up is not how a healthy relationship works.

"And this upset you?"

I grimace. "She's the first doctor I've ever felt comfortable with. The only woman I confided in, and told all of my...um, *secrets*." I glance down at my bandaged arm and then back at him. "I thought she cared..." I can hear my own voice rising, but I barely recognize it.

Nick rubs one hand along my leg and thigh and grasps my shoulder with the other. "Babe, I'm sure she does care."

I shake my head furiously as the tears wet my nightgown. "You see, there's where you're wrong. The second she could find a way to remove me from her life, she did. Just like everyone else. And then after I ran out of her office, my mother called. Told me how horrible I am as a daughter, demanded I move back home, go out with that man..." I ramble on. What I don't realize is the beast awakening in the man next to me. I'm so focused on getting it all out, easing my conscience for a moment, I don't notice what I've said until the pressure on my thigh turns almost painful, and I glare up at Nick.

His eyes are daggers of rage, and his mouth is formed in a scowl. "Your mother normally say off-color things to you?"

I nod, afraid to say anything more.

"Set you up with men you don't want?"

I nod again.

"She hurt you with her words a lot?"

More nodding.

Nick stares into my eyes, and I swear he's seeing straight through to the barely flickering light of my wounded soul. This man can ruin me with one look. One word. A simple touch of his hand. I want him desperately, but he's better off not wanting me. I could so easily imagine a good life away from all the despicable things surrounding me if I only had him. I'd give it all up. The money, the status, anything to have him. Except, I'm not enough. He deserves perfection, not a broken shell of a woman with nothing more to offer than a scarred body and torn heart.

He looks at my face and focuses on my bandaged hand. Every so slowly he lifts my hand, placing it into his. With a featherlight touch, he runs three fingertips up my exposed inner arm. When he reaches the first hidden line, he traces its length. A shiver ripples through me.

"What brought this on?"

I choke on a sob but don't so much as flicker my gaze away from his. He waits patiently. "My mother was angry when I slipped and collided with a waiter at a social function. He dropped several glasses of wine and champagne. My lack of grace took away from her function and laid waste to a disaster people spoke of later. She didn't like that and made sure I knew it."

He squints, his pupils narrowing to tiny dots. He brings his fingers to another jagged scar. I'd opened that one twice, which is why it's more raised than the others.

"This one is worse," he says conversationally, but each finger to one of my sins is opening me up anew; the physical manifestation of the blood not being present doesn't matter. It's the raw truth that leaves with each confession.

I shake my head. "No. Sometimes I reopen them. It makes a bigger scar," I admit, still holding his gaze.

Nick's lips curl into a frown. "And this one?" He reaches another one.

"I missed Hannon."

"And how did missing your brother turn into needing pain?"

Needing pain is not usually how I imagine others would describe what I've done. It's absolutely the exact right description for why I do what I do, but it's not often that someone understands it so completely.

I shrug, not wanting to answer.

"Words, Honor. You owe me that." And he's right, I do. He's here, still with me, and I don't know why he hasn't left the room and run as far away as he can get from the broken mess that I am.

I lick my lips and let my heart offer a response. "At least if I have pain, I feel something other than grief. Sadness. The worst is when I just feel numb. The pain takes that all away, and for a time, I feel..."

"Relief."

I suck in a sharp breath and pull my arm away. My heart pounds a beat so hard in my chest, I can barely breathe. "Nick..." I nearly suffocate with the power that single word holds.

Nick grabs my hand and holds it between both of his before running his hand back down my arm to feel each scar. "I know a thing or two about needing to feel something, Dove. Watching men die for their country, my brethren, men I worked with, cared for, and then lost within a blink of an eye. It changed me. Gutted me in ways I can't begin to explain. It's why I lift iron. Punish my muscles. And when that's not enough, I get into the ring, punch any man who dares to get in and fight. It may not be cutting open my skin, but it hurts, every day. I need the pain to keep the demons away."

I gasp, his words digging so deep within me, I don't know

where he begins and I end. I sit up and lock my hands around his neck, needing him closer, plastered against my body. The urge is overwhelming. He must feel it too because he stands, scoots onto the bed, and tucks me along his chest. His chin rests against the crown of my head, surrounding me fully with his embrace.

"Honor, I get you on a level no man will ever understand. And I want to teach you healthy ways to get through your depression, anger, and grief so that the bite of the razor doesn't call to you. Never does again." He clears his throat. "Would you let me inside, let me help you deal with these wounds?"

Let him inside.

Help me.

It all sounds so surreal. The only man who ever cared was Hannon. And what Nick shared, he does understand, maybe better than I do.

"Why?" I need to hear what is compelling him. What's inside this good and honest soul that wants to trudge into the ugly unknown with me.

"Because when I'm with you, my demons disappear. You do that for me. Your presence, your smile, the goodness I see every time I look at you. It's as if you were put on this earth for me and me alone. You're my broken dove, but together, we'll fly free. Free of the pasts that haunt us." Nick runs his fingers through the tendrils of my hair before continuing. "It may be selfish of me to want you close, to be that shoulder you cry on, but babe, every time I hold you, a little of my own hurts fade away."

I close my eyes and nuzzle my nose against the center of his chest. "I want you, Nick, but I don't want to bring you down." My voice quavers and shakes.

He tips my chin up with his thumb and forefinger. "Hey, you only lift me up. Remember what I said: We brave it together; we fly free together. You and me. Maybe that's why I'm attracted to you. Aside from your gorgeous face and big tits, that is." He grins and kisses my forehead.

A small chuckle slips from my lips, and I can hardly believe I'm in a hospital bed, snuggled into the most amazing man's chest, after having suffered a tragedy I didn't mean to inflict on myself, and here I am laughing. Not hardy-har-har type guffaws, but like the light flickering in the center of my chest is getting bigger and brighter. And it's all because of this man.

"Do you think you can do that? Let me be there for you?"

I press my lips together and think about what he's offering. It's almost too good to be true. "I can try." I'm almost afraid of the words as I whisper them, not wanting to do anything that could let him down again.

"That's the best I can hope for. And while we're doing that, we're going to work with Moe to figure out your therapy."

I frown. "Moe?"

"Monet Hart. She's Moe to all of us."

I nod.

"Have you called her? Does she know you're here?"

I shake my head and snuggle close, suddenly so tired. My mind feels like it's been on a merry-go-round, which hasn't stopped spinning in days. I just need a moment to breathe.

For long minutes, Nick runs his fingers through my hair and holds me close as best he can around the IV and bandages. He kisses the top of my head and whispers. "I'm going to be here for you. I promise you're not alone anymore."

His words sound like a benediction, a promise. I curl my

fingers into the soft fabric of his T-shirt, take a deep breath, and sink into his embrace. "Please don't make me love you..." I sigh. "I'll never recover when you leave."

Nick's arms tighten around my body, and he tugs the blanket over us both. "Not going anywhere. You rest, get better so I can take you home. We'll worry about everything else one day at a time. One day at a time."

The last thing I hear is Nick's steady heartbeat lulling me to sleep, and I feel the press of his lips against the crown of my head.

CHAPTER FOURTEEN

Mermaid Pose (Sanskrit: Eka Pada Raja Kapotasna)
This pose will open your heart and chest, expand your flexibility, and you'll look beautiful doing it. This pose is an advanced level pose and a variation of pigeon pose. Start this pose by placing one leg out behind you. Bring the other knee in front of you in a bent position so that the heel of your foot crosses under the body. Then bend over your knee, learning to stretch that hamstring, quad, and leg in a different way. You can use your hands to press the upper body up and arch back as much as you are comfortable. Once you are flexible enough, you can bend the back leg up, foot pointed to the sky, and grab onto the foot during your arch.

NICHOLAS

"Nick? What can I do for you this morning?" Monet

answers my call on the first ring, sounding chipper and friendly.

"Hey, Moe, it's uh..." I run my fingers through my hair and look over my shoulder at my girl sleeping soundly in the hospital bed. "It's Honor."

An audible gasp comes through the line. "Oh no, please tell me she's okay. When she left yesterday, I tried calling, but..."

"She's in the hospital." I clear my voice. "Alive."

Thank Jesus, Mary, and Joseph.

"Nick, I'm sorry. What happened yesterday..." Her voice trails off, losing momentum.

"What *did* happen yesterday?" I urge, a hint of anger and accusation filling my tone.

"You know I can't discuss client sessions."

"Moe, she took a razor to her wrist. Bled all over the floor of her bathroom until the maid found her. Now, I don't give a flying fuck about your ethics and shit! What I need to know is what are you going to do to help me turn this around?" I growl into the phone, barely containing my anger. I want to pound my anger into the wall in front of me, but instead, I curl my hand into a tight fist and hold it there.

Breathe. She's okay. You're here with her. She's safe.

"My God." The way her voice shakes, I can tell she's deeply affected. There's no way that Moe doesn't care for Honor. I glance over my shoulder, taking in her white-blond hair, pale skin, and delicate features. She's innocent, hurting, and needs a lot of help. Help I'm determined to get her.

"Yeah, and she thinks you fucking abandoned her."

"I did no such thing." Her tone is indignant. "She wouldn't let me explain, but it's not uncommon for a doctor to need to excuse themselves from giving treatment when they can't be objective." She takes on her doctor speak, but I don't give a shit. All I care about is answers. How to get Honor back on track and getting the help she obviously needs.

"Nick, I offered to refer her to another doctor. My own, in fact. A female doctor she can connect with, someone I trust implicitly."

"Fine. Great. Get her to the hospital." I start pacing the corridor, ideas skipping through my mind. I make a mental checklist of items I can work on toward getting my girl back to a good place. "I want a set plan before they release her."

"They're going to want a psych consult anyway. I'll come and ask Dr. Batchelor if she's available to come too. Introduce her and schedule her sessions." She sniffs, and her voice lowers. "I'm really sorry, Nick. I wish I could do more. No, I *will* do more. I like Honor very much, and if the fear in your voice is any indication, you do too. Which means I'll likely be seeing her more often in a social capacity."

I grit my teeth. "Count on it. And one more thing. What's the deal with her mother?" I remember back to the short conversation we had about her mother telling her what to do, who to date, and that she was a lousy daughter. A loving mother wouldn't do that. She might attempt to set you up on dates with her friends' kids or prod you about your love life and having babies, but not once has my mother ever talked down to me like I was an awful child or horrible human being. "I get the feeling that some of this shit burning up inside of her has to do with her relationship with her parents. Especially her mother."

"Nick..." she warns. "I can't discuss this with you."

Hot, blazing anger bubbles up and prickles along the surface of my skin. "Fine." I grate through my teeth. "Just tell me, is it bad?"

"Nick." The sadness in the way she says my name says it all.

"It's bad. Is she more than verbally violent toward Honor?"

"You know I can't..." Her voice cracks, and I can hear how torn she is.

I close my eyes, press my hand to the wall, and drop my head down in front of me. "I need to know if I should be calling her family, letting them in on what's going on."

"Absolutely not." Monet's reply is firm and resolute. Heat swarms over my body as the knowledge that my girl has been hurt beyond a mere tongue-lashing burrows in. The sensation settles inside my gut and twists and turns like a tilt-a-whirl.

"Moe, did her mother lay a hand on her?"

"Please stop." Monet is crying over the line, likely warring with her ethics and her desire to protect her patient and help her friend.

"Fuck." The woman puts her hands on her. "Her father?" I growl, barely able to function as this news sinks in.

"Nick, I don't know," she whispers, all hope gone from her voice. Which means she really doesn't know. They probably haven't talked about him yet, or maybe he's a good guy. Only time will tell.

"I'll see you soon."

Monet clears her throat. "Yeah, okay."

I punch the off button and lean my forehead on the cool plaster. Her mother is verbally and physically abusive. Her father is an unknown.

"Nick?" Honor calls out from the room behind me.

I take the few steps needed to enter. "Hey, Dove, I'm here."

Her lips tremble. "I thought you'd left me."

"No, babe. Not going to leave you. Just making a phone call and didn't want to disrupt your sleep."

She nods and twiddles her fingers. "Has Sean been in, mentioned when I could go back to the hotel?"

Hotel, not home.

"Shit. You haven't found a place yet, have you?"

She shakes her head. "It's okay. All the things I want and need are at the hotel. One of mine."

"Where were you living before, and what do you mean one of yours?"

Honor shrugs in that nonchalant way that is an attempt to change the subject. Not gonna happen. I'm not letting her off the hook on anything anymore.

I wait patiently until the silence becomes uncomfortable.

"I was living with my parents before...uh...well, just before." She picks up a lock of her wavy blond hair and runs her fingers over the strands in a repetitive nervous gesture. "You know Zero Tower?"

"That swank hotel downtown? Shit, that costs like eight or nine hundred a night?"

Her forehead crinkles. "Is it that much? I'll have to talk to my people. That seems exorbitant."

This time I'm the one crinkling my forehead in confusion. "Your people?"

"I own that hotel and a few others. I'm currently living in one of the four penthouses."

I tip my head back and look up at the ceiling. "You're living in a hotel."

"It's what I have." Her voice cracks, and she looks away.

That's not where you go to heal. She needs a home. A place where someone can dote on her, bring her soup and lasagna.

"You're not going back there."

She bites her lip and looks down at her lap. "I don't have anywhere else. I can't go back to my parents' estate. I just... I can't do it, Nick." With the way she's twisting her fingers and tightening her hands, I'm able to read between the lines. She's afraid.

"Fuck that. You're coming home with me."

She lifts her head and her eyes light up. "Really? You'd want me there?" The happiness that pinks her cheeks is something I want to see every day of my freakin' life. My heart races, and I come to her side, curl a hand into her hair, and hold her against me at her nape.

"Yeah, babe. I want you to come home with me. Let me take care of you. Plus, my work is right under my apartment. I'm not scheduled for another class at Lotus for the next three days. And even if we need more time, Gracie can sub for me."

She looks back down at her lap, and I tilt her chin with my thumb.

"You're too good to me." Tears fill her eyes, but she doesn't let them fall.

I tap both of her lips with my thumb, wanting to kiss away her sorrow. "Not possible. Besides, I want you in my home and between my sheets. I think I'm the lucky one in this scenario." I offer a sexy grin in order to get her mind off the potential downside of suddenly sharing space with one another. I've never done that with a woman before, but for some reason, with Honor, I'm not scared or nervous. Right now, it just feels right.

Honor offers one of her beatific smiles, and I swear it mends a crack in my heart. Yep, healing her is going to heal me. She's what I need. I send up a prayer to the big fella upstairs that I'm man enough to take care of her, to get her through this rough patch and out the other side.

After Moe and her doctor friend get here and we settle up with the doctor about her being discharged, I'm going to call for reinforcements. When my ma finds out my girl is hurt, she's going to be all over bringing food and pampering her, and she hasn't even met her. That's what a good mother does and what Honor deserves. If she's not getting it from her mother, my mother will be all over it. Not to mention Grace, Dawn, Angela, Cara—even Faith will want in on the action.

Honor Carmichael is about to experience the full Salerno effect far sooner than she thought.

★ ★ ★

The apartment is dark when I unlock the door and gesture her inside. One of the hotel staff packed up her belongings from the hotel room and met us at the gym.

"Go ahead and get settled on the couch, and I'll bring in your suitcases."

She nods but doesn't speak. Ever since Moe came to the hospital, apologized for whatever happened between them, and introduced Honor to Dr. Batchelor, she's been quiet. Contemplative. I didn't leave the room when she spoke with them, and my girl didn't ask me to. If I'm going to help her, I need to be there for her at all times. I held her hand as the good doctor spoke calmly, confirmed that Honor didn't actually intend to take her life. Her sessions have been bumped up to twice a week, and she's now got a weekly lunch date with Monet.

I've never been a bigger fan of Monet than when she held

AUDREY CARLAN

Honor's hand, told her that it wouldn't be right for her to be her doctor, and that instead she wanted to be her friend. Then she asked her to lunch for later this week. Honor seemed to be surprised that Moe wanted to spend social time with her but happily accepted the date. They hugged, cried, and then Dr. Batchelor set up a regular weekly schedule right onsite.

I drag the suitcases and a couple shoulder bags up the stairs and directly into my bedroom. The apartment is rather large since it runs the entire span of the top of the gym, but it still only has one walled-in bedroom and bathroom. The rest is completely open, almost like a loft. The kitchen needs work—the white cabinets are old and beaten up, but the appliances I scored from the former owner were new. That was a plus. Especially the stove. I love to cook, and the oven and range are pretty stellar.

Right then my stomach growls, and I realize I should probably cook us something to eat.

I enter the living space, and Honor is leaning against the arm of the couch, a throw blanket wrapped around her shoulders, her knees drawn up to her chest. Her eyes are closed, and her head is resting on her knees.

"Hey, Dove, you want to stretch out, take a nap while I fix us something to eat? You hungry?"

Her eyes open lazily. "I like your home."

Home. There's that word again. I wouldn't consider my bachelor pad a home, but it's comfortable and suits me well enough.

"Yeah? What do you like about it?" I want her talking, not spending too much time escaping into herself.

"You can put your feet up on the couch and cuddle in."

"Well, yeah, that's what couches are for." I chuckle.

Her lips purse. "You have pictures of your family in frames all over the place. Shows that you're loved."

I glance around and note the cluster of family photos on one wall. "Ma brought those pictures and hung them there." Checking out the room, I glance at several other framed pictures of my sisters, the Lotus House gang, Mila and her family of three. "The rest are images people gave me. So I kind of cheated in my decorating prowess. Most of the furniture was my sister Dawn's. When she and her husband bought a new home, they gave me their hand-me-downs. It was ideal at the time because I'd just bought this place. Eventually, when I buy my own house and settle down with a woman, we'll get things together. I figure that's the way it should go, yeah?"

No response there, just a shrug.

"You like grilled cheese?" I ask, and a smile forms on her lips.

"Very much, though I haven't had it in ages."

I grin and head into the kitchen to prep and get her a glass of water. "Let me guess. Since college?"

She smiles softly and stands, clutching the blanket around her shoulders. "Yeah," she whispers. "My family isn't big on comfort foods."

I raid the pantry and pull out some bread and then open the fridge, where I find a thick block of cheddar cheese and butter. Once I've got the goods on the table, I pull down some glasses, pour her some water, and bring it to her. "What kind of meals did you grow up with?" I ask conversationally.

"Uh, whatever our chef made. Not something a child would normally eat, that's for sure, but Hannon and I got used to it. On a particular gourmet meal evening, we'd sneak down after our parents went to bed and raid the fridge. Usually Chef would leave us premade peanut butter and jelly sandwiches, cheese and crackers. That kind of thing. He knew we didn't want to eat rich, five-star meals but our mother and father wouldn't have it any other way. They considered it training for our future."

Her story makes me sigh long and hard from deep within my chest. "You haven't had it easy."

She huffs. "On the contrary. Some would venture that I've had it very easy. Rich family, expensive education and clothing. What more could I want?"

"All of that doesn't make your life easy, Honor. Money doesn't solve the heart's problems. Besides, all the money in the world can't replace the loss of your brother."

Honor looks down at the counter and runs her finger along one of the grout lines in the tile. "No, it doesn't."

"Will you tell me about him?" I genuinely want to know about the man who has such an emotional effect on my woman's life.

Her head shoots up. "You want to know about Hannon?"

"Was he important to you?"

"The most important person in my life."

I smirk. "Okay, then. I'd like to know about him." I take a few steps to a drawer and pull out the cheese slicer. "What was he like?"

Honor braces her elbows on the counter and rests her chin in her hands. "He was amazing. Everything I'm not. Funny, extroverted, and he loved life. He never took a moment for granted. Then he met Sean, you know, Dr. Tillman."

I nod, encouraging her to continue.

"Our lives finally started to make sense. I was in my master's program for business. Hannon started working for my father right after his bachelor's."

Grabbing the butter, I slather one side of each slice with a thick, creamy layer before setting the two sides on the griddle next to the stove.

"Did he like working for your dad?"

"Actually, yes. Hannon was an overachiever. He excelled in everything he did and always found a way to have fun doing it."

I slice several pieces of cheese and arrange them on the bread. "And what was the age difference between the two of you?"

"He was my twin."

I was not prepared for her answer. Those four words slam into my heart like a sucker punch to the chest. I drop the tops of the bread on one another and turn the knob to get the griddle hot. "Aw hell, Dove, I didn't know that. Fuck. Fuck!" The sorrow ripples off her in waves, slamming into me, and I imagine losing Dawn. We're a year apart, and that would gut me. I walk over to my girl, turn her on the stool, push her knees apart so I can fit my body in between, and wrap her in my embrace. "I'm sorry. Fucking sucks you lost the closest person to you. But I'm proud of you for being strong."

She clutches at my back. "I don't feel strong," she whispers against my chest, holding me tightly.

"I know. But one day soon, you will be, and I'll be standing right there with you, holding your hand."

She lifts her head and rests her chin against my chest. "Thank you for bringing me here. You didn't have to, but I'm grateful."

I kiss her on the forehead and then briefly on the lips. There's a hint of her mint and vanilla taste clinging to her mouth, making me want to kiss her more fully, but now's not the time. She needs to feel safe and protected. Not groped and taken advantage of.

I hear the sizzle of the bread, turn, and groan. "Shit!" I flip the bread over, and though it's a little darker than I'd like, it's still edible. "Whew!" I wipe my forehead. "Close call."

She chuckles, and it's music to my ears.

For a few more minutes, we chat about the gym and the yoga studio while we eat, and I give her the rundown on my family. Mostly all the overbearing but well-meaning women. Once done, I grab her hand and lead her over to the big leather couch. I sit down at one end, hold out my arm, and pat the space in front of me between my legs.

Honor hesitates, putting her finger up to her mouth.

"Come on, Dove...I won't bite. Much." I grin and waggle my eyebrows.

She rolls her eyes and gets settled, her back and side mostly against my chest, her head cocked to my chest.

"Nick, I'm, um, not sure it's a good idea that I go on Sunday." She glances down at her bandaged wrist and hand and then back to me. She's referring to dinner at my folks'. My family was expecting to meet the woman I've been hiding. Grace has already spilled the beans about Honor, and Ma's losing her mind that she hasn't met her yet.

I shake my head and cuddle her closer. "Babe, they are not going to judge you. No one's walked a mile in your shoes. They are not perfect, nor do they claim to be."

"And I'm not Italian."

"Now *that* we're going to fib on," I respond flatly.

Her eyes widen. "Really?"

"Really." I chuckle. "It's just easier."

She nods and rests her head against me. "It's so peaceful here."

"It can be. The building has good insulation, so even during the day, you can't hear the gym downstairs. Speaking of the gym, did you want to rest here tomorrow or come down?"

She hums, and that sound goes straight to my dick, stirring it from a peaceful rest. Then Honor wiggles against me, her hip rubbing along my cock, bringing him to full mast. I hiss a breath of air, and she stops moving. Her eyes are so round and big when she realizes what she's caused, but she doesn't move a muscle, as if she's afraid to.

I tug her against me harder, give one shameless thrust against her, and growl into her ear. "Ignore it. When you're around, it has a mind of its own."

"But if you need something..." she starts to offer, but I shut it down flat.

"No. No way, no how, is our first time together going to be the night you come home from the hospital. Now tomorrow, all bets are off." I grin and nip along her jawline until I get to her mouth, where I take her lips in a lush, wet kiss. She opens for me instantly, swiping her tongue against mine and moaning deeply. I tunnel my fingers through her hair and shift her weight and legs, bringing her to a straddling position, and then pull my lips from hers.

"I want you, Nick. So much." She gasps.

I softly head-butt her forehead with mine. "And I want you. More than anything. I want to bury myself so deep inside you I get lost in all that's you."

She moans and curls her fingers into my hair.

"Doesn't mean we can't play a little though, now does it?" I waggle my eyebrows and focus on her beautiful face and slender neck, thinking about where I'm going to kiss and bite her skin first.

Her response is to rock her hips against my cock in a grinding, devious motion. "Like this?" she whispers against my lips and mewls when she presses her body hard against mine.

"Fuck yeah." I grab a handful of ass and roll my hips until her eyes close and her mouth opens on a gasp.

Her slim hips switch from a series of circular motions to grinding back and forth along my cock. I can just imagine my length between her puffy pink lips, making me hard as a rock.

"You feel so good sitting on top of me, dragging your body over my cock." I kiss a line down her neck. "But I need a small taste."

She nods and sighs while I get to work on the buttons down the front of her shirt. I get them undone and praise the good Lord above that her bra clasp is in front. It's like she wore it just for me. Which she likely did not, but a guy can dream.

I squeeze each globe, appreciating how the flesh spills over my hands. "Beautiful," I whisper and nuzzle between the two, dipping my fingers in between to unlatch the clasp. Her tits practically bounce free when I release the hook, gifting me far more than a handful, with two pretty, pale-pink nipples that look perfect for sucking. I grip both breasts, making sure to run my first and third fingers along each side of her pea-sized tips so I can pluck and hold each tit at the same time.

She moves her hips in a less organized fashion, losing her rhythm, going wild for me.

"That's it. Want to see you lose it with nothing but the friction of my cock between your legs and my mouth on your tits."

"Oh my...Nick." She tips her head back as I cover one of

her succulent nipples with the heat of my mouth.

Her body jolts and stills. She brings her hands to my head and holds me there while I suck the hell out of her breast. Each tit is warm, soft, and tastes like heaven. There's a hint of that fresh flowers scent that clings to her naked skin, making me want to drag my tongue all over her. One day, I will do just that, only not today. Today is for healing. Making her forget.

"You like when I put my mouth on you?" I pinch the areola at the top and bottom of each nipple and flick the erect nubbin until she's a frenzied mess of need and want.

"I'm gonna...oh, my God." Her hands go for my head, to maneuver me the way she wants.

I let go of her tits in order to secure her arms to her sides. I'd hold both wrists behind her back, displaying her perfect breasts for my taking, but since she's hurt, I'll settle for immobilizing her arms to her sides.

"Honor, I'm in control in the bedroom. It would be wise for you to get that in your head now." I hold her arms to her sides but lean forward and suck one of her nipples again. They've already gone from the palest pink to a cherry red. I admire my work. "Keep your arms to your sides or on my shoulders in order to ride the length of my dick. Those are your options," I instruct, and her eyes darken, swirling with unspoken lust as she lifts her hands to my shoulders.

"That's good. Now, do you want me to make you come, Dove? End this horrible couple days feeling good?"

She nods frantically and licks her lips.

"Words, babe." I suck on her breasts and bite down on the tip.

"I."

I lave the nub with the flat of my tongue.

"Want."

Switching breasts, I suck that nipple hard, letting it go with a pop.

"Your."

I bite down on the swollen tip.

"Words."

Her nails dig into my back, and her hips thrust forward. "Yes! Please. Do something, anything."

On that request, I wrap one arm around her back and bury one hand in her hair, where I grip it by the roots, arching her spine toward me. She comes willingly, presenting her big tits and body for my taking.

"Fuck, yes." I tug on her hair, and she cries out with the bit of pain I've caused but presses down along my cock over and over. She bucks and grinds her sex wildly, until together we're a panting, sweaty mess.

I remove my hand from behind her back, tunnel my fingers down into the front of her yoga pants and inside her panties, and press two digits deep, swirling my thumb around her clit. It's hard as a rock and hot to the touch.

She cries out with pleasure, her pussy convulsing around my imbedded fingers, her body arching beautifully. I take as much of her breast into my mouth as I can so I've got a piece of her everywhere I can hold. My mouth on her tit, my fingers deep inside her slit, and her arms wrapped around me. I press up against her curves, the movement taking me over along with her.

I take her mouth and kiss her hard, pressing my fingers up and in until her body locks around mine. My own arousal is racing through my system, drawing up and down my limbs, igniting a passion so intense, I know I'll be ruined from it. I shudder, my orgasm rippling along my spine, down into my cock and balls, and shredding me completely.

I lay my lips over a pillowy section of her breast, bite down on the soft globe, and then suck as hard as I can. Her sex tightens around my fingers, and I fuck her with them while I'm still coming until she goes off a second time, her body wrung so tight, I can barely keep hold of her. But I do. I'll never let her go. Not ever.

When she has passed the pinnacle of her release, her entire body slumps against mine in a panting, loose-limbed heap. I remove my fingers and wrap my arms around her, cuddling her close.

"You're safe with me. I'm going to take care of you."

She nuzzles against my neck. "You shouldn't have to."

"I want to." I run my hands up and down her back. "But you know what?"

"What?" Her words are whispers of air against my heated neck.

"You're going to have to take care of me too."

Her body stiffens before she lifts her head and looks at me with the most soulful gray eyes. "I'd like that more than anything."

"Good, because you're not going anywhere for a long time, maybe not ever."

"As long as I've got you, I could live with that." She smiles, and I could almost swear that smile was a promise.

I tip her head toward my chest. "Rest now. I've got you."

CHAPTER FIFTEEN

THROAT CHAKRA

The throat chakra couple will typically have vast musical, artistic, and poetic tastes. Their ability to see beauty and delicacy in everyday things allows them to have happier, more fulfilled lives. It is not uncommon for a person driven by the throat chakra to be a natural singer. These people will often be told they have "God-given talents" that others don't have.

HONOR

Dear Hannon,

I made a terrible mistake a week ago. I hurt myself and the man I care very deeply for. It was much worse than I've ever done before. I didn't mean to take it so far. If you were here, you'd have been so angry. But you're not here, Hannon. You left. I have to live with the decision you made each and every day.

It's hard not having you here to talk to, to hug, to love. To know that my brother is by my side...

How could you?

I know you didn't want Sean hurt, but he's not the only one you left behind. He's not the only one who loved you. I'm your sister, your twin, the other half of your soul. You destroyed me when you took your life. And now, I'm left to pick up the pieces of mine, one shard at a time, not knowing how to put myself back together.

Nick is helping.

If I didn't know better, I'd think he was an angel, a saint sent down from above in order to help me see there's a beautiful life to live if I just reach out and grab for it. He's teaching me this. Every day.

I wish you could meet him. You'd have liked him. He's rough around the edges and bossy. So bossy, but it doesn't bother me. It shows he cares. I don't know what he sees in me, because he deserves a perfect woman, a whole woman. Yet he won't walk away. He tells me time and time again that he's going to stay.

I'm scared, Hannon, because I'm starting to believe him.

I miss you.

I love you.

Your sister,

Honor

I tuck my journal under the mattress by the side of the bed I've been sleeping on. A full week has passed since I was released from the hospital and moved into Nick's apartment. My injuries are healing well, and they barely hurt. Nick tends to my bandages each morning and every night like my own personal physician. He's amazing. Never making me feel less than for what I did. He just accepts the things he cannot change and moves on. I want to learn from him.

We've spent the week moving around each other in harmony. Making meals, working in the gym, side by side. I've never felt more happily settled in a routine. Twice a week, therapy with Dr. Batchelor, who is easier to trust than I thought she would be. Lunch with Dr. Hart, who insists I call her Monet or Moe like everyone else. I can sense her sincerity to be friends with me. I may invite Grace next week. They already know each other, and Grace has been calling my phone nonstop all week with requests to meet up. All of which I've denied, wanting to let my wounds heal a bit more figuratively and literally. Overall, it's been a wonderful week. Being with Nick, spending time with him in his home, is easy, simple, and feels right. I don't know how he feels about it yet, but he seems content. Definitely not eager for me to find a place of my own. Every time I suggest it, he tosses the paper aside and tells me to just relax and enjoy my time with him.

Stepping out of my clothes and into the shower, I turn the water on and adjust to a barely scalding setting before I get under the spray. The instant prick of pain that sizzles along my skin offers a touch of bliss. Would this be one of the healthier ways to deal with my need for pain?

I pour shampoo into my hands, rub them together, and slather my hair with the flowery scent. Nick loves the way I smell. He tells me all the time. I also have a bit of an obsession with his citrus and leather scent. He uses some type of hair product that his friend Genevieve sells to him that, mixed with his natural scent, turns into an orangey smell, but the leather... that's all my man.

My man.

I laugh deliriously as I rinse out the shampoo. Nick's shower is incredible. The pressure is fast and hard. He says he had to upgrade the shower when he moved in because he works his body hard in the gym and needs the water therapy. In my opinion, a large tub would do wonders, but he'd need to renovate the bathroom to do that. Of course, I could do that for him. Maybe as a thank-you present for helping me through this past week.

Storing the idea away for another time, I start to sing. The shower is the only place I can be free enough to let the music inside me out.

I hum the tune at first and then get louder with each verse until I'm belting through the lyrics for "Wild Horses" by the Rolling Stones. The song moves my heart in ways so many others haven't. Words of suffering and pain have always resonated so clearly with me over the years. I've got my eyes closed when I sing my heart out to the last line.

"Fuck, Honor!" Nick's voice startles me and makes the images the song inspired disappear instantly inside my mind. "Babe, you're a songbird."

Nick steps into the shower completely naked. It's not the first time I've seen him naked, but this time feels different. More meaningful. The energy around us both is hypercharged and magnetic.

Nick brings his hands to my waist and tugs me flat against

him. "You can sing like angel," he whispers in awe.

I shake my head. "No, I can't. I just..."

He runs a hand up my bare back, causing goosebumps to rise over my skin even against the heat of the water. "Yeah, babe, you are. Fucking incredible. We've gotta get you singing on stage."

My eyes practically bulge out of my head, and I try to back away, but he doesn't allow it. "No, no, no, not possible."

His lips twist into a wicked, sexy slant. "Oh yes, anything's possible, Dove. Anything. Sing something else for me?"

I cringe. "Here? Now?" I run my fingers down his sculpted arms, arousal flickering through my body at his nearness.

"If you do, I'll reward you," he taunts in a husky timbre while bringing a hand down and squeezing bare ass. The movement forces his hard length against my belly, and I moan, knowing just how badly I want him inside me. He's been denying me all week, stating that he wanted me fully on board mentally and physically when we took that last step. I've almost been to the point of begging for it, I want him so badly.

"Will you fuck me if I do?" I raise my eyebrows and purse my lips, waiting for his answer, hoping for the response I want.

He cocks his head to the side and gets his face low enough to look me in the eye. "No, Dove, I'm not gonna fuck you the first time. I will make love to you, though."

A ribbon of heat flutters along the surface of my skin and flushes my cheeks.

"Sing to me."

"What do you want me to sing?"

He holds me close, our bare skin touching from knee to chest. I tremble against him, but he's there to keep me upright. "Our song."

"Which is what?" My voice shakes, wondering how he sees us. What song he'll chose that speaks of what this thing between us feels like for him.

"Hallelujah."

I swallow around the lump in my throat, and the steam billows around us in the confined space. I close my eyes and start to sing the song that would change me for the rest of my life. When I get to the part about the woman in the moonlight, I tip my head back and give it my all, each verse ringing through the bathroom walls. Nick's hands move over my body as I sing. Caressing, worshiping...loving.

A certain verse speaks of my own tale of broken love with my parents, my brother, myself. This time, I sing of love from my heart, for the man cradling me, bared in body and soul. I'm learning anew what love can truly be if it's given freely and without limitations.

By the time I get to the end of the song and sing the very last hallelujah, his lips are on mine. Nick ushers me against the wall of the shower, drinking deeply from my mouth. His hands cradle my face as he kisses me. He doesn't have to speak to tell me what this kiss means. I know from each press of his lips to mine, his tongue to mine, this is it. This is when our bodies, our hearts, and our souls will connect in an unbreakable bond that will span time.

He kisses me so hard and so long, the water goes cold. He moves back a few inches, holding my face with one of his hands.

"We're starting over. Both of us, right now. No longer are we alone. When I take you, I'm claiming you. We no longer live alone because we live for each other. Support one another in all things. Be there for the good and the bad."

"Sounds like a proposal," I barely croak out.

"Call it what you want. I have no doubt we'll get there too. For now, we live for the other. Promise me, Honor. You'll live because I need you alive."

"I love you, Nick." The words come out at the same time two tears fall from each eye. One for him, and one for me.

His smile is as bright as a new day. Full of hope, wonder and, dare I say, love. "Good," he says, and for now, it's enough.

Nick turns off the water, grabs my hand, opens the shower door, and pulls us both out. With gentle movements, he dries me with a towel, each pass of the fabric as though he's fanning the flames of lust. I close my eyes and enjoy this moment of devotion. I've not felt anything like it before, and I want to remember every last second.

Without delay, Nick has scooped me up, walks me into the bedroom, and lays me on the bed that's quickly becoming our bed instead of just his bed.

"Do you have any idea how beautiful you are?" He shakes his head as his gaze runs over every bare naked inch of me. "I don't even know where to start." His voice is rough and laced with desire.

I point to my lips. "How about here?"

He smiles and straddles my body, not bringing his big bulk over me, just hovering before he takes my lips. His tongue peeks out, running along the length of each lip before flicking against my teeth when I smile. Who knew Nick would be a little playful as well as dominant in the bedroom? All too quickly, his playful side disappears, and his mouth devours mine, sucking, nibbling, biting until my lips feel swollen and bruised.

I gasp when he plucks at my bottom lip and pulls back; his normally light eyes are dark and focused. He grabs my hands with both of his and lifts them above my head. "Hold on to the

231

headboard and don't let go until I tell you."

"What happens if I let go?"

"Defy me and find out," he warns, and I make a mental note to hold on to the headboard as tightly as I can. The last thing I want is for him to stop touching me, and the worst he could do to me would be that. I'm so primed and ready for this next step in our relationship. I physically *need* him.

I grip the wooden rungs and arch up, presenting my breasts.

He grins salaciously. "An offer I can't refuse." And before I can take a breath, he's got one of my nipples in the wet warmth of his mouth. It's heaven and hell all at once because I want to touch him, hold his head to my breast while he ravishes me.

Nick laps at my nipple with the flat of his tongue, making it throb and ache deliciously. He wraps his other hand around my neglected breast, pinching and plucking at the erect tip to the point of pain.

"How does that feel?" He sits up and works each peak until a burning sensation ripples from them throughout my body, creating a euphoria I've never known.

"Mmm, good." I gasp and arch into his touch when he pinches harder.

"You try to get closer when I press harder. Do you want more?"

"Yes! God, please."

He pinches and twists my nipples until they are fiery hot pokers. Rivers of pleasure dance through my body and to the place between my legs.

"Please, Nick."

"Oh, Dove, I'm going to enjoy hearing you beg in the future, and I'll do it until your throat is raw. Now, though, I'm just figuring out some of your thresholds. This pain makes you feel alive, does it not?"

The concept slams into me like a hose putting out a fire. "Oh, my God!"

He grins devilishly and plucks at my burning tips again until I have to shut my eyes tight from the delightful pain.

"I told you, there are more ways to get what you need. Honor, I'm going to make you hurt so good. Give you a healthy outlet for that ache inside."

I nod, tears filling my eyes and falling down my cheeks. This man accepts me. Understands my need and wants to fill it, not stop it.

Nick swipes my tears away before nudging both of my knees with his. I do one better, spreading myself wide open for him. An offer.

His lips go into a flat line, nostrils flaring, and eyes intent between my open thighs. "You giving me this?" He cups my sex roughly, dangerously. I want so much more.

My silence is defining.

"Words, Dove. Right now, I'm going to bury myself inside you, and I need to know that it's mine, when I want it, how I want it. Just like your heart...your broken soul. I'm taking it all."

"You can have it," I whisper, more tears falling.

Nick leans over to the side table and pulls out a condom. I stop his hand and shake my head. "I'm safe and clean."

"You letting me have you bare?"

"You want all of me?" I firm my jaw and lift my head, feeling prideful and beautiful.

"Fuck, yeah."

"I want all of you."

Once the word leaves my mouth, he notches his thick cock at my entrance, wraps both of his hands around my hips, and slams home. I cry out at the intrusion, his mighty length large and thick inside my walls. I suck in several breaths and shimmy my hips, attempting to accommodate his girth, but I'm not sure anything would do. He's huge. *Everywhere.*

Nick lays his body over mine, curls a hand under us to grip my bum where he curves his hips, and tunnels his cock deeper. I ease my head back and push down with my hips, wanting him inside as far as he can go. I bite my lips with the pain that move brings, washing over my lower half like a true bathing of his soul into mine.

"You will take all of me, Dove." He growls and sucks on a sensitive spot at the base of my neck.

I'm awash with overwhelming sensations of pleasure, pain, need, and desire. I raise both of my knees up his sides. He takes that opportunity to press against the back of my thighs and thrust deeper.

"Sweet heaven," I call out, gripping the rungs of the headboard so tight I'm sure I'll have indentions in my palms.

"Fuck yeah it is. Warm, beautiful heaven. Jesus, Mary, and Joseph, I should have taken you sooner." His voice is raw, gritty, and coated in lust.

I smile against his neck and lay a round of kisses on every patch of skin I can reach. He groans and swirls his hips, crushing my clit in the process. My entire body goes stiff as an orgasm races through me. My toes curl, and my fingers tighten around the wood above my head as I go off.

Nick runs his hands up my arms and unfurls them from the rungs. "Hold me, babe. Touch me."

Glorying in the ability to finally put my hands on him, I

run them all over his sweat-misted back, feeling each bump of his spine. He fucks me hard, lifts up off my chest so I can see his magnificent body. His shoulders are wide and full of sinewy muscle. Each pec is a hardened square with a brown, almond-shaped nipple I'd like to lick and bite. Down farther is sheer male perfection. He works hard at keeping his body healthy and toned. I draw a fingertip down the center of his chest and over each brick of his eight-pack.

"Everything about you is hard," I whisper, touching all over his upper body.

He smiles, opens my legs wide so my knees fall out to each side. He takes his thumb and swirls it around my clit, which reacts like a lightning bolt to the rest of me. I jerk and tremble, the pleasure obliterating all thoughts besides ramping up for another explosion.

"And everything about you is soft. Your body..." He runs his hand over my inner thighs, up my abdomen, and to my breasts, where he gives them a little squeeze. "Your heart." He comes over me and kisses the skin above my heart, which repositions his dick in such a way to torture me with pleasure.

I moan and grip his hips, wanting him to stay where he is. His dick is gliding along the most perfect place; I feel like my insides are going to explode in sheer ecstasy.

"That the spot?" He kisses me as I sigh and moan into his mouth.

Nick uses his talented hips, rotating and stirring his length inside me, crushing that hot bundle of nerves with each rotation. I curl around his body, bringing us as close together as we could possibly be.

He fucks me slow and long, until I'm panting, squirming, pushing, and pulling for that last little bit that will send me over the edge.

"Gonna love you like this forever, Honor."

"Nick!" I tip my head back and let out a long breath of air as the orgasm pounds through me.

He picks up the pace with his hips, hammering into me in short bursts. His mouth covers mine, and his massive body locks around me. His cock seems to get bigger, thicker, until both of us fall over the edge of the cliff into nothing but ecstasy.

"I love you, Honor. I fucking *love* you," Nick whispers in my ear as his body shudders and his release fills me.

Closing my eyes, I hold this man to my body and open the broken parts of my soul, allowing this moment to fill some of the empty holes.

"I love you too."

★ ★ ★

A pounding on the door breaks through the warm haze of sleep swarming around me. Nick's naked body is pressed up against the back of mine, his arm locked around my waist. I press against his back, snuggling closer as the knocking sound comes again.

"Nicholas Salvatore Salerno Jr.! You better answer this door for your mama, or I'll call your father and have him break it down!"

I sit up like a shot in the dark and pull the sheet up to cover my chest. Nick rolls over and starts laughing.

"What's going on?" A nervous panic swirls around me instantly.

"My mother is here." He chuckles and scrubs at his eyes.

"Why?" I rub my head, our lovemaking flickering through

my mind like a sexy movie on repeat.

Nick gets out of bed stark naked. I admire his form longingly, my gaze focusing on his thick cock and sculpted muscles. My mouth waters at the idea of bringing him into my mouth, making him crazy for me. Taking him over the edge into bliss.

He narrows his eyes and points a finger. "None of that," he says, sounding more Italian in that moment than I've heard him.

"What?" I blink innocently.

"Looking at my cock like it's your next meal." He grips his length and gives it one long stroke.

I moan, and he shakes his head. "Fucking knew it. Perfect goddamned woman. Wants me to fuck her face even when my mother is banging at the door."

The reminder of his mother has me scrambling out of bed. "It's not my fault all of your maleness is so...so you!" I wave my hands and look around the room, finding my yoga pants on the floor and one of his shirts. I tug them both on as he zips up his jeans and walks bare-chested out of the room.

Oh, my God. He's got nothing but a pair of jeans on, and he's going to answer the door. His mother is going to know what we did.

Like his mother doesn't already assume.

"There you are. I thought I would have to call the cavalry out on you," I can hear his mother say from the other room.

I take a few precious moments to run my fingers through my hair and find a speck of courage to walk out and meet his mother.

"Where is the girl? I want to see her. You can't hide her away in your love nest forever!" she scolds.

I take that moment to exit the room. I wave shyly. "Hello."

Nick's mother is more beautiful than I imagined. She's small, curvy, and stunning. Her hair is as dark as Nick's and her smile just as kind.

She lifts her hands to her heart in a prayer position. "Jesus, Mary, and Joseph! You are real! And so beautiful!"

Guess that answers where Nick got one of his favorite religious sayings.

"Come, come child, let me get a good look at you."

I pad close and stretch out my hand to shake hers.

She shakes her head. "No, no, no. That's not how we greet one another in this family." She holds her arms out and embraces me in an all-encompassing hug. "I'm Josephine or Jojo, or Mama. Whatever ever makes you comfortable, my darling girl." She pulls back and holds both of my cheeks. "My boy has done well. Son, she will make me beautiful grandbabies."

I'm certain my eyes are about to pop out of my head, and I cough.

Nick laughs. "Yeah, Ma, she will." He answers as if it's every day that you introduce your girlfriend to your mother and blatantly admit to the prospect of having children. We haven't even talked about kids. We just admitted we loved one another.

Oh, my God! We admitted we loved one another.

In all the touching and lovemaking, that little admission slipped to the wayside. Now that I'm awake and standing in front of his mother, the memory of him whispering he loved me is running rampant in my mind. Did he mean it? Was it something he said in the heat of the moment?

Nick comes over and tugs me to his side, looping an arm

around my shoulders and kissing my temple. "Ma, this is my girl, Honor Carmichael. Dove, this is my mother, Josephine."

"It's so good to meet you, Josephine." I grip Nick's waist and hold on tight.

"So, tell me, Honor, are you Italian?" she asks while lifting a bag off the floor and walking into the kitchen. She starts unloading several Tupperware containers onto the counter.

"Um..." I try to come up with the right words, but Nick cuts me off.

"Five percent, Mom." He winks at me.

His mother beams. "I knew it." She wipes her hands on a dish towel and throws it over her shoulder. "Now, you both look hungry." She gestures to the stools at the bar. "Sit, sit. I will feed you, and you will tell me all about how you met and fell in love."

I shakily make my way to a stool and gratefully sit down before I fall down. I am not used to a mother who not only cares this much but makes a point to insert herself into her children's lives because of concern and love instead of status and keeping up with the Joneses.

His mother opens all of the Tupperware she brought, gets the plates, and dishes out more food than I can usually eat in two days, let alone one meal. Lasagna is cut and steaming hot. A bowl of minestrone soup, thick slices of garlic bread, and some steamed fresh veggies are sitting in front of me, making my mouth water. I haven't smelled food so good in ages.

Nick digs in like nothing is strange about his mother popping over, laying out a feast, and grilling him about his girlfriend. Without knowing what else to do, I tuck into the food and answer Josephine's questions as best I can.

When she leaves, she hugs me not once, but twice, and

kisses me on both cheeks.

Nick walks his mother down and out of the gym. She must have a key if she was able to reach his door inside the building. Thankfully she doesn't have a key to the inside, or she'd have found us in a more precarious position, and I would have died from sheer embarrassment.

"My mother likes you," Nick says as he comes back from downstairs.

"I like her. She's full of happiness and love. What's not to like?"

"Care to tell me about your mom?"

Instantly, ice fills my veins. My mother is nothing like the loving, joyful woman who pushed her way into Nick's home so she could make sure he and his new girlfriend were okay. My mother doesn't even know where I am, and she probably doesn't much care.

"Not today. I want to end this day on a happy note."

He comes over to me and tucks me against his chest. I wrap my arms around him and know as long as I'm in these arms, I'll be fine. Nothing can hurt me here.

"Okay, Dove. But soon, yeah? You have to let me in on the good, bad, and ugly."

I nod and hold him tighter. "Soon."

"How's about we cuddle up and watch some TV like an old married couple?"

I chuckle into his chest. "Sounds perfect."

CHAPTER SIXTEEN

Cow Pose (Sanskrit: Bitilasana)

Getting back to the basics, cow pose has the yogi dropping the belly low while the hips and bum rise up, along with the head and neck. Keep the shoulders hip distance apart and press into the hands and arms getting the most from your stretch.

NICHOLAS

Our convoy stops suddenly. "Master Sergeant Salerno, there's something up ahead."

The skin at the back of my neck stings, and the hair stands up. We were supposed to be alone. This trek has been hidden from our enemies for a year now, and we've had zero problems.

"What do you see, Private?" I gesture to Danielson, a young twenty-year-old from Kansas. He's got eyes on the desert ahead. We'd been driving along a path cut near a long line of

boulders, scoping out enemy territory. This is the first time we've seen any movement along this route.

The sky is pitch dark, but a faint light can be seen ahead. I squint, focusing on the light.

"Not sure, looks like two women in burqas stuck in the desert. The van they're standing near has the hood up, Sergeant," Danielson reports.

One of our jeeps goes on ahead, and that sensation I get when things are about to go tits up hits me again. "Keep your eyes on them. Something doesn't feel right."

"Master Sergeant, we've saved some women before. The guys could use this pick-me-up. Been a long few weeks."

I nod and grit my teeth. "Eyes on." One of our jeeps meets the two women, and our men jump out of the cars.

"Women are holding their hands up," Danielson reports back.

A niggle of frustration and fear digs at my psyche. What are these two women doing out here alone in the desert at night? Could be refugees. We've seen that before too.

Just as I'm about to use the two-way radio to check in on my men, Danielson gasps.

"No, oh fuck! Get out of here!" Danielson screams.

I grab the binoculars and watch as two men come out from behind the car. One is holding a rocket launcher, the other a machine gun. The women drop to the sand as the gun blasts through my four men. They didn't even have a chance to lift their weapons in defense.

"No!" I roar as a light sparks in the distance, and I watch as a rocket is launched into the second vehicle in front of me.

The jeep is blown to bits along with eight of my men. Just gone in a flash.

"Gas it. Get to the rocks!" I instruct, pulling out my weapon and firing alongside Danielson. Enemy fire prattles against the jeep, the sound of metal on metal piercing my eardrums. Bullets continue to fly as my driver gets us to the section of rocks that will ultimately be our escape route. I've got my sights on one of the men as another of my men goes down, taking out the radical with the rocket launcher.

"Fuck. No!" I slam my hand down on the seat in front of me. Danielson doesn't say anything, his head flopping from side to side as another one of my men gets us out of the line of fire.

"Danielson!" I scream, pulling myself toward the front of the jeep to find him bleeding from his neck, his body littered with bullet wounds.

"No!"

"No!"

★ ★ ★

"Nick, honey, I'm here. Wake up."

I'm shaken awake, and I can see nothing but a white halo and darkness.

"You're okay!" Honor touches me, but I push her back with one hand, not sure exactly where I am. Sweat tingles against my skin as I turn toward the mattress and slam my fist into it over and over. The images are so real. Death and loss all around me.

"They're all fucking dead!" I cry out and punch the mattress again. "I couldn't save them."

A small, cool hand flattens against my back. "Nick, honey."

I turn around fast, scoop her up, and hoist her over me. She straddles my legs and rests her head against my beating heart.

"You're okay. I'm here." She kisses my chest over and over.

"They're all gone," I whisper, holding her close.

"I'm sorry."

"I couldn't save them," I say, tears falling down the sides of my cheeks like a pussy.

She doesn't judge me. Not her. My Honor sits up, wipes the tears away, and kisses me until all I can see, hear, and feel is her wrapped around me.

"Nick, you're saving *me*. Every day I'm with you I feel alive."

I hold her close and cry against her neck, letting out the anger, rage, and grief. She holds me, never letting her grip soften until I've cried all the tears I can. There's no more left.

"Maybe I'm the one who needs saving," I whisper against her temple.

She nods. "We can save each other."

"I love you, Honor."

Her body softens and relaxes against mine. "I love you, Nick."

After a few long minutes of just being with one another, Honor sits up on my lap, curls her fingers around the hem of her tank, and rips it over her head. Her pretty breasts glow pale white in the moonlight.

I cup both of them and swipe my thumbs over her nipples.

"You can take it out on me," she offers.

"Take what out?" I'm not sure where she's going with her statement.

"You're angry and upset. Whatever is hurting you. Use it to hurt me."

I grip her hips, close my eyes, and suck in a full breath and let it go, along with the wonder that is this woman. She's always surprising me with her selfless acts.

"Do you need me to hurt you good, Dove?" My voice is as rough as sandpaper. How she could know I need this is beyond me.

She bites down on her bottom lip and nods.

"Words. I need your words." My jaw feels tight and ready to crack rocks with my teeth at how much I want to take her up on her suggestion.

"Yes, Nick. I want you to use me to feel better."

I sit up, and she slides down my thighs and comes face-to-face with me. "What if I told you I want to hit you? Spank you until your white ass was red with my handprints and then fuck you until it hurt to walk tomorrow."

Her pupils dilate, and she lets out a little moan alongside a wiggle of her hips. That move makes my Johnson perk up and take even more notice than when she sat in my lap and bared her tits.

"I see you like that idea."

"Yeah," she murmurs, as if saying it out loud will make the idea disappear at any second. She'd be wrong. I've been dying to get my hands on her ass, and tonight, I need her submission. Need her to give me full control of her body and her pleasure.

"Get up, take off your panties, and present your ass to me. Get on all fours in the center of our bed."

She moves quickly, scrambling off my legs. So eager, my girl.

I watch her like a hawk as she slips off her simple cotton panties and crawls to the middle of the bed. She gets into position, and I have to grip my cock and press hard to stave off the desire to come. My nerves are rattled, and my palms are itching for a fight, but every breath she takes eases the tension from my nightmare. Brings me back to the place where it's only her and me in this room and the beauty that we are together.

I remove my boxer briefs, place a knee on the bed, and ease my hard dick in between her ass cheeks. I close my eyes and groan around the pleasure that simple act provides. She pushes back on a moan, wanting more.

"Did I say you could move?" I use a stern and forceful tone, reminding her exactly who is in charge tonight.

Her body stills magnificently.

"Dove, I'm going to do things to you tonight that will make you scream, cry, and possibly beg for more. If at any time you don't like something or want to stop, you just say *stop*. Specific safe words won't be necessary between us. I plan to learn your body, your wants and desires as if they are my own. Your pleasure will be my pleasure. Your happiness is my happiness. Your tears are my tears. Understand?"

"Yes, Nick."

"Are you ready to take a little pain?"

Her head drops between her shoulders, and a calm wave of energy rolls off her form. "So ready."

And right then it dawns on me that, seeing me break down, being there for me, my violent response, probably triggered her own corporeal need.

I rub my hands along each plump globe. Her ass is heart shaped and silky smooth. Not for long. I grin, levering one hand around her hips, the other along her cheeks. Then I pull back and lay the curve of my palm against the roundest part in a fast, firm smack. She squeaks, her body pushing forward momentarily before she eases back. I give her another, and another, until I've got a cadence of whacks going. Top, down, left, right, other side. She cries out, louder in the bedroom than she's been before, and I want so badly to make her scream. Force the demons rolling around inside her to make their way out, for at least one night. Give her peace.

"Does it hurt?" I smack her in a new position, wanting every inch of her ass red and throbbing with a beautiful ache.

"Yes!" she cries out as I smack the part where ass meets the back of the thigh. I rub my hand around each cheek, appreciating the heat.

"Have you had enough?" I growl between clenched teeth. I'm so focused on her body, on each sway of her hips moving closer to my punishing hand, proof she's enjoying every second of her submission. Her tits are bouncing below, both tips erect, begging for attention. When my hand hits her skin, she makes a little noise in the back of her throat, the same noise she makes right before she comes, only this sound is shorter, more staccato. My girl is loving her spanking as much as I love giving it to her.

She shakes her head.

"No?" I confirm to make sure she's heard me.

"No. More. Harder." Her voice is caked with longing.

"You want harder than my hand, Dove?"

Her body twitches at my question. "Please, yes. Hurt me good, Nick. It's so, so good."

My body trembles at the magic of this moment. I like gifting pain, whether in the gym by working over my members or in the ring by battling it out, but what I haven't had since the early army days is a willing masochist. Someone who enjoys the pain I inflict and begs for more. As with any true gift, it has to be appreciated, respected, given with care and concern, and reciprocated. I intend to always be the man to give this woman what she desires. What she craves.

Walking up to my closet, I pull a belt off a hook and fold it in half. "You sure you want more? My leather belt here would love to kiss your ass, but you need to be sure."

Her voice is dense with lust. "I need it. Please," she pleads.

"Dove, I love hearing you beg." I toss the belt over my shoulder and rub my hands down her back, under where I can tweak and pull at each nipple, and then back around.

She shivers at the loss of my touch, making my dick weep with the need to be inside her. I stroke my cock a few times, allowing the beast a little me time before I dispense a lashing to Honor's perky reddened ass.

When I've calmed down a bit, I take the belt and lay it over her back, each side dangling over so she can see the object of what will soon be her affection. She trembles and shimmies. I cover her ass with kisses, licking against the hottest bits of flesh and then delving between her thighs to taste her honey. Her arousal is dripping down her thighs.

"You fucking *love* my hands on you." I grip her reddened cheeks hard, spreading them apart so I can have deeper access to her pussy.

I lick her from her clit to the tiny hole that puckers and winks. I swirl my tongue around the dark rosette, and her body arcs into cow position, wanting more.

"One day I'm going to take your pretty ass too."

She moans. "Yes, please. Whatever you want."

Nothing but pride enters my chest and swarms around my heart with her light. She's it for me. This moment, tonight, seals it. I could never want or love another the way I do her. Never. My heart, my head, and my cock know it as fact. The next step will be making her accept it.

"Good girl." I pat her ass, take a few more long licks, coating my tongue in her sweet nectar, before I pull back, grab the belt, fold it in half, and lay it firmly against the center of my girl's ass in one stinging crack.

She shrieks with the first blow, but I let my arm fly, giving her three more in quick succession. Her entire body is trembling as white rectangular welt lines appear on her ass. They are a stark contrast to the marks from the spanking I'd given her minutes before.

I rub her ass as the tears come, and she sobs. "Yes, yes, yes." Each word is a chant, and it's so beautiful, I can't take a minute longer of not being inside her. I line up my cock, spread her lips so I can get as deep as possible, and slowly enter her, inch by inch, until my pelvis is smashed against the heat of her ass.

I tip my head back and cry out at the glory, the sheer rapture of bonding with her on this plane of existence.

"Oh, Dove, you are my salvation."

With no words needed, I lean over her body, kiss her neck, her spine, and cup her breasts. I pluck and pull at her overly sensitive nipples until the walls of her sex lock around my cock and she's coming. Splendidly. My entire body is humming with energy. The gift that she's given to me tonight is coating every pore with pure love and devotion.

Honor was created for me. To take my hand in all things, pleasure and pain, equally harmonious.

Her body is trembling so much, I grip her chest and haul her up to her knees, letting her lean back against me as I take her. Every stroke of my dick is better than the last. My heart is full inside my chest; my mind is focused on nothing but her and the pleasure between us.

I bring one hand down her front and find her clit hiding in the wet thatch of curls. I pinch her hot bundle of nerves, and she roars, tears dripping down her face onto her chest.

"Nick, God, Nick." Her head lulls to the side as she gives herself to me.

I'm a greedy motherfucker, and I want more. I rub her clit and fuck her hard, holding her pinned on my cock. She takes me like a champ because that's what she is. My champion.

Fire burns up my legs from holding the position, and my cock is as hard as granite and ready to blow. My girl is loose-limbed but holding on, her arms around my neck as I fuck her into that ethereal place where nothing exists but serenity and pleasure.

I want one more out of her. As her body shakes in my arms, my balls draw up tight, and I grit my teeth and power her down on my cock until we're both screaming out in euphoric release.

For what feels like eternity, I gently thrust into her, not wanting to leave the safety of her body, but I realize I've become selfish. My girl is a complete ragdoll. She may have even fallen asleep with my dick inside her while leaning against my chest.

I kiss along her neck and rub her body where I can reach. Her breasts, belly, hips, thighs, and up to her face. She hums in delight, the only sign she hasn't passed out completely.

"Did that hurt good?" I know the answer already.

"Better than good," she mumbles and then sighs.

I chuckle, pull out, and lay her onto her stomach. Once she's set, I whisper in her ear. "Be right back. Gonna clean you up and get some lotion."

She hums again but doesn't move. A love so pure and profound fills my heart. When I met Honor, I knew there was something special about her. I also knew there was a troubled side. I didn't know how far that side to her went, but I'm finding the side that loves life, and loves me, is far brighter and bigger than the negative voice inside her.

I've taken it as my personal goal to show her what's out there to live for. She's incredible at the gym. Whipped my office into shape in a week without any help. I've brought more money and members in this week than I have in the last three, and I owe it all to her. She's filled with marketing ideas, runs the money end of things so effortlessly, and seems to enjoy doing it. I know I should be paying her, but she knows I can't yet afford it. Not that she needs it.

I don't even know what she's worth monetarily, but I know it's a lot. Frankly, I've never cared much about money. As long as money doesn't get between us, we'll be fine.

And that voice of hers. What she doesn't know is that I've secretly told Atlas about her. Not that she's mentioned a deep-seeded desire to become a singer or anything, but he had a great idea about getting her to do an open mic night. Come out of her shell a bit more. All part of my ultimate plan to give her the tools she needs to live life to the fullest. Try new things. Live the life she was meant to live. To believe there is more out there than what she's lost.

She hasn't talked much about it, but I know the loss of her brother has been devastating. I can't begin to understand what that would be like losing one of my sisters, and they're not even my twin. We haven't shared everything from inside the womb and beyond. To suffer a loss like that would be catastrophic, but I'm going to teach her to find her own path. And I hope that path will continue to be with me.

After tonight, the gift she gave, the trust... I lean my hands against the sink basin and stare at my reflection. I've never known such love. To allow me to lose myself in her after the hell I suffered in that nightmare...to react so perfectly to every blow. I shake my head.

"I'm gone for this woman," I tell my reflection.

Then I grab the arnica and a wet washcloth to go take care of her.

★ ★ ★

Honor spins around in my rolling office chair, smiling. I love seeing that smile on her face. That once haunted look—the one she had when I found her in the hospital bed—has almost completely faded. She's not entirely a new woman or done a full three-sixty, but she's changing, growing more confident every day, and I'll do anything to help it continue.

"What's the smile for, Dove?" I come around the desk and kiss her.

She's breathless when she finally responds, her eyes a little glassy. Fuck, I love that too. The fact that every time I touch her, she loses herself. Makes me feel like a god on high, knowing I have that effect on her.

"Um..." She shakes her head. "I've been looking at the books, and everything is totally in the black! Your loans are all paid on time. You're bringing in some real money, as in money you can use to start a savings account. Isn't that great?"

I tug on her hands and pull her up to my chest, where I hug her and spin her around. "Really?"

She beams. "Yes!"

"Awesome news, babe."

A pensive look flashes across her face. "You can totally add more memberships, and then you'll be way ahead on your profit margin. I can work on some marketing plans, we can discuss advertisements in the local newspaper, and..."

I stop her from continuing, with two fingers to her lips. She quiets abruptly and frowns.

"Babe, I can't add more members."

"And why not?"

"We don't have the room. The gym's at capacity most nights. Where would we put the people?"

A somber mood settles over her. "That sucks."

"Sucks?" I snicker, pretty sure that's the first time I've ever heard her say that phrase.

"Yeah." She wraps her arms around my neck, and that feeling of contentment oozes over me like a nice warm shower spray.

"No worries. Let's just enjoy this win, yeah? Tonight we have a celebration to attend with my friends. Are you ready to meet them?"

She shrugs and looks down and away. I grip her face and force it up with my thumb to her chin. "Hey, none of that." I kiss her lips until a little brightness enters her eyes.

"What happens if they don't like me?"

I shake my head. "Dove, it's not possible. You're hot, smart, sweet, considerate, kind, and hot."

"You already said hot."

"You're so fucking hot, it warrants saying it twice." I punctuate my comment by sliding my hands down to her rear and goosing her good.

She howls and smacks my chest but does it while smiling. Mission accomplished.

"Fine, it will be fine. Go away and get your work done so I can start looking for my own place."

I snarl under my breath. Every time she mentions leaving me, I get pissed the fuck off. I like her in my space. I've told her that a hundred times, but she keeps coming back to this. It's time I ended this train of thought for good.

CHAPTER SEVENTEEN

THROAT CHAKRA

An individual driven by the throat chakra tends to be naturally poetic with their words. That person understands the power a word, song, or sound can hold over others and chooses them carefully and wisely.

HONOR

Nick crowds me and then lifts me up by the waist until I'm sitting booty to his desk. When I'm settled, he raises up my loose skirt enough that he can spread my knees and insert his body between them.

"We're not doing this right now," I warn, my voice cracking while my body temperature spikes. My nipples get in on the action too, hardening into tight little points. Instantly, the space between my thighs flushes with heat, readying for whatever he wants to do to me.

He grins wickedly. "If I wanted to fuck you right now, you'd take my cock. End of." His words are a decadent caress of my libido.

I lick my lips and focus on his mouth. He's right of course. The second he insinuates any mention of sex or touches me in a suggestive manner, my body's traitorous reaction is to go soft and open up. If I didn't know better, I'd swear he's brainwashed me into being his willing sex slave. Not that I'm complaining. It wouldn't be a bad gig. Definitely a position I'd excel at.

He bites my bottom lip playfully. "See, just mention sex, and you turn sweet on me. Right now, though, I've got an important point to make, and I want you to listen. Really hear me."

I swallow, worried that he's going to say something about not needing me in the gym now that his profit margins are up, or maybe he wants me out of his home sooner rather than later. A whirlwind of possible bad outcomes spins like a top through my subconscious.

Nick curls both of his hands into my hair behind my neck. "Get out of your head, Dove. Nothing bad is going to happen. You and me, we're solid. Okay?"

The breath I was holding leaves in a rush. He always knows just what to say to make me trust him, to put me at ease. "Okay. We're solid," I repeat, needing to say the words and hear them in order to continuing believing they are real.

"What I wanted to say is that it pisses me off when you talk about leaving the apartment. Do you not like the space?"

I cringe, and a pinch of tension fills the space between my eyes directly above my nose. "Oh my heavens...no! I love it!"

It's more a home than anywhere else. I think the phrase, but I don't say it, the fear of revealing too much this soon clouding my judgment.

"Do you not like sharing space with me? A bed, a kitchen, a bathroom?" He nudges his head against mine.

I grip both of his wrists where they are holding me. "Being with you, sharing your space, has been the happiest I've ever been. Nick...I love you." I kiss his lips so he can feel the power with which I'm speaking and feeling.

"Then why do you keep trying to leave?" A sadness flashes across his eyes.

His question shocks me as though I've been tased. "What?"

He sighs heavily, and I suddenly want to rub his shoulders, take some of the weight from them.

"Stop trying to move out." He makes an animal-like snarl. "Just stay. Live with me. Make this our...for-now home."

Our for-now home.

The words ping around my mind until they eventually sink in. "You want me to stay..." A million butterflies take flight in my stomach.

"Stay forever," he says. But that's not what floors me; it's the truth burning in his eyes.

I don't know that there's anything I can do or say to express how much him wanting to share his home, his gym, his life with me, means. So I do what I do when I can't find the words. I nod and look away.

Nick chuckles, kisses my forehead, and then head-butts me. "Dove, you gotta give me the words. I need to know what you're thinking. I've just asked my girlfriend to move in with me. Yeah, it's fast, but I don't give a flying fuck. I want you. You want me. We're happy. The end. Okay?"

I laugh in the space of our little huddle. "Okay, Nick. I'll stay."

He grips my hair harder, tugging on the roots, which has the instant effect of me focusing on nothing but him—his voice, his nearness, only him—and kicking my arousal up a hundred notches.

"You'll stop talking about moving?" He tightens his fingers at my scalp.

I inhale and then form my response so he knows I'm serious. "No more. That's it. I'm fully living with my boyfriend." I'm incapable of holding back the smile saying that to him brings.

He turns his face to the ceiling, arching his body closer to mine so more of him is pressed against me. "Jesus, Mary, and Joseph. Fuckin' A. I thought you'd never quit talking about it. How's about you consider buying something else?"

The suggestion weaves through our plastered bodies, and I nudge back to search his eyes. "Like what?"

He shrugs noncommittally. "Whatever floats your boat. You want to start looking at businesses or doing something with your degree, look around. What makes you happiest right now? What gets you excited to get out of bed? What would better you and the lives around you?" He removes his hands from my hair and drags them down my back to squeeze my hips. "When you find that, scoop it up and make it yours. It's what I did."

Nick backs away from my body and physically closes my legs on a groan. "Hate to shut the gate to heaven, but I've got a member coming in for private boxing lessons. You good?"

"Yes." I smile, truly feeling the effervescent sensation that everything is just and right in my world. "Really good. Roomie."

He cups my cheek and kisses me long and hard before

pulling away. "I'm glad you're staying."

"Me too," I say as he makes his way to the door of his office.

"See you at home?" He winks and grips the handle.

His excitement and humor make me brave enough to say what I'm thinking. "See you at home, my love."

"Love that, Dove. Keep it up."

"What?" I clasp both of my cheeks, smiling, and run my fingers through the hair he messed up with his big man paws.

"Your smile. It could change the world."

I close my eyes and let him leave, or I wouldn't have been able to.

When he's gone, I flop very unladylike into the office chair and slowly spin around in circles. The questions he asked are running a track race around my mind.

What makes you happiest right now?

Nick makes me happy.

What gets you excited to get out of bed?

Nothing. Nick is walking sex on legs.

When I have to get out of bed, though, working for Nick in the gym gets me moving. Managing his administrative needs, his money, maintaining the work behind the man and what he does here.

What would better you and the lives around you?

Now that's the question I don't have an answer to. I lift a pencil up and worry it against my bottom lip.

What would better Nick's life and therefore my own?

His happiness is paramount to me. Making him proud, showing him what I can contribute to our shared lives and this new relationship. I want to hold on to him more than anything.

Maybe I need help?

★ ★ ★

"So what you're saying is, you and my brother straight-up shacked up...*already*." Grace shoves a hunk of salad into her mouth, dropping bits of nuts and a tomato in the process.

I close my eyes, not wanting to answer her question but also not wanting to see how horrible she is at eating leafy greens.

"No. Well..." I start.

Monet puts her hand on mine where I'm clutching my napkin in a death grip. "Honor, you did just inform us both that you and Nick have decided to share space, as you put it. Am I correct in that statement?" My friend sits back and rubs her very pregnant belly in circles.

I tap the stem of my wineglass a few times while I get my bearings. "Yes," I answer flatly.

"And how is that not shacking up?" Monet smiles widely and takes a sip of her ice water.

"Told you!" Grace points at me with her fork, no longer dangling food off it, thank God.

I frown. "I guess it is. Okay, technically, Nick and I have agreed to live with one another. But that wasn't what I wanted to talk about."

Grace snorts around her bite of garlic bread. I swear, that girl...

"Let's talk about how ecstatic Ma is going to be when she finds out that you've moved in with Nicky. This is going to be an epic Sunday dinner! I can't wait!" Grace shimmies in her chair, bouncing happily through life without a care in the world.

Crud. I hadn't thought about the fact that Nick would likely want to tell his family we've moved in with one another.

Or I should say, I've moved into his place. I haven't even met the whole family yet, only his mother and Grace. Now we're going to dinner and likely making a big announcement. That's not very normal when you are first introduced to one's family. *Hi, I'm Honor. I've shacked up with your son in a matter of a month of knowing one another.*

I groan and plop my head into my hand, leaning against the white tablecloth. The restaurant is lovely, halfway between the gym, Lotus House, and downtown. The sun is shining, and it's a wonderful day to be outside. Briefly, I watch the people walking down the street, wondering if they are warring with feelings of inadequacy or if it's just me.

Monet clears her throat, bringing my attention back to the two women sitting with me at lunch. She eases to her side and grabs my hand. "Honor, you'll be fine. You already said Josephine loves you."

"Likes me! Nick is the one who said she loves me. I don't know her well enough one way or the other to make that determination."

"Puh-leeze! Ma's bringing you homemade dinners every couple days. She doesn't do that for just anyone. Her food is her fortune, and you're getting it on the regular. You feel me?"

I roll my eyes, and Grace laughs and points her fork at me again, this time with pasta dangling precariously off it. "Totally loves you. Did she mention grandbabies at any point?"

"Er...perhaps."

Grace's eyes widen to the size of our salad plates. "She did! Was that on her last visit?" Her tone is bordering on hysterical and excited. Hysterically excited, I presume.

I think about it for a moment. "No, it was on her first visit. And the second, actually."

"Shit! You are so fucked! Mama wants you spittin' out blondies ASAP!" She snort-laughs this time.

My head starts throbbing, and I press two fingers to each temple and rub in frantic circles.

"Grace, you're freaking the poor girl out. Mama Josephine is just excited. Don't fret, Honor. It's good that she likes you. Really good. If she didn't..." Monet makes a face as if she's just eaten something disgusting. "Anyhoo, what is it you wanted to discuss with us?"

I tell the two about Nick's suggestion about finding out what gets me out of bed and makes me happy, but most importantly, what I thought would better my life and the lives around me.

"And that's the problem. I have no idea. I never have. That's why I've floated around from one charity function to another with my mother. I had nothing better to do. No talents or skills outside of being a rich girl who stands on the sidelines and looks pretty at parties."

Monet vehemently shakes her head. "Not true. You are a college-educated woman with two degrees. That takes skill and effort. Do not sell yourself short because you haven't found your calling. There may have been some bumps in the road after you graduated, and you're feeling uncertain about what's next, but you have made immense strides in finding the things that bring you joy. Remember that. You'll find what it is you are meant to do." She finishes breathily, practically panting, as if it took serious effort to get all of her words out.

The poor thing. I can't imagine what it would be like to be pregnant, have a being living inside me. *Nick's baby.* Then again, if it was Nick's child, it would be perfect. Dark skinned, dark hair, light eyes. Full of love and a good life. He'd make it so, and I think he'd teach me along the way.

Grace finishes her bite and bursts my baby-making bubble, bringing the topic back to the matter at hand. "But you love working at the gym, right?" Grace asks pointedly.

I brighten, and a smile spreads across my face at the mere mention of the gym. "Yes, and it's totally in the black and making a profit. Only it's a shame that he can't take on more members and make a far larger profit. So many would benefit from his training, experience, and service."

Monet taps at her bottom lip, her coal-black eyes flashing with worry. "Why can't he add members?"

"Unfortunately, space in the facility is limited. He'd have to expand, and he definitely doesn't have the capital for that type of venture or the square footage. It's not a small gym, but it's not as big as the regular franchises."

"It's awful how franchises steal all the mom-and-pop business." Grace groans.

I can imagine the frustration of coming from a family that has a boutique winery. "And see, that's the thing. What Nick offers is special, and people aren't canceling their membership. He's absolutely closing in on capacity. Soon he'll be turning people away." I frown.

Gracie shrugs. "Well, you have tons of money. Why don't you buy the building next to his? I heard a rumor that the owner wanted to retire, but the offers weren't good enough on his building for him to do it. A lot of people don't have the coin to renovate. They look for buildings that are turnkey." She pouts and stabs at her lunch.

A light bulb goes off in my head. "Are you referring to the juice and smoothie bar or the laundromat?"

"The laundromat." Grace's entire face illuminates as her

excitement grows. "It's huge." She spreads her arms out wide. "And it has another storage building behind it and a loft on top."

Interesting. Our apartment shares a wall. "Does the owner plan to stay in the loft?"

"Not last I heard. Wanted to move to a retirement community up north on a golf course." She grins. "Old people love to golf, I hear. Not my parents. They love to drink wine, play music too loud, and get all up in their kids' lives."

"Really?" The hamster starts spinning its wheel.

"Really, my parents are like an octopus with its eight arms when it comes to their kids. Just wait, they're gonna cling to you and want to know everything about you. Then they are going to tell you how to live your life differently...the way they want." She laughs.

I shake my head. "No, I meant the retiree, but now you've got me scared of your family again."

Monet bumps my shoulder. "Looks like you've got some research ahead of you. Exciting proposition, perhaps."

"Yes, yes I do. Grace, do you think you could introduce me to the owner?"

"Sure. I've met him a bazillion times. Done laundry at his place for Nick when he has the loaner towels to wash."

Now that the idea has taken wing, a niggle of anticipation prods me like a little devil with a pitchfork. What if I paid to expand the gym and the apartment? It could be *my contribution* to what he's already built, expanding our lives together. I could run the business easy enough when it's double the size. Nick would make a mint, and we could have a much larger home, including a whirlpool tub for his aching muscles, a walk-in shower, more bedrooms. A reading room with a library full of books. The options are endless.

If it works out, it will have to be a surprise. Something I do all on my own so Nick knows I'm not a loser—that I'm capable of much more than he's seen of me in the past. I also have to do it for me. To prove to myself I'm not worthless. Just because my brother took his life doesn't mean I have to give up everything in mine.

I may have been Hannon's twin, but we're not the same. He didn't fight our parents when they threatened to end Sean's career, have him fired from the hospital he loves, because they are donors and on the hospital's board of directors.

He gave up.

They broke him and have spent years trying to break me. No more. I'm going to make this decision for myself, for my love, and for my future.

I can't wait to get to work.

★ ★ ★

Nick opens the door of a bar named Harmony Jack's and gestures for me to enter. Behind us are his friends Atlas and Silas, as well as Amber and Dash. At first I felt weird seeing Amber outside of the hospital, but she hasn't brought up what occurred a few weeks ago, and neither have I. Her doing that for me added a level of trust toward Nick's friends that I'll hold close to my chest. The people he shared his time with were incredible. All of them. Unfortunately, Monet, whom I've come to consider a close friend, was exhausted after the launch-party dinner we attended for a new album Atlas and Silas put together. They'd nabbed some local talent, and the album Atlas wrote and the kid sang was hitting charts across the States.

The entire party had been exciting and stressful at the same time. Nick was amazing, though. He didn't leave my side all evening and made a point to include me in conversations with all his friends. Now, we're hitting what he calls the chill-time-after-the-party party at his favorite bar.

I'm not a big bar frequenter, but as far as places to imbibe, this place has a cool, hip vibe. Blue lights flash across a stage where a male and a female are singing a rock version of Sonny and Cher's "I Got You Babe." Across from the stage are several pool tables and some sort of long table with rolling discs on it. I'll have to ask Nick what game it is.

The group heads over to a section of tables that have a reserved card on them. A petite woman with short spiked purple hair and a curvy body approaches and hugs Atlas. "Where's that sexy wife of yours? Don't tell me you left her at home where I can't drool all over her?" She pouts prettily.

Atlas tips his head back and laughs, hugging the woman again. "She's taking care of Aria Monet, my even smaller fiery Latina."

"How old is that sweet thing now?"

"Pushing eighteen months. Getting into all kinds of trouble...just like her mama."

The woman smacks his bicep like an old friend. "It's good to see you, man. You gonna play?"

His eyes flash to Nick's and then mine. A strange foreboding falls over me momentarily.

"Nah, not tonight. Just going to enjoy the music and check out new talent."

"Cool." The pixie-like woman shakes hands with Dash and Silas, hugs Amber, and then turns to Nick and me. "How's it hanging, tough guy?" She puts up her hands and pretends to make some jabs at Nick's muscles.

He battles her hands for a moment. "Long, thick, and a little to the right. Maybe you should ask my girlfriend that question."

Her eyes widen, and she smirks. "Girlfriend, eh? That's a first." She smiles widely and genuinely when she extends her hand toward me. "Jacqueline. I own this bar, but my friends use just Jack."

I offer my hand. "Good to meet you, Just Jack."

She shakes my hand and pulls me in for a hug. "Quick, this one. Smart and looks like a fuckin' angel. How'd you score something so sweet?" She's speaking to Nick, but her gaze is roving up and down my form. I'm pretty sure she's checking out more than my outfit.

I shimmy from one foot to the next in my pencil skirt and silk white blouse. Nick thought I looked like a naughty librarian, so I put my hair up in a loose bun to aid in his fantasy. He liked the look so much he bent me over one of his gym benches and fucked the daylights out of me before we ever even made it out of the building. At the end of our lovemaking, he reddened my ass with a series of spankings so hard I'd have no choice but be reminded whose body my ass belonged to. I've been twitching with the memory all night, readying for round two back at home. The alcohol in my system from the party, the flickering lights above, and this woman's suggestive comments are not helping the need flooding inside me.

Nick loops an arm around my waist and tugs me to his side. "Hands off. Get your own angel. This one's mine to dirty up with all the devilish things I can think of. Aren't you, Dove?"

Thank God the lights are flashing in a dark room, or my

cheeks would be shining cherry red for all to see. I nod and sidle up to his chest.

The conversation changes quickly and drinks are ordered. I sip on a whiskey and 7UP, my new favorite drink in the entire world, and sway to the music. Until all of a sudden, I'm being led by Nick, the lights around me flashing, the music thundering inside my heart. Nick walks me up a set of stairs to a DJ's booth.

"What do you want to sing, Dove?" Nick gestures to an iPad that has songs listed from a prerecorded track of songs.

"What is this? What are you talking about?" I ask, not sure what's going on.

"Karaoke. You're gonna use that songbird voice of yours and show these people the God-given gift you have. Spread your wings, baby. Try something new." He beams.

As the mention of what he just said takes hold of my liquor-infused brain, the floor falls out beneath my feet.

CHAPTER EIGHTEEN

Saddle Dive–Variation of Airplane Pose
(Sanskrit: Dekasana)

Aerial yoga participants often feel like they are defying gravity as so many of the asanas are done above the ground. This pose in particular gives the yogi the feeling of taking flight. It's an intense shoulder and upper body stretch. This position will help teach balance and work your core. Beginning yogis start with the silks stretched out across the abdomen, hips, and some of the quads until their body is ready for a more intense stretch.

HONOR

"Baby, it's not a big deal. You've got the pipes. Just close your eyes and pretend like you're singing in the shower," Nick offers what I feel is rather terrible advice.

Something inside me snaps. I can feel my nostrils flaring as I size up my boyfriend. How could he do this to me without asking? Drag me up on stage as if singing in front of a crowd is not a huge, momentous occasion. I hope he can feel the heat from the laser beams I'm shooting him. His lip curls, and his sex-laced pucker forms across his lips. With one of his hands, he cups his package suggestively.

Through my anger, I clench my teeth and point at his chest...hard. "How dare you!" I whisper angrily. "My singing is not something I'm ready to share with the masses. When I sing, it's private. For you, and you alone." Adding pressure, I dig my pointer finger into his sternum. Take that!

"Ouch, babe. Lay off. Relax." Nick grabs my hand and twists it behind my back, forcing my upper body to connect with his. A little of the tension within me eases away at our shared proximity. God, I love and hate that about him. He can manipulate my body and mind with a single touch.

Nick's eyes turn hard, and he uses the darker, more dominant tone that makes my panties wet and turns my mind into a puddle of mush. "You *will* do this, Honor." That tone sears through me, and I want to beg for a single ounce of pain I know his hand can gift me.

Even irate, I'm at a loss for how to proceed. I don't want to disappoint him, but I'm scared. "Nick." I say his name with a warning—against what, I'm uncertain.

Twisting me into a position behind the curtain, away from any onlookers, he corners me in a dark cubby. Once there, he makes quick work of the top three buttons of my blouse, easing his hand in between the fabric and under my bra, where he takes my nipple between two fingers. With force and intent, his fingers act like tiny little clamps, pinching the tender flesh in an iron grip.

I moan and tremble against the onslaught of pleasure, going perfectly slack against his form. His command over my body and my mind is unbelievable. In this moment, I'd do anything to please him and, therefore, please myself. Ever since he started introducing me to small amounts of D/s play in the physical sense, I've been able to let go. Release the anxiety and fears inside me, giving it all up to him. I allow Nick to take care of me, learn what I need, and give it to me in all things. Before him, I didn't know this type of connection with another person existed. He understands my need for pain, for release, giving him the power to mold me into his willing and worshipped submissive.

"That's right." His dark stare locks me into compliance. "You are going to do this for me but, more importantly, *for you*. Show the world how talented my girl is. And when you have, I'm going to take you home, make you cry, and fuck your remaining fears away. Got it?" He pinches the erect flesh until I cry out with the burning pain. No one hears because the music is too loud, and Nick muffles my scream with his sinful mouth.

He flicks his tongue against mine, invading my mouth with deep, draining kisses. All along he tweaks and pinches my nipple until my body is no longer my own. My hips are grinding, my pelvis aching to drag along his firm length, all but begging to be taken. In a flash, he pulls away, removing his hand and putting me back together one button at a time. I pout, not wanting to be dressed but rather taken out of this bar and undressed.

"You ready to sing for me, baby?"

I nod because right now, I'd do anything for this man.

"Words, Dove."

My vision is blurry as he cups my face and lays a series of kisses from my temple, down along my cheek, landing on my lips. "You are gorgeous. You sing like an angel. Share it with the world. Be different, baby. Take chances."

I wrap both my hands around his neck, lift up on my toes, and kiss him once more.

He pets my cheek. "Live the life you are meant to live."

Live the life you're meant to live.

He's said this before, but it's never been so prevalent and important. There's no reason why I can't get up there and sing. No reason to be afraid of what people are going to think, because only two people matter. Nick and me. Monet and Dr. Batchelor have been urging me to take more chances, put myself out there. This could be one of those times. Nothing can hurt me here. Nick would never allow it.

"Where are you going to be?" I ask frantically, needing to know he'll be close.

"Wherever you want me." His fingers dig into the back of my neck, massaging, centering, grounding.

"Right below the stage where I can see you. Then if I get scared..." I trail off.

"I'll be there to catch you. Always. Now sing me a song, Dove."

I smile softly and nod.

He leads me over to the table, and I scour through the list and find the perfect song. If my man wants to test my limits, I'm going to test his.

The song..."Fever."

For a couple of minutes, I breathe in and out, using the yoga-style breathing I've learned in my study with Nick and Grace. The performer before me finishes, and the DJ hands me the microphone. I walk slowly to the single stool and mic stand at the center of the stage. A blue-tinted light shines down from above, casting everything in an ethereal glow.

The lights change, turning into a more golden hue, making me feel more spotlighted. Nick's large form becomes visible below, standing right where he said he'd be. He's a wall of muscle and man. Sharp, edgy, Italian features that ooze sexuality from every pore. His tight black dress shirt shimmers when the light catches it. He crosses his arms over his chest and stares. Those pale-green eyes, haloed by sculpted eyebrows, would look menacing if I didn't know him better. Only I do, and I can see in his stance that he's in full command, using his sex appeal and stunning features to pull me out of a place of anxiety and fear to one of sex and sin. He knows exactly how to push every single one of my buttons, but right now, I'm going to turn the tables on him. Show him the kind of woman I want to be for a man like him. A woman he can be proud to have on his arm, in his bed, sharing his life.

The first base notes of the music plunk out through the loudspeakers, and I start by swaying my shoulders and then pair each beat to a kick of my hips. While singing the first breathy lines, I trail one hand behind my head and run it down the back of my neck toward my front, over the side of my breast, easing it down my ribcage and lengthwise along my hip and thigh. I squeeze my legs, swiveling them left and right, the power of the song making me hot and bothered—or it could be the man I'm singing to who is doing that to me. As I belt out the words about loving my man and the feeling I get when he's holding me, my voice comes out a cross between a Peggy Lee version and a younger, more unique sound.

Nick's eyes have not left me for a single second. Everywhere I put my hands, his gaze follows. He licks his lips, bites them, and curls one inside his mouth as if he's barely able to contain his own hunger.

I get into the lyrics, losing myself in the sensual nature of the song, the man in front of me, and the heady beat until I've sung the last word. I'm breathless, my head to the sky, the lights coating me in warmth, and for a moment, I don't hear anything. All sound is lost. A stillness, a peace and quiet settles over me in a rowdy bar in downtown San Francisco. It's that same essence of tranquility I get after I've cut myself or Nick has spanked me into oblivion. Here in this place, there's nothing but freedom.

All too soon, it's gone, and I'm bum rushed by an explosion of applause. It feels like my eardrums are going to implode with the strength of the response from the audience below. I can barely take it in because I feel as though I'm flying, soaring above everyone, including myself. For the first time in forever... I'm proud of myself.

I look everywhere, not believing what I'm seeing and hearing.

"Uh...thank you. Thank you," I sputter into the mic before walking it over to the DJ.

"Lady, you're the shit!" he says. "Anytime you want to sing, I'll move your ass up to first spot. Anytime. Multiple times. Whatever. Damn, that was good."

I shyly thank him and head toward the stairs. My guy is there at the bottom, waiting for me.

He holds his arms out, and I rush down the stairs and fly into them. He spins me around and holds me so tightly, I can't breathe. I don't even care because he's laughing in my ear and swinging me. Nick sets me on my feet, cups my cheeks, and kisses me one, two, three times. He loves doing things in threes.

"So damn proud of you, babe. My God. You're a star!" He kisses me again, and I loop my arms around his back, enjoying the powerful excitement rushing between the two of us.

I did it! I finally did it, and for the first time in my life, I'm proud of myself.

"Come on. After that, you need a fresh drink! Damn, my woman is a songbird." He chuckles and leads me over to the table with his friends.

All four of them stand up and clap heartily. I feel a heat suffuse my cheeks, and I cower against Nick's chest.

"No way, nuh-uh. You're gonna take your applause like a champ, babe. That was fan-fucking-tastic. I knew you were good, but that's a whole new level. Tell her, Atlas!" He gestures to his friend.

"Seriously, Honor, do you want to sing professionally?" His wild hair flops into his eyes, and he pushes a lock back. It stubbornly falls into his face again.

I shake my head, feeling a little dizzy with all of the attention on me.

Silas McKnight, a hunky black man whom I found out owns Knight & Day Productions, stands up. "Girl, you've got a true gift. Not something we see every day, and *believe me*, we're always lookin'."

"Thank you." I nudge Nick and gesture to my empty glass.

He whistles, lifts his arm above his above his head, and waves two fingers to Jack, who's behind the bar. She dismisses the line of people standing in front of her, pours a fresh glass of champagne, and taps a new beer for Nick before hustling over.

"Really amazing. Feel free to clean those pipes out whenever you get a bee stinging your ass." She hands us the drinks. "Girl, with your face, that body, killer voice...hell yeah.

It's good for business. This is on the house." She buses the table, winks at me, and then takes her leave.

"So she's into women, then?" I ask the group, and all of them dissolve in a fit of laughter.

Nick shakes his head. "My dove, so innocent. Yeah, babe. She's into chicks not dicks."

"Cool." I sip my champagne and let the chilly bubbles slide down my parched throat. Nick lets me go so he can visit the bathroom while Silas makes his way over to me.

"You really do have a beautiful voice. I'd sign you in a minute if you're thinking about going pro."

I cross my arms around my body. "Not really a stage and lights kind of girl. Singing is something I do for stress release, but I don't feel that calling."

"What do you do, if you don't mind me asking?"

I glance toward the bathrooms to check if Nick's still gone. "I've been helping Nick manage his gym, and the work is rewarding. Plus, I get to help Nick, which makes me happy."

He nods and takes a pull from his beer.

"And I'm working on another secret project now that's keeping me busy."

Silas smiles and looks at the stage as if he's gauging the talent, his hazel eyes a stunning contrast against his mocha-colored skin. If I had to guess, I'd say he's probably not a hundred percent African American. The other half could very well be Caucasian. Whatever it is, his mother and father did well in the genetics department, because he's extremely attractive in that smooth and suave *GQ* way. I prefer my men brute-like, bossy, and Italian, but I know a lot of women would not turn down a date with him.

As I'm about to ask him if he's seeing anyone, Dara

Jackson from Lotus House makes an appearance, pushing through the crowd. Her dress is a tight, shimmery blue number that barely covers her booty. And this woman has a whole lot of booty. Long, dark waves of streaked brown and blonde hair trails down her back in big curls. Once she's given hugs and says hello to Dash, Amber, Atlas, and Nick as he returns right on cue from the bathroom, Nick hooks her arm and brings her over to where Silas and I stand.

I glance at Silas, and I swear his tongue is hanging out of his mouth. His eyes are all over the sexy newcomer.

I nudge his shoulder. "Hot, huh?"

"So hot," he whispers back, and I laugh at his obvious discomfort.

Dara is all big smiles, pouty lips, and giant Caribbean-blue eyes. They are so intense, I wonder if the color is real, or maybe she wears contacts for fun or to mess with peoples' heads.

Nick lets Dara go and loops an arm around me. "Hey, babe, you know Dara Jackson from Lotus House."

I smile. "I do. Good to see you again."

She glances at Nick and his possessive hold on me. "Glad you scooped up your man. I'm sure there are yogis everywhere crying into their soy chai latte over the resident hottie being off the market."

"Absolutely off the market," Nick confirms and then curves his head toward mine and kisses me. "We're living together now too." He says this with pride and another kiss. The man is definitely not concerned about public displays of affection. I'm getting used to it, but for Nick, I'll manage any discomfort.

"Righteous. And who is this tall, dark drink of heaven?"

Her hand extends toward Silas.

He takes hold of her hand, brings it up to his lips, and kisses her knuckles. I swoon right along with Dara, who sways closer toward him.

"I'm Silas McKnight. I work with Atlas."

Right then, Atlas clasps Silas on the back. "Don't let him fool you, Dara. He's my boss. The dude is rich, available, and a hard worker." He clocks Silas on the arm. "Don't say I never did nuthin' for ya, buddy, but I've got to get home. Mila says Aria is awake with a fever and calling for her daddy. My girls call, I'm out. Bye, guys. Great job tonight, Honor. Really killer voice. Hope to hear it again soon."

Silas ruffles Atlas's hair. "Catch ya Monday. Don't be late... again!"

Atlas chuckles, lifts a hand above his head, and waves as he exits. Dash and Amber are quick to follow.

"We've, um, got plans tomorrow. We should, uh..." Amber twists her lips in a pensive gesture.

Dash chuckles and hooks her around his waist. "I promised my wife a handful of orgasms tonight. It's been a long week for her. So we're headed out."

Amber's eyes widen. "My goodness. I can't believe you just said that! Dash!"

"Little bird, everyone here tonight is going to go home and fuck like rabbits. We're no different. Am I right?"

Nick coughs into his hand. "I'm hitting my girl for sure." He twists his head to where his lips rest against my ear. "With an emphasis on the hitting part," he whispers, and a bout of strong arousal slams through my system.

"Yes, please," I murmur back.

"I think we all need to head home." Nick sets down his

beer, grabs my glass, and adds it to the ones on the table.

"Guys, I just got here!" Dara pouts.

"I'm happy to keep you company." Silas offers his hand.

Dara smiles, and he leads her over to an empty table before waving to Jack.

"See ya!" Nick says and tugs on my hand before I can even say goodbye.

"Nick, I didn't say goodbye!"

"Too much time. I need you naked and biting down on my shoulder while I ride you wild. No time to waste."

The image of me bare, riding him instead, his huge length piercing me deeply, has me positively panting. "Maybe I want to ride *you*. After the spanking, of course," I say in my most sultry and submissive voice.

He growls one single word that has my toes curling and my heart pounding.

"Deal."

★ ★ ★

Our family's Realtor meets me at the laundromat next to Nick's building a few days later. His suit alone costs twice as much as what Nick pays for his monthly mortgage on his business and home.

Mr. Harbinger wipes a single finger along the top of one of the washing machines. "He's offering to let you keep all of the equipment and buy the property as is." He scowls and flicks his fingers.

"Yes, I know; we discussed it. I'm going to keep two of them for washing towels, but the remaining lot of them are being donated to local shelters, missions, and charities that need them. A lot of them are brand new and will do some good for the community," I explain happily.

Mr. Harbinger frowns. "Are you completely sure you want this property? I can find you far better in more affluent areas."

I tilt my head. "Another area won't work. I'm expanding my boyfriend's business." I hook a thumb over my shoulder toward the wall that is shared with Nick's gym.

"The gym? Your significant other is the gym owner next door?"

I smile widely and with pride. "Yes. And the loft. I'm going to hire some of our people to tear down the wall between the two lofts above our gym. It will triple the current size of our home."

"You *live* here. On this street, above a filthy gymnasium of men who pound each other with their fists for sport?"

His statement rankles, and I'm unable to keep the glower from appearing across my face. "Mr. Harbinger, you really shouldn't judge a book by its cover. The neighborhood is fine. I know practically everyone now. And Nick takes care of me. Besides, the guys who come to the gym would never let anything happen to me or any woman. It's perfectly safe."

"What do your father and mother think about this?" he asks haughtily.

I shrug. "I don't know, and I don't care. Do you have the paperwork? I'm eager to sign and get moving on this project."

He huffs, sets his briefcase on one of the washing machines, and pulls out a stack of papers with yellow tabs where I'm to sign.

"You're paying above market value." His tone is conciliatory and condescending at the same time.

I snicker. "I know. Old fella wants to retire. Who am I to

deny him what he thinks the place is worth? And I'd have paid more because I want this...very much."

Mr. Harbinger pushes up his rimless glasses. Nothing on him is out of place. He has snow-white hair, slicked back to perfection. His suit is pressed, nary a wrinkle to be found. Scanning him up and down, I note that he fits into the life my parents have but not mine. Not the life I'm making for myself here in Berkeley with my Italian Stallion.

I take the pen he offers and sign away for the property. I cannot wait to tell Nick about my plan. It's going to be amazing, but first, I need to donate all the extra equipment and get it cleaned out. Especially the loft. I'm going to hire two teams to outfit the loft at the same time that work is being done below. Then maybe once this half is complete, Nick will let me update the rest of our home.

A stab of anxiety pricks me as I hand the papers to the Realtor.

What if Nick doesn't like the idea of expanding our home and his business? Maybe he won't want to share his dream with me. It's definitely a very big risk I'm taking with a man's man type like Nick. He's got a dominant personality in and out of the bedroom and a true old-fashioned family. He could very well not take kindly to his woman making changes like this without telling him.

I pluck at my lips with thumb and forefinger. Mr. Harbinger snaps his briefcase closed, comes to me, and air kisses both sides of my cheeks. "If that's all you're buying today, I'll take my leave."

I chuckle. "That's all for today. Thank you."

"Until next time." He half bows, which I've always thought was really weird. I'm not royalty. My mother, on the other hand, loves his formality. Me, I just appreciate that he takes care of everything and does it quickly.

As he leaves, I look around at the brightly lit laundromat, trying to imagine it as a gym. I can totally see it, but the real question is...will Nick?

My heart says he will; my mind fears he won't. There's only one way to find out.

I think back to the conversation I had with my new doctor, Shelby Batchelor.

"Worst-case scenario, he says no, and you resell the property. No harm, no foul."

No harm, no foul. She also reminded me that the greatest achievements in life often come when taking the greatest risks. Nick has absolutely been my biggest leap of faith, but this, this will be his. He'll have to agree to commit to me and this relationship for the long haul. As he's mentioned before, it's moving fast, practically at the speed of light, but I can't deny what we have is real. It's honest, and it's good. With Nick, I'm beginning to feel like I have a purpose, alone and with him. I haven't had that before. Nick pushes me all the time to come outside of my box, climb without being afraid of how I'm going to get down. He's teaching me that life is worth living. And I can't do that holed up in my room or at a stuffy charity ball or political function. Life is to be seen outdoors and communing with the ones you love. Breaking bread, spending time, supporting each other's dreams.

I hope Nick can see that this expansion is me supporting his dream and finding my own.

I just have to have faith.

CHAPTER NINETEEN

THROAT
CHAKRA

*The throat chakra couple is a rare couple to come across.
They tend to be very talented people. They spend their time
in careers or positions they personally and emotionally feel
connected to, as if they were "meant to" serve the world in
that chosen capacity.*

NICHOLAS

Flying blind. That's what it feels like as Honor leads me
blindfolded through the gym's door and outside to the busy
street. I assume she's going to put me in her car, but instead
she walks me to the right. The Bay Area wind whips my hair
around and puts goosebumps on my bare arms. I'm wearing
nothing but my track pants and a ribbed tank, my standard
work attire.

"Dove, where are you taking me?" One of her hands is

tight around my waist and the other pressing against the center of my back.

"Shhh...and no peeking. It's a surprise. I told you already!"

I chuckle but follow along, trusting her to not smash me into a wall or a car.

"Okay, stop right there," she says, and then all I hear is the sound of a door being unlocked, a bell tinkling against glass, and her labored breathing.

Honor grabs my hands this time and leads me into a building. We didn't walk that far, so I can't figure out what she's up to.

"Are you ready for your surprise?"

"From you? Born ready." I pucker my lips as if I'm expecting a kiss.

She giggles, and it's the most beautiful sound in the world. Her warm lips press against mine, and I take advantage, pulling her into my arms, where she gasps, opening her mouth, inviting me in. I plunder her mouth with my tongue, not giving a fuck if there are people where she brought us or what. If my girl is going to get close, put her mouth to mine, I'm going to fucking kiss her full out. End of story.

After long licks of her vanilla and mint taste, I pull away. "Great surprise."

She laughs and smacks my arm and then rips the blindfold off my face. I blink against the suddenly bright lights of what used to be the laundromat next door. Now the machines have all been removed, the walls have been painted with a fresh coat of gray paint with black, red, and white stripes running down the center. Just like the color scheme in my gym.

I look around, contemplating what I'm seeing. The once laminate floors are a brushed clean concrete. Next to one wall is an exact replica of the free weights set-up I have next door. Another area has several shiny black and red punching bags lying on the floor like sentinels waiting for orders. Mirrors span one far wall where red protective mats are stacked ten high. Another section has a table in the center with unopened boxes of new gloves, headgear, fighting pads, knee pads, and everything else we have over at my gym. Only there's twice as much.

"Babe, what am I looking at?"

I spin around and find her with her arms crossed protectively over herself and finger and thumb at her mouth, plucking her lip nervously.

She flings her hands out as if she's drying them off. "Okay." The one word is abrupt and filled with what can only be panic. "You know how you told me to find what makes me happy, what gets me out of bed, and what would better my life and the lives around me?"

For a moment, I rescan the room. "Holy..." I cover my mouth as I walk around the huge space, taking it all in. It's at least twice the size of the current gym but bare of any real set-up or machines.

"You're what makes me happy, Nick."

I focus on the matching color scheme, the new equipment. "Jesus..."

"And you and the gym are what makes me excited to get out of bed in the morning."

"Mary..."

Her voice cracks. "And I want to better your life, *our lives.*"

"Joseph." I gasp, push both hands into my hair, and tug at the roots. The prickle of pain centers me.

"Nick...I want you to expand the business. Um...I want

you to expand it with me."

I give the room one more gander, and then all my attention is on her. The most precious, selfless, giving woman I know. My heart pounds, the surface of my skin prickling with an electric energy I'm not used to. There is so much I want to say, but the words feel jumbled and coated with intense emotion.

I pause to take it all in, breathe through the overwhelming feelings skittering along every single one of my pores.

"You did this for me?" I can hardly recognize my own voice as I barely get the words out.

She nods.

"Words, Dove. Right now!" I shake my head. "Babe, need to hear every single word in your head. Don't leave anything out."

Tears spring to her eyes, making them seem glittery, as though I'm looking into two matching crystal balls.

My girl stands tall, lifts her chin, and clasps her hands loosely in front of her. "Yes. I did this for you. For us. And for me. If you want, I would like to help expand the business into this building. I've already bought it, the back lot, and storage space and the loft above it. I want to expand our home so that it's no longer our for-now home but our forever home."

Our forever home.

"You want to saddle your horse in my stable for good."

She nods.

"Tie your hitch to my truck."

She nods again, but her gaze never leaves mine.

"You want to do all of this, with me, out of everything else you could do in the world with that money you have."

"It's nothing without you. This is the first place I ever felt free to be me. You taught me that, Nick. You gave me the tools to find what I want to do. I want to use my business skills and manage this gym. Expand it and our home. With you. That will make me happy."

I chuckle and take the ten steps needed to stand directly in front of her.

"So we're going to go into business together. You and me, partners?" I hold out my hand for her to shake. She puts hers into it.

When she tries to let go, I stop her.

"We're going to build our forever home...you and me."

Her response is like watching an angel spread her wings for the first time. Nothing but magnificence in her smile, the light in her eyes, and her reddened cheeks. I can see the happiness radiating from her face, which also makes me head over heels for her.

"There's only one problem..."

Her eyebrows furrow. "I've taken care of everything so far..."

"We're not married."

She licks her lips and takes a slow breath, glancing away and then down at her shoes. "Well, um, that's okay. Lots of people start out their lives unmarried and wait until the time is right."

"The time is right," I deadpan.

"It is?" Her question reveals surprise.

"It's right now."

Her eyes get teary again. "Nick..."

Right then and there, I get down on one knee. "Honor Carmichael, I love you. Not a person in this world would have ever done this for me. *For us.* You could have anyone, anything..."

"But I want you." Her voice is a whisper in the wind.

I grin huge. "Let me finish."

She swallows and a tear falls. "Okay."

"You could have anyone, anything with the resources you have, but I will tell you this one thing right now. No man will ever love you the way I do. I will put you and your happiness first in all things, the same way you just proved you will for me. There's always been something special about you. From the minute I laid eyes on you, I thought to myself...she can't be real. And you are. More real than anything else in my life."

Even though I'd been thinking about making her mine for good, this is still sudden, so I don't have a ring. I pull my dog tags from around my neck, the ones I've had with me through all the good, bad, and ugly, and I hold them up to her.

"This will have to do for now, but I will get you a ring that shows my commitment to the world. This is my commitment to you. I've worn these every single day for the last eleven years. They represent honor, but I don't need them anymore. You're the only Honor I need." My eyes moisten, and my throat clogs with emotion.

Tears fall down her cheeks, and she gets onto her knees and holds my cheeks in her tiny hands as I place my dog tags around her neck. "I love you." Her declaration is accompanied by a watery mess of tears.

"Marry me." I press my forehead to hers. "Be my forever. Marry me."

She nods.

"Dove..." I warn.

"Yes! Yes, a million times over, I'll marry you."

"Fuckin' A. You'll marry me. My goddess, my angel, my Honor."

"I'll marry you, Nick," she repeats, as if she also needs to hear it multiple times to believe it's real.

"Over my dead body!" a woman screeches from the entrance to the building about twenty feet from where we're kneeling.

I fling my head around and find what has to be an older replica of my woman standing next to a tall, dark-haired man. They are both wearing stuffy suits and matching sneers.

"For heaven's sake, Honor, get up off this disgusting floor and step away from the filthy mongrel groping you. Don't act like a dirty tramp. I've raised you better than to canoodle with people who are below your status and beneath your caliber of pedigree."

The words burn me like verbal fire, and I can only imagine what they are doing to my girl. I pull her to a stand. "I'm guessing you're the mother? The father?"

"We're Timothy and Judi Carmichael, and we're here to remove our daughter and prevent a lifetime of mistakes. Come now, Honor."

Honor's body goes statue still in my arms. Her skin turns cold and her eyes seem distant.

"Babe, you okay?"

"Don't let them take me," she pleads, her lip quivering.

She's scared of them. Physically trembling in my arms. Oh, hell no! No woman of mine is going to live in fear, especially of her parents.

The couple enters the space, the door swinging shut behind them.

"Look, Mr. and Mrs. Carmichael, you busted in on an extremely private moment between me and your daughter. As I'm sure you heard, I'm now her fiancé. You can deal directly with me. Not her." I put my arm over her shoulders and keep her close. She clings to my side.

Her mother rolls her eyes and sighs. "Timothy, we don't have time for this. We have the dinner with the Braxtons. Leonard, their son, is expecting her. And look at her." The woman's lip curls up as if she's smelling something funky. "She looks like a heathen. We'll have to stop at home, get her dressed, hair and makeup done, and move quickly in order to be on time."

"Leonard?" I jolt, my spine, straightening while I fist the hand not holding Honor possessively.

This time her father speaks up. "That is the man to whom she will be marrying. It's best for business and our familial relations. I'm sure you understand that...Mr. Salerno, son of Nicholas Salvatore Salerno Sr. of Salerno Hills winery, a boutique vineyard outside of the city. Most of your family works there, correct?"

"So you've looked me up. Good for you. How does what my family does have anything to do with the fact that I, Nicholas Salerno Jr., am marrying your daughter with or without your permission?" I smile, lips closed, trying not to lose my cool.

Her mother shakes her head. "Reading between the lines is not these people's strong suit, Timothy. Lay out the consequences so we can be on our way."

At that comment, Honor bolts from my side and stomps over to her mother. "You wouldn't dare hurt his family over me. The pathetic offspring, the one you wished was in Hannon's position instead of your prized son." Honor's tone is full of spitfire and rage. I love every second of it.

With a quickness I didn't expect from a small refined woman, her arm comes out, and she smashes her handbag across Honor's face. I watch in horror as Honor tilts and sways to the side, about to fall. Her mother catches her by her hair, twisting her arm around the long waves and forcing her neck back. Honor falls to her knees. "I will ruin this man's life and family if you don't heed our request now and get up, get in the car, and move back home until we can plan a wedding for you to Mr. Braxton."

"The fuck you will," I growl and grab on to her mother's arm, squeezing it, letting her know with one grip that if she doesn't let go, I'm going to break her arm with my bare hand. "Let go of my woman. Now." There is so much hate in my words, I don't even recognize myself.

Mrs. Carmichael releases Honor's hair, and she falls to the floor. I lift her up by her underarms and push her behind me. "There's nothing you can do to me or my family that would ever have us running in fear."

"Try me," Mrs. Carmichael says. "I know your family owes money to the bank for the land that winery sits on. Would be a shame if those loans all of a sudden fell through."

"And I'll pay them!" Honor fires back.

Her mother's eyes narrow into tiny slits. "You'll be cut off."

What comes out of Honor's mouth is downright effective and surprising. Laughter. She starts laughing. Hysterically. "You think you can cut me off from my trust? The inheritance set up by my grandfather, my great-grandfather. You can cut me off from any monies you and Father were going to leave in your will, but I don't need it. Do you not realize, Mother, that I'm worth more than you and Father put together? I have Hannon's money too. All of his inheritance was left to *me*." She points to her chest and continues her rant. "I can buy the

Salerno family a thousand wineries and still leave my future children billions!"

"And what of the Salerno reputation? I will tell everyone..."

Nick slices the air with his hand. "Shut the fuck up, old woman. Nothing you could say or do would tarnish my family's good name, but go ahead and try. We've been pushed down for generations by snooty socialites like you, and we're still going strong. What you might want to be wary of, however, is my Uncle Franky. Italian Mafia. He doesn't take too kindly to having his family threatened."

Finally, the father steps into the fray. "That is enough. I've heard enough. I know I've not been around my daughter or been much of a father to her and Hannon because I was working, making sure their legacy was set for their future, but you seem like you genuinely love her."

"I do, sir. Not that it matters what you or your vile wife think."

Her dad lifts his hand to stop me speaking, and it carries enough weight that I shut it...momentarily.

"Judith, I don't care who Honor chooses for a husband. You told me that she wanted to marry Leonard and convinced me that it would be good for business. I agree that it would, but if she's unwilling, there's no reason to continue this conversation. I've got work to do."

"But your campaign for governor. Your daughter can't be seen slumming it with the depraved bits of society. Whatever will people think?"

"My publicist can deal with anything. Besides, he looks like a nice, healthy young man. Far from depraved."

"Father, if you want to speak to me again, don't ever come back with Mother." Honor comes from behind me, but I keep her an arm's distance away from her parents.

"Mother, I'm done with you and your verbal and physical abuse. Your hatred of me. *Everything.* You made my life a living hell. You threatened my brother's boyfriend with everything that mattered to him. Hannon killed himself because of you! And you don't even care!" Honor screeches like a siren. "What kind of mother does that to her only son and daughter!"

"Don't be ridiculous." Her mother yawns and waves a hand in front of her face.

"It is true. He would be alive if you hadn't gotten involved. You forced him to leave Sean because of his sexual orientation and how that would look to Father. Hannon idolized him. Wanted to be exactly like our father in business, and you took it all away. All of it! I hate you!" she cries, tears falling down her face. "I hate you so much. I want you to leave and never come back!"

"Hannon was gay?" her father blusters, a shocked expression marring his face.

Whoa, nelly. He didn't know.

"No, he wasn't. Just go wait in the car, Timothy." Judith pushes him toward the door.

"Just stay out of my life," Honor reminds her mother.

"Honor, I'll be in contact." Her father grabs her mother's hand.

"Timothy! You can't possibly allow her to stay here. She's our daughter, for crying out loud. We *own* her!" she cries as he pulls her toward a black limo idling at the curb.

"I want to know everything about Hannon's death..." is the last thing we hear before he opens the car door and ushers his wife inside.

When the limo drives away, Honor spins in my arms,

plants her face against my chest, and sobs. I hold her, letting her cry as long as she needs to.

"It's over. They're not going to hurt you anymore," I whisper into her ear while caressing her back. After lifting her into my arms, I carry her out, lock the door, and then pocket the key. I walk through my bustling gym, but no one stops me. The anger on my face, the possessive caveman lock I've got on my woman, ensures me a straight shot to our apartment with no interruptions. I take the stairs up, get her inside, and settle her on our bed.

She cries for a long time, so long the day turns to night right before my eyes. I've got her cuddled up against me when I realize her tears have turned into tiny hiccups against my chest.

"Do you think my mother is going to come after your family?"

I close my eyes and rub her arms. "No, I don't. It sounded like your father hadn't been made privy to a lot of the information. And although he made it clear he wasn't there for you and your brother in a parental capacity, he definitely holds the reins over your mother. He seemed surprised about Hannon."

She nuzzles against my sternum. "Yeah, I had no idea it was Mother alone. The letter that Hannon left me before he died told me that Sean had been threatened and the details of what had been said, but he never specified it was only our mother. I should have known. Father never cared enough to get involved in our personal lives. His only sin was not being there. What our father concerned himself with was where we sat at the table at a business function or on a board of directors. For my father, work is everything. Family comes second. But he had a special connection to Hannon. When he died, he did what a man like him does. He worked harder. Barely ever came home for the first year."

"Still, he was absent for you. He didn't know what was going on between you and your mother. Her abuse. Babe, I'm sorry you had to go through that. Tonight, I came the closest I ever have to punching a woman in the face when she hit you."

Honor pats the skin over my heart. "I'm glad you didn't. She would have sued."

I chuckle. "It would have been worth it."

She sighs. "No, it wouldn't."

"You would have bailed me out of jail."

Honor smiles and nods. Her famous nods.

"I'm sorry about today." I run my fingers through her hair.

Her body tightens up around me. "Sorry about everything?" Her voice shakes when she asks.

"Not the part about making you my wife, about growing this business and our home together." I finger the dog tags around her neck. They look good on her.

She smacks my chest. "Nick! You had me scared out of my mind just then!"

I roll over her and kiss her silly. "How about now? Still scared?" I peck her lips.

"Maybe a little." She squirms under me, wiggling her sexy body against mine delectably.

Cupping her face, I press my forehead to hers in a soft head-butt. She giggles, and it's exactly what I need to hear right now.

"You're going to be my wife. We're building our lives together. Nothing else is more important than that."

She wraps her arms and legs around my body, clinging to

me. "Nothing more important."

"Except for one little detail. A challenge, if you will. Think you can handle it?" I tease before laying down a series of kisses between her breasts, nudging her shirt and my tags away so I can get me some tit.

Honor hums low in her throat. "For you, I can handle anything."

"Now that's my girl." I nudge her bra out of the way with my nose and suck her pretty pink tip into my mouth. She moans and arches into me.

"What's the challenge?" She sighs and runs her fingernails along my scalp.

My dick punches against my track pants at the sensation of her fingers on me. I thrust my dick against her core, grinding until we're both moaning.

"Nick..." my sweet girl says in that way that makes me want to strip her naked and fuck her to kingdom come.

"Well, there's one person we still need to get through on this marriage deal."

I lift up far enough that I can watch her face. Her legs drop down to the bed. "Who?"

I grin. "Ma."

Her eyes flash with fear.

"Dinner, tomorrow. We tell them that we've moved in together and we're getting married. All of them."

A wave of panic hits my girl's face, and she shakes her head.

"No, no, no. You need to tell them by yourself!"

I chuckle and pin her down, grabbing both of her wrists with one hand so I have the other free.

"Dove, together. We do everything together now,

remember."

She purses her lips prettily. "'Cept maybe this one thing?"

"You're cute when you're scared."

"Am not," she huffs.

"So cute. And so mine." I lean down and kiss her, making sure to taste every inch of her lips, teeth, and tongue. Her lips are swollen and bruised when I'm done with them. "Tomorrow," I repeat.

"Tomorrow," Honor responds in a hazy, sexed-up tone.

"You are downright easy, babe. I fucking love it. Time to reward you." I drop her hands and run my hands down her body, where I pull off her yoga pants and underwear at the same time.

"Spread 'em, and don't be shy, or I'll bust out the crop and use it on your clit."

Her entire body shivers underneath my hold.

"I see you like that idea." I cock an eyebrow, waiting for her reply.

"Mmm-hmm," she mumbles, her hands going to the edges of her knees, where they are open for me.

"You want the crop tonight?"

A breathy "yeah" leaves her mouth.

"My dove wants to be bitten."

"Nick..." She sighs as I make my way off the bed and over to the closet, where we have a drawer full of our new purchases. Crops, paddles, belts, cuffs, blindfolds, toys, and more.

I grab the crop and smack it against my palm once. "Take off the rest of your clothes. Spread your arms and legs, and don't move. I'm going to work you hard tonight. Get every ounce of that experience with your mother out of your system and remind you who owns this body, mind, and heart. You got it?"

She scrambles to remove her shirt and bra. Like the good girl she is, she spreads out her legs and arms.

"Thank you, Nick."

Music to my ears. Now it's time to give my woman the release she needs. Help her let it all go so the only thing that remains in her mind is our love, life, and the future we're building.

CHAPTER TWENTY

Inverted Butterfly (Sanskrit: Badhakonasana)

The health benefits to this pose are endless. The most important being improved circulation, decompression of the spine, detoxing of the tissues, and promoting healing of all kind. Inverted positions are a great resource for the body, and yoga teachers everywhere will encourage some time upside down. In this position, you place the silk in a tight band at your hips. Stretch out the legs wide at first, and using your arms, walk down the silks until you're upside down. When you're comfortable, you can bend the knees and touch the soles of the feet, toes, or wrap the feet around the silks. Let hands fall or place them at heart center.

HONOR

The silks slip through my fingers as I curl my legs around

them, my lower back cradled, and I flip upside down. The hammock holds my weight so I'm hanging high enough off the ground that I can easily touch and flatten my palms against my mat but not so low my head is at risk of touching. While hanging, I count to thirty before widening my legs to balance my weight and lift forward with my arms, gripping the silks and easing back up.

"Yes!" I smile and twirl in the hammock.

Behind me, I hear the door lock. Nick just finished teaching the last class for Sunday night, the one he likes to do right before heading to his parents' for dinner.

"Great job, Dove. Now stand up."

I do as he instructs, thinking he's going to lead me into practicing a different aerial yoga pose. The silks sway behind me.

"Remove your pants."

His comment knocks me off guard. "Nick?" I turn my head to where he's standing behind me. He places his hands on my waist; they are warm and comforting.

"You heard me, Dove. Remove your pants and underwear."

The way he said it was not a request but an order. I glance over at the door and window; both are closed, the drapes hiding us from view.

"We're the only ones here. You know I'm the last one at Lotus House. Now strip." He clucks his tongue.

I swallow the lump of nerves and ignore my racing heart. Nick slips away from me as I push my pants and panties down and kick them away. He goes over to the stereo and chooses a song. Feeling brave, I lift my arms and tug my strappy sports bra over my head. When he turns around, I'm gloriously naked.

The piano notes of the song start, and I inhale long and

slow. Hozier's "Take Me to Church" blasts through the speaker, taking my fear and soul with it.

"Fuck! Amen." He stands there on the raised stage looking like a golden god or a bull ready to charge. His upper body is bare, and his lower half is only covered by a pair of black linen pants that are tenting in the front quite magnificently.

My breath stutters as I raise my hands above my head and grab the silks so I don't fall over at the raw masculinity in front of me. The music he's chosen weaves through my subconscious, speaking of church and bedrooms and worship. And that's exactly the way Nick looks at me. With a worshiping stare.

While the first chorus hits, I compare my Nick to the words the songwriter uses. Each one so fitting. With my focus only on him, I watch Nick curl his fingers into his waistband and push his pants down. His long, thick cock stands at attention, looking larger than normal. A spot at the top glistens under the track lighting above, and I want so badly to lick it off. My mouth waters at the sight of his essence coming to the surface. He's so virile, sexually powerful, a god in the bedroom.

"You've got me hard and hungry." He strokes his length from root to tip and back down, masturbating with little care to how much I want to do that for him. "Put the silks to your lower back and repeat your position."

I open my mouth, but nothing comes out. The music's getting louder, and the graphic visual the artist presents permeates my mind like a dirty karma sutra yoga scene.

"Now, Dove. Don't make me wait, or I'll deny you lashes later."

A spike of frustration jabs my chest. The dirty dog *would* deny me if it meant he got to be the one to hold it over my head like a pleasure-stealing ninja.

He continues stroking his length with one hand and gestures in a circle with one finger at the hammock behind me.

Leaning back, I shimmy the gossamer, soft fabric into position. Once I've got it tucked to my lower back, I use my hands to grip the fabric. Then, I lift my legs, open them in a wide V in the air, and let my back and head fall toward the floor on one fluid movement.

"Jesus, Mary, and Joseph." Nick bursts into action, moving fast as I spin around. My sex is completely exposed, my legs out, the silks holding me open and in position. Nick stops behind me. *Behind me, damn it!* Where I can't touch him. Both of his hands wrap around my ankles.

His length prods against my ass, and I mewl with need for him. Nick runs his fingers down my legs, and I can't help but tremble. I shoot my arms out in front of me to hold the floor so I don't lose my position or fall on my head.

"How long do you think you can hang like this?" he asks low, his voice uncontrolled and unlike anything I've ever heard from his lips before.

"Maybe two or three minutes before I get light-headed," I reply as his fingers reach my center, smoothing through the wetness he finds. "Oh God," I gasp, wanting to close my legs, but I can't because if I do, I'll fall on my face.

"Your body is a vision." He runs his hands up and down my legs. "Smooth." He kisses my ankle. "Toned." A kiss to the inside of my knee. "Pale white." Another kiss touches my inner thigh, so close to where I want him most. And yet, I'm also afraid to have him there for fear I'll lose my mind.

Arousal roars through my system like a wild animal. I flex my toes and dig my fingers into the mat below.

"And all mine," he whispers before I feel his mouth on my sex.

Wild, animalistic pleasure assaults me. I become dizzy, my hands pressing into the mat so I'm pushing up as he's pushing down. His thumb twirls around my clit in devious circles, and I am humping his face and the air recklessly, lost in a tumble of sensation as he sinks his tongue deep inside me. I howl at the intrusion. He flutters and flicks the talented muscle, working me into complete and utter oblivion. And then he amps it up a notch when he pinches my clit...hard. I scream, my body jerking as though it has been electrocuted, but he doesn't stop feasting. He moans loudly, smashing his face between my legs as if he wants to be smothered in me, in my taste. I lift one hand to his head and ride the remaining waves of my orgasm.

When I'm boneless, he pulls away, helps me up, and pushes the silk along my back and just under my bum so it cradles my body. Dreamily, I lie back, supported by the hammock, but Nick has other ideas.

"No rest for the wicked, baby." He spreads my legs and adjusts the silks so I'm tilted and my pelvis is lifted up to his perfect height. As I lock my legs around his waist, he centers his weeping cock at my center and power drives in.

Full. I'm so full, I arch my upper body and grind my heels into his lower back.

"Fuck, yeah. Now hold on to the fabric, Dove, because I'm about to take you on one helluva ride."

That is the only warning I get. A second later, he is gripping the silks and powering me on and off his cock in fast, spearing jabs. I can see a full few inches of his cock as he eases my body forward and back. Inside, I am a mass of contradiction. Full, empty, choking with his size, and bereft. Over and over he pounds into me, each thrust harder than the next, taking me to new sexual heights I'm not sure I'll survive.

Nick shifts my legs from around him so my heels are wedged up against my sides and inside the silks. The new position is vulgar and filthy. He pulls away, his dick falling from me as he assesses his handiwork.

"Look at you, strung up and open for your man. Ready to take my cock, my fingers, or my mouth. This pretty, wet pussy, open all for me?"

Apparently, I've made the error of not answering fast enough, because before I can formulate an answer in my sex-induced haze, Nick has straightened his hand, fingers out flat, and he draws his arm back and spanks me right between the legs.

I whimper with the first lash.

"All." He smacks me again, my clit turning fire hot with the second blow.

"For." Nick doubles his force, and my body rocks with the rebound of his slap.

"Me!" He growls and smacks my sex three times in quick succession.

My body is unable to catch up with the overwhelming pain and pleasure that is shooting through my system. He doesn't let up. Before I can take a breath and process the fiery spanking of my most private part, he lines himself up again and thrusts his cock deep. So deep I lose my ability to breathe.

"Jesus, fucking woman. I love you so damn much," he thunders as he wraps his hands around my ass and forces me so deeply onto his cock, I could swear I feel him in my chest.

I explode around him, the pleasure so acute it splinters from where we are connected, through every limb, taking me away. Far, far away. My mind instantly shuts down.

My entire being and world shrink down to one solitary person. Nick.

Every touch.

His kiss.

Nick's love.

He hammers into me, racing to find his own release, and through it, I again find mine.

And again.

And again.

I can't stop coming. It's like my entire body is an exposed nerve and Nick is pricking it repeatedly with a pointy needle. One wave of heaven rolls into another.

When Nick is done torturing me with orgasms, he wraps his arms around me, hugging me closely while still imbedded, his manhood a massive force between my thighs. I follow his lead by draping my legs and arms around him. Face-to-face, heart-to-heart, mouth-to-mouth, he gets up on his toes, his body arching sublimely, his cock a weapon of pleasure inside me. Every inch of his strong, muscled body convulses and quakes against mine, exposing his vulnerable, softer side. I hold him tighter, reveling in the feel of this man giving it all... to me.

"All for you," he whispers, forehead to mine, the puff of his labored breaths coating my lips in warm air. "Everything I am, all that I will be, is all for you."

★ ★ ★

NICHOLAS

Honor is a wreck of nerves as I lead her up the steps toward my family home. "Relax, Dove. They're all going to love you. Gracie and Ma already do. The rest is a formality, just trust me." I curve an arm around her waist so we're walking together in matched stride.

She knots her fingers together and then presses a wild lock of loose hair behind her ear. "It's not that I don't think they'll like me."

I stop at the crest of the staircase and turn toward her. "Then what is it?"

She looks down at her sandals and plucks at her flowy dress. The fabric has bursts of brightly colored flowers in a variety of pale pinks, greens, and blues. Her skin positively glows against the backdrop. Two tiny strips tie at each shoulder, leaving her arms bare. Since her stint in the hospital, my girl hasn't so much as scratched her skin, and though I liked the henna she used to decorate her arms with, her scars are out in the open and barely visible. I've taught her that it's an opportunity to either open herself up to that person about her past choices and share who she was and how far she has come or to change the subject. The choice is always hers.

I run my fingers over her scarred arms like I have many times in the past weeks. I've done it so often, she doesn't even blink at my touch, but for me, it's a reminder that she's alive, she's here, and she's mine to protect and keep safe.

The chain from my dog tags catches the light and sparkles against her skin. The beads of the necklace are visible, but the tags are properly hidden between her breasts. Every time I take a gander and see my tags nestled between her billowy goodness, a contented sigh comes out of me. I can't help it. It's the alpha dog in me howling with approval.

"I'm worried that they are going to think things are moving too fast, and in normal circumstances..."

I shake my head and place both hands on her shoulders, grounding her to this moment. "None of that. I've told you before. My mother and father had one date. A month later, they were married. Three months after that, they were pregnant with me. Babe, this family does fast. You know what they say... never let a day go by. Get it? Dago?"

She titters behind her hand. "Not nice. You kiss your mother with that mouth?"

And there's her sense of humor. Finally!

I hook my arm over her shoulder and keep her close to my side. "Dove, it's going to be great. Don' worry ah-bout it. *Capisce?*" I say while contorting my hand as if I'm pinching salt between my fingers.

She giggles, and I bring her to the door and open it for her. "Ma, we're here!"

"In the kitchen!" she hollers from the back of the house.

I know by all the cars in the driveway that everyone's already here. I planned it that way to make it easy. The goal tonight is to get Honor to connect with my family and to let all of them know about our future plans.

Taking Honor's hand, I lead her back to the kitchen. The volume of chatter ceases to a complete dead silence as we enter. So many gazes land on us, it feels like the Spanish Inquisition.

Ma comes over to Honor, wooden spatula in hand, apron

on, and her arms open. "Honor, my sweet girl, come, come, give your mama a hug."

Honor preens under the praise, and it makes my heart happy for her. The debacle with her parents yesterday proved that she won't be having her family around anytime soon, if at all. Still, all is not lost. My family will pick up the slack and then some.

Gracie hugs Honor next and gushes about how pretty her dress is.

I whistle when the chatter picks back up in the kitchen, making it impossible to hear one another. It's not a small kitchen by any means, but with this many bodies in it, with *Italian* boisterous voices, it can be damn near deafening.

"Hey, hey, everybody. I've got an announcement, and I don't want to have to repeat myself ten times. So let's all play nice and listen."

"Get on with it, Nicky. We're starvin' here!" Lo, my sister's husband, calls out.

I shoot him a dangerous glare. "Zip it. I want to start by introducing you to my girl, Honor Carmichael. Honor, over in the corner there is my sister Dawn and her husband, Lorenzo, but we all call him Lo. They are expecting their first baby, and we're all fucking ecstatic!" I smile huge at my baby sis. She places both of her hands on her abdomen and grins. Lo covers her hands with his.

"Good to meet you," Dawn says.

"Next in line, you've got Angela and her boyfriend, Javier, who has been draggin' ass with making an honest woman out of my sister. He may need a talkin' to," I snarl at my sister's man.

He raises his hands in surrender. "Back off, *amigo*. I've suggested marriage many times, and this one seems to want to wait for some magical time off in the future. I'm just biding my time."

All eyes go to Angela. Her face flushes red. "I, uh... I'm young! Ma, I didn't say not ever."

Our ma is shaking her head and flinging her saucy spatula around her head like a crazy woman. "Jesus, Mary, and Joseph, and God above, please knock some sense into my child, for she knows not what she does."

"Sorry, man. Angela, you and me, talk. Later."

She groans. "Fine."

I shake my head of the craziness that is my family and move to the threesome sitting around the table where a blond-haired girl is coloring in a book. "Over there is my sister Cara and her *live-in* boyfriend, Scott, and his daughter, Kaylee."

"What! You're living in sin with my daughter!" Mama screeches, about to burst another vein. She lifts her hands to her heart in prayer. "Blessed Mother, protect and lead my daughter to making good choices and her boyfriend to putting a ring on her finger." She makes the sign of the cross and leans against my father. He wraps an arm around her shoulder.

"It's okay, *tesora mia*. We will have a talk with these ungrateful children and show them the way," my father coos to my mother.

I cough into my hand because if I didn't, I'd crack up. Everything is going exactly as planned. Nailing everyone to the wall before I get to my news so it won't seem so shocking. So far, it's working perfectly.

"Okay, now we get to the twins."

Honor interrupts me. "You're twins?" She points to Grace and Faith.

Faith laughs, and Gracie falls all over herself giggling.

"No! They call us twins because we're less than a year apart."

"Oh, Irish twins," Honor adds helpfully, or rather unhelpfully, because Ma jumps on it in a second.

"We are not Irish! A hundred percent Italian! Screw the Irish!" Ma raises and shakes her spatula like it was a golden, mighty fist, sauce dripping down the side of the spoon.

I lift my hands. "Easy, Ma. It's an expression."

"I'm sorry, Mrs. Salerno," Honor says quickly. She's going to do so well in this family.

"It's okay, angel." Ma tuts like she's precious china. I agree with the precious part, though, so I don't say anything.

"All right, so now that we've introduced you to everyone, we have our own announcement."

Magically, everyone is silent, even though Angela and Cara are giving me death glares. A second from now, it won't matter.

I curl an arm around Honor and take a deep breath. "I've asked Honor to marry me, and she's agreed. She's moved into my apartment, and we're expanding Sal's Boxing Gym & Fitness and the apartment. Honor has bought the laundromat next door, and well...that's it." I get the words out in one rushed breath and look at my girl and not the shocked faces of my family.

"I've never loved a woman or been happier in my entire life. I hope all of you will show her the same love and respect you've shown me and make her part of our family."

For an entire minute, not one person speaks. The only sound comes when Ma drops her death grip on the sauce spatula, and it falls to the floor, sauce splattering everywhere, and then spreads her arms out wide and screams.

"Oh, my God! My dreams are coming true! My Nicholas is

getting married!" And then the dramatics build as she drops to her knees, turns her face up to the ceiling, and prays. Out loud.

"Thank you, Jesus, Mary, and Joseph for this blessing you have brought upon our house. In the name of the Father, the Son, and the Holy Spirit, I praise you! Amen! Amen! Amen!"

Dad moves to help her get off the floor, but he doesn't move fast enough. Ma springs up and into my arms, tackle-hugging me. "Nicky, you've made your mama so happy, baby. So happy. And she's perfect!" Ma stretches out a hand and curls it around Honor's chin. "May you give me many grandbabies!"

Honor smiles and nods in her way.

"You'll start right away...yes?" She grabs Honor's arm and pulls her into our hug huddle.

"Marriage first, Ma," I remind her.

"Yes, yes, marriage first." She pulls back, tears rushing down her cheeks, and she claps. "Salvatore! You bring out the good stuff. We are celebrating!"

"Woman, you're always celebrating!" he jabs back but heads toward the cellar door anyway.

After Ma finally lets us go, each of my sisters gives us their blessing and congratulations. Even Angela and Cara, who I kind of threw under the bus, have nothing but love and excitement to offer us.

Once my dad brings up several bottles of wine, opens and pours hefty full glasses, and passes one out to each of us, he clears his throat.

Dad doesn't give speeches often, preferring to speak to us one-on-one when he has something to say, but in this moment, we all pay attention. He lifts his glass, stretches out his arm, and makes a slow circle, pointing his goblet at each one of us, making eye contact in the process.

"To my wife, my girls and their chosen mates, my son and his bride, all of you here today are now a part of the Salerno family. We fall in love hard...we give love deeply...and we give it for life."

Honor squeezes my hand. I bring hers up to my lips and kiss right over her new shiny diamond ring we picked up this morning.

My father continues. "As you have chosen us, we have chosen you. We are family. *Dio benedica la nostra famiglia.* I love you all." He raises his glass and then takes a sip of the lifeblood of our family. Our wine.

"Dio benedica la nostra famiglia!" each of the Salerno members repeats and then takes a sip.

"What does that mean?" Honor asks.

"It translates to, God bless our family."

"God bless our family," she repeats.

"I love you, soon-to-be Mrs. Salerno," I whisper.

"I love you calling me Mrs. Salerno." She smiles, and my world lights up.

As I stand around my family, chatting up each person, sharing stories of how Honor and I met, how we're updating the gym and the apartment, it becomes real.

For eight years, I served in the army, trying to find my place, to protect and serve. Three years out, and I've built a business, found the woman I want to spend my life with, the person I now live to serve and protect. Everything I went through, the ups, downs, hardships, and losses, have all led me to now...to her.

EPILOGUE

HONOR

One year later...

The grass is cool and crisp under my feet when I kick off my shoes and settle down into it, sitting cross-legged.

"I know it's been a long time since I've visited. I'm sorry." I pluck at a few grass blades and twist the strands between my fingers.

"Sometimes it's hard to come here. Before, it was one of the only places I could go to feel close to you. Now it seems unnecessary, because I can feel you everywhere. In a song, a meal, a book I've read, the pictures all around my house." I toss aside the grass and fiddle with the lace at the hem of my dress instead.

"I talk about you all the time. To Nick, his family, and my

friends. I have a lot of friends now. Nick says it's time we bring you into the light. You're not a secret. I'm not ashamed of you, but for a long time I was...angry with you. So angry. I blamed you for leaving me behind. For not taking me with you. For not being strong enough to fight. That was wrong of me. I know better now."

The wind blows my curls into my face. I push a lock back behind my ear and focus on the engraved granite slab a few feet from where I sit.

Hannon Timothy Carmichael
Beloved son and brother
10/3/1990 – 7/4/2014

"I miss you every day, Hannon. Some days it's hard to breathe, but when that happens, I have Nick to breathe life back into me. He reminds me of all the beauty I have to live for, and he's taught me to fight for those things."

Tears fill my eyes and spill over my cheeks. "I'm better now. Happy. I'm married, we have a successful business, but more importantly, we have new life to celebrate."

I wrap my arms around my blossoming belly. "It's twins." The tears fall unchecked. I don't even try to hold them back. "Boys. Two boys. And I wanted to tell you first before we told anyone else."

I clear my throat. "One will be named Nicholas Salvatore Salerno the Third." I rub my hand over one side, finding what I'm pretty sure is a set of feet. Moving along my bump to the other side, I feel a curved lump that I know is my other son. "And his brother will be named Hannon Sean Salerno. After you and the man you loved most. I want our children to know who their uncle was. That he was a good, smart, kind man who sacrificed it all for love."

A sob slips from my lips, and I hunch over, but before the sorrow engulfs me, a long leg appears on each side of my body, and I am embraced by the most comforting arms.

Nick presses his scruffy chin into my neck and inhales and exhales, over and over until I've paired my breathing with his and calmed down. He tips my head, wipes both of my eyes with his thumbs, and kisses me softly. "You okay?"

I nod.

"Dove..."

"I'm okay. I miss him so much. I wish he could be here to meet you, to see how good my life has turned out...to meet our boys." I suck in a shaky breath, and more tears fall. "It's not fair."

"No, it isn't, but every year will get just a bit easier. You'll never stop missing him, and the hurt will never go away completely because his loss is a hole that can't ever be filled." Nick gently head-butts my forehead with his. "Eventually the wound won't feel so deep."

I kiss him softly and twist back around to face my brother's gravestone.

"My sins are no longer silent, Hannon, and neither are those of our parents. Your goodness and beauty will be carried on through me and your namesake. Be still, brother... Find your peace."

I let Nick hold me for a few minutes until the boys start boxing one another inside my belly.

"Whoa! I think it's time to feed these little buggers." Nick places his large hands over our children and kisses my temple. "Come on, Dove. Time to go celebrate Independence Day with the clan. Ma's cooking up a feast, and you know how she fawns over you."

"She just loves me because I'm giving her grandchildren."

Nick swings our arms, leading me to the car. "There are worse things. Besides, wait until they find out we're having not one boy but two. Ma may have a coronary."

I frown. "You think?"

He opens the car door and helps me get inside and buckled up before racing around his Chevy and hopping in. "No! That woman is going to live to be a hundred."

I sigh. "I'm not sure it will really be that big of a deal."

"Babe, we're giving my mother and father guaranteed continuation of the Salerno name. Dawn had a girl. We are so going to be the favorites right now. Let's eat it up and take as much advantage as possible!" He laughs, puts the car in gear, and motors down the road.

"This is true. You can't really beat that logic." I smile and lean my head back against the headrest.

"Nope. And when she finds out we're naming one of the twins after my father and me..." He grins huge. "We're going to have a million get-out-of-jail-free cards. You're going to be the most loved daughter ever! Including her own."

"Wow. This is good news," I say rather uncertainly.

He grabs my hand and laces our fingers tighter. "This is blockbuster news, babe. I'm so fucking happy. I can't wait to be a father."

"You're going to be an amazing dad, Nick." I stare at his handsome profile, thinking back over the last year.

Only a few months after we announced our engagement did we turn around and have our wedding. There was no reason to wait, and money wasn't a problem. We married right on the family property near the vineyards. After the wedding,

Nick announced he wanted me to get off birth control pills. We discussed it, agreed that we wanted a big family and, again, didn't want to wait. We were pregnant less than two months after we said *I do*.

"You think?" Nick grins and glances over at me and then quickly puts his attention back on the road.

"I know." I rub my hand over my belly once more. "It's like your dad said: You fall in love hard...you give love deeply...and you give it for life. Our boys will only know love like that."

Nick lifts my hand and kisses my fingers and then places our hands on top of my belly. "I know you're going to be a spectacular mom."

His words choke me up and start the water works once again. *Damn hormones.* "Why?"

"Baby, your love is endless. For me, my family, our friends. If you give half of that to our children, they'll be the luckiest kids in the universe. And I know you're going to do right by them because you already love them."

I wipe away the tears with my free hand. "I do. I love them so much."

"Love is all anyone could ever need...and hot sex. And pasta. Let's not forget the pasta."

My mouth waters at the thought of Ma's spaghetti and meatballs. "Ooooh, pasta."

Then the reminder of Nick taking me from behind while I was up on all fours in our bed this morning. "Ooooh, hot sex."

Nick burst out laughing.

"Oh, my God! I just thought of the best idea." It's like a light bulb flickered on right above my head.

"What's that, Dove?"

"Hot sex while eating pasta!" I grin and lick my lips.

"Perfect fucking woman, my wife." He lifts my hand and kisses the back. "Absolutely perfect."

THE END

Want more of the Lotus House clan?
Continue on with Dara Jackson
and Silas McKnight's story in:

Intimate Intuition
Book Six in the *Lotus House Series.*
Coming May 8th, 2018

EXCERPT FROM
INTIMATE INTUITION

A LOTUS HOUSE NOVEL (BOOK #6)

THIRD EYE CHAKRA

The third eye chakra is the sixth chakra in the body. It is located in the brain at the brow, above the top of the nose. In Sanskrit, it's called Ajna. This chakra is considered the part of the body that can transcend time.

DARA

Positive. Plus sign. In the modern world, the addition symbol is literally *positive*. As in *more*.

More quantity.

More happiness.

The white stick with the pink plus symbol glaring at me evokes the exact opposite of more. Next to the plus is a second window with two lines—in dramatic opposition to the glaring addition symbol I so desperately want to be a *subtract* symbol.

A negative.

The two lines infuse everything with glaring, unavoidable clarity—and mean only one thing.

Pregnant.

I close my eyes, sigh, and lean back against the bathroom wall. It's been three weeks since I laid eyes on him. Two weeks since I'd given up hope he'd call and explain himself. One week since I missed my cycle. Now here I am, knocked up with the product of a one-night stand. Only this isn't just any one-night stand. We have mutual friends. Several of them. Of course, they have no idea we spent a drunken night of carnal delights with one another. No, they are none the wiser.

Technically, my friend Nick did ask how "drinks" went with his buddy. As usual, I played it off like it was just another night. Nothing special. Definitely nothing to talk about.

As if I would discuss the feel of his lips trailing down my neck.

The way his hands curved perfectly around my naked breasts.

Our endless worshipping of one another.

Except how can they all not know?

We couldn't get enough of each other's bodies. We were careful, using condoms every single time. Completely on top of it. Literally. Went through a half dozen of them throughout the night. But one round...the condom broke. At the time, it wasn't a big deal. We were drunk as skunks and feeding on flesh and booze. It took a lot of meditation and thinking back through the haziness to even remember the incident, as inebriated as I was. By the time I recalled the slip, it was too late. The day-after pill wouldn't have worked. I know—I asked the pharmacist. Three of them. At different locations. And my gynecologist.

Until this moment, I had been banking on my good luck. Except I've never been lucky. Not in love and not in life. At least not in my formative years. I started out in foster care and a girls' home for orphaned kids, no family to speak of, until I was eight years old. Then out of nowhere, a round black woman with big cheeks, dark eyes, and an easy smile picked me out of a lineup of children in my age group to sit and talk with. I knew from the other kids, when one of us was pulled out and talked to, it could mean ending up in a home. It was all any of us ever wanted. Still, one of the scariest days of my life was meeting Darren and Vanessa Jackson.

Until now.

For a week, the Jacksons came back to the home to visit with me. I guess they were making sure we were a good fit. I clung to Mrs. Jackson during our visits. I'd always wanted a mother, someone to look at me with soft eyes and a smile. Once our week was up, the Jacksons both held my hands and asked me if I wanted to come home with them. *Live* with them. I couldn't have known then it would be the best thing that ever happened to me.

I distinctly remember looking up into Mrs. Jackson's eyes and then Mr. Jackson's, trying to discern the significance of what was happening. All I could do in that moment was ask an awe-filled question.

"You want me?"

They assured me that, yes indeed, they very much wanted me to be their child. They took me to their expansive home in Berkeley, California, and showed me a room painted in a soft yellow with sunflowers scattered throughout. I was in heaven. Two human beings who wanted me, craved having me as their daughter. They worked, fought, and paid through the nose to adopt me officially. I had a family.

As I stare down at the three positive pregnancy tests, I cup my hand over my belly and cry. Big, heaping sobs. I've wanted nothing more in life than to be a baker and a mother just like my adopted mother, Vanessa Jackson. To show my child from the second it took its first breath I would always want her and do right by her—or him. Unlike my biological parents, I would *want* to give a child the love and family the Jacksons gave me.

And while the tears fall down my cheeks, I vow to my unborn child I will do exactly that. Regardless of whether or not Silas McKnight wants any part of his child's life, I'll be everything our child needs and more.

Positive.

Plus...one.

★ ★ ★

Three weeks earlier...

Harmony Jack's is packed to the gills with bodies as I enter and push past a beefy, handsy fellow. Mentally, I chastise myself for my choice of attire, but the sparkly blue, micro-mini dress called to me. So the hem sits just below my ass...big deal. I work hard in the studio to keep my shit tight. Aside from my ba-donk-a-donk. It seems there is nothing I can do about the size of my ass. Squats, leg lifts, and an endless circuit of yoga poses with an emphasis on slimming the glutes does absolutely nothing but make my bum higher and tighter. I've since given up on trying to slim it down and now focus on flaunting the hell out of it. If a man doesn't want tits and ass, they can get to steppin'. *Ain't nobody got time for that noise.*

I see my crew at the back of the bar. They look like they

are hugging Honor, Nick's woman, for some reason. As I wiggle my way through the dancers and partygoers, I see Nick and wave. He pulls me into a hug. I turn around and snuggle Dash and his wife, Amber, and then Atlas before Nick hooks his arm with mine and leads me toward where Honor is standing next to a fine-as-fuck black man. His mocha-colored skin positively gleams under the flashing lights of the bar as I give him the once-over. He's dressed to impress: black slacks, a royal-blue dress shirt tucked in, with a thin leather belt around his trim waist. I can tell by the V shape of his upper body he's likely packing some seriously tight muscles under those threads. When I make my way up his form and my gaze lands on his face, his bright smile positively blinds me.

"Lordy..." I whisper under my breath as Honor leans into the fine man's space and says something I can't hear.

Still, I watch as he nods and does his once-over of my body, from my spiked silver heels up my bare legs to my cleavage-bearing chest, before landing on my face. He licks his lips and bites the bottom one. I'm positive my panties have dampened from one damn perusal.

I lift my hand to push my suddenly heavy locks off my neck so I can get a little air on my overly heated skin.

"Hey, babe, you know Dara Jackson from Lotus House." Nick lets me go and loops his arm around Honor.

She smiles softly and glances at me. "I do. Good to see you again."

I glance at Nick and note his rather possessive hold on the blonde and can't help but offer encouragement. I want to see my friend settled and happy. Honor seems to give him that. And I know for a fact she needs him. Shy, sweet, and naïve. Plus, her aura is starting to shimmer with a glowing pink, meaning these two are about to have some serious fun!

"Glad you scooped up your man. I'm sure there are yogis everywhere crying into their soy chai latte over the resident hottie being off the market." I laugh and wink at Nick.

"Absolutely off the market," Nick confirms and then curves his head toward Honor's and kisses her. "We're living together now too," he says with pride and another peck of his woman's mouth.

I sigh. I love seeing Nick so taken with this woman. It gives me hope the right man is out there for me too. Not that I've had a good one yet.

The man standing next to Honor clears his throat, reminding me of his presence. Not that I could forget. He's ridiculously attractive, and his light eyes have not left me since I arrived. Hell, I could feel those hazel gems running all over me while I greeted my friends a few minutes ago. Now, it's no different. He's not even trying to act cool. Confidence. I like that in a man. Almost as much as I like a body that won't quit and a smile that could melt the panties off any sista in here.

"Righteous." I grin at Nick before turning my attention lazily to hot stuff. "And who is this tall, dark drink of heaven?" I extend my hand.

He takes hold of my hand. The instant our palms touch, a sizzle of magnetism starts my hand chakras spinning in the opposite direction, my body's way of trying to pair instantly with his energy. *Interesting.* More interesting is when he lifts my hand to his mouth and kisses my knuckles. I swoon in my spiked heels, nearly falling over, but his tight grip won't allow that, and I sway toward him.

"I'm Silas McKnight. I work with Atlas." He gestures over to our friends behind me.

Right then, Atlas claps Silas on the back. "Don't let him fool you, Dara. He's my boss. The dude is rich, available, and a hard worker." He clocks Silas on the arm. "Don't say I never did nuthin' for ya, buddy, but I've got to get home. Mila says Aria is awake with a fever and calling for her daddy. My girls call, I'm out. Bye, guys. Great job tonight, Honor. Really killer voice. Hope to hear it again soon."

I frown. Honor sang? I would have liked to see and hear that side of the sweet woman.

Silas ruffles Atlas's hair, making me smile. There's a brotherhood there. If Atlas let Silas touch him in such a casual and friendly manner, he must be well-liked. "Catch ya Monday. Don't be late...again!" Silas warns, and Atlas chuckles, lifts a hand above his head, and waves as he exits. Dash and Amber are quick to follow.

"We've, um, got plans tomorrow. We should, uh..." Amber twists her lips in a pensive gesture, but her aura is spiking red-hot, readying for a romp with our resident Tantric yoga teacher who also happens to be her husband.

Dash chuckles and hooks her around the waist. "I promised my wife a handful of orgasms tonight," he says with absolutely no concern for decency or etiquette. Such an endearing quality in my friend. "It's been a long week for her." He nods to his wife. "Means we're headed out."

Amber widens her eyes to the size of dinner plates. "My goodness. I can't believe you just said that! Dash!" She smacks his arm with righteous indignation.

He nuzzles her temple. "Little bird, everyone here tonight is going to go home and fuck like rabbits. We're no different. Am I right?" he asks our group. I'm not touching that statement with a ten-foot pole, because it has been too damn long for me.

My dry spell is closing in on ten months, and I need to get me some. I glance up at Mr. Tall, Black, and Handsome, assessing my chances of a sexy romp with a stranger. It's not the first time—although, I don't make a habit of sharing my body without strings attached—but something about this man has me squeezing my thighs and fanning my face. I'd like so very much to take a bite right out of him. Plus, he must be solid if my friends like him so much.

Nick coughs into his hand. "I'm hitting my girl for sure." He twists his head so his lips rest against Honor's ear where he whispers something I can't hear in the overly loud bar.

"Yes, please," Honor murmurs, and her pink energy starts changing to the same bright red Amber's was a moment ago. Nick, on the other hand, is a straight fireball of energy. Always is. Everything he does is accomplished with a thirst for life and an unmatched exuberance.

"I think we all need to head home." Nick sets down his beer and grabs his girl's glass, adding it to the ones on the table.

"Guys, I just got here!" I offer my best pout, knowing it's going to be useless with this much sexual energy bouncing between my two friends.

That's when Silas offers his hand. "I'm happy to keep you company." He grins, and I place my hand into his once more. Again, the hand chakras start buzzing. I briefly wonder if he can feel it. "Come on." He leads me over to a quieter area with a hand to my lower back. I glance over my shoulder and realize all of my friends have left me high and dry.

Brats. Really, I can't blame them, and at least I get a hottie out of the exchange.

Silas offers me a corner booth seat. I grab the hem of my micro skirt and sit down, situating my legs so they don't show too much but leave very little to the imagination. His gaze takes in my bare thigh as he settles into the booth next to me, sitting so close, our knees touch.

"You work with Atlas?" I start off the conversation, wanting to get the basics out of the way. It's not as though I want to jump him straight away...but I kind of want to get to the good part a lot faster. Figure out if he's a psycho or not before I jump his bones.

He lifts a hand up and flicks his fingers at the bartender. Within what feels like seconds, she comes over with a glass of champagne, which he hands to me, and a full pint glass for him.

"Sorry, the women were all having champagne earlier, and I figured you looked a little parched. Champagne okay?" he asks. His voice is a low rumble, which sends my earlier arousal from a five out of ten to a nine out of ten.

"Uh, yeah. Never heard of anyone turning down the bubbly before." I take a sip, allowing the sweet taste to permeate my dry mouth.

He sips his beer and then licks his upper lip. I'm instantly fascinated by the small movement, wanting so much to lick that same lip myself but knowing it's far too aggressive at this stage of the evening.

"Ah, back to your question. Atlas and I work together, yes." He leans back into the booth.

"He said you were his boss."

He nods. "True. Really we're all part of a big team at Knight & Day Productions."

I smile. "You own the company, don't you?" I cock an eyebrow, waiting to see if he'll start to boast and fall all over himself telling me how amazing he is, how much money he makes, blah blah, like every other successful man I've dated in the past.

Silas lifts his hand and rubs at his bottom lip with his thumb before glancing away momentarily. "Guilty. But only because my father retired and I'm the eldest son. Couple of my siblings work the business too. Then we've got incredible talent like Atlas Powers. He and the team as a whole are why we're so successful."

Now that response I did not expect. To downplay his status in the company...

I shake my head and smile into my drink as I take a sip.

"Tell me about you."

I swallow the rest of my bubbly before answering. "For that, we're going to need a bit more alcohol. As in shots."

His eyebrows rise nearly into his hairline. "Shots?"

"Yep."

Silas leans closer, placing his arm on the back of the booth so his face is near enough for me to hear him whisper into my ear, even over the boisterous chatter and music. "You planning to get me drunk and take advantage of me, Ms. Jackson?"

Feeling bold and brave, I turn my head so our cheeks are touching, and I know he can catch a long whiff of my perfume. I lift my hand and link it around his neck, holding him in place.

"You can't take advantage of the willing, Mr. McKnight."

His body trembles as I scratch my nails lightly along the back of his neck.

"No, I guess not. You offerin' up a night of bliss?"

I grin against his cheek and use my patented sexy lilt, the tone that usually gets me what I want with the opposite sex. And right now, it's a hot night with one Silas McKnight. "Order up the shots and we'll find out."

"Anything you say, my queen."

Continue reading in:

Intimate Intuition
A Lotus House Novel: Book Six
Coming May 8th, 2018

ALSO BY AUDREY CARLAN

The Calendar Girl Series

January (Book 1)
February (Book 2)
March (Book 3)
April (Book 4)
May (Book 5)
June (Book 6)

July (Book 7)
August (Book 8)
September (Book 9)
October (Book 10)
November (Book 11)
December (Book 12)

The Calendar Girl Anthologies

Volume One (Jan-Mar)
Volume Two (Apr-Jun)

Volume Three (Jul-Sep)
Volume Four (Oct-Dec)

The Falling Series

Angel Falling
London Falling
Justice Falling

The Trinity Trilogy

Body (Book 1)
Mind (Book 2)
Soul (Book 3)
Life: A Trinity Novel (Book 4)
Fate: A Trinity Novel (Book 5)

The Lotus House Series

Resisting Roots (Book 1)
Sacred Serenity (Book 2)
Divine Desire (Book 3)
Limitless Love (Book 4)
Silent Sins (Book 5)

Intimate Intuition
(May 8, 2018)
Enlightened End
(June 26, 2018)

ACKNOWLEDGMENTS

To my husband, **Eric**, who understands I don't intend to be locked away in my office every day. I'm working so hard to set us and our boys up for the future. I want our retirement years to rock! Thank you for being so understanding. I love you.

To my editor **Ekatarina Sayanova** with Red Quill Editing, LLC...I love how you connected with Honor and Nick so completely. You give me hope with each book I write.

To my Waterhouse Press editor, **Jeanne De Vita**, I'm thrilled you loved this book. Your changes as usual were thoughtful and helped make the novel sparkle. Thank you.

To my one and only pre-reader **Ceej Chargualaf**, I'm pretty sure this novel would not have been completed on time without your encouragement. Reading my raw chapters one at a time has to be painful. It would literally kill me to wait, not to mention wading through all the errors prior to editing. All I can say is that I'm so incredibly thankful for your commitment to me and my stories. The feedback and thoughtful replies you give for each chapter keep me writing. Period. There is no one like you on this earth.

Jeananna Goodall, my wonderful and efficient Personal Assistant, thank you for keeping my ass in check! I swear I'd be bouncing all over the walls without you to keep me sane. I love your happiness and ability to see through to the light at the end of the tunnel. I need more of that, and am so appreciative I have that in you.

Ginelle Blanch, **Anita Shofner**, and **Tracey Vuolo** you are amazing bad-ass betas for different reasons. Ginelle, you find errors two editors don't find! Your meticulous attention for detail is such a gift. Anita, you keep me laughing with your reactions to every chapter. Tracey, I love the way you get mad, happy, sad, and find all the best teasers! Keep it coming. Ladies, these books would suck without your feedback. Thank you.

To the Audrey Carlan Street Team of wicked hot Angels, together we change the world. One book at a time. BESOS-4-LIFE, lovely ladies.

ABOUT AUDREY CARLAN

Audrey Carlan is a #1 *New York Times, USA Today*, and *Wall Street Journal* bestselling author. She writes wicked hot love stories that are designed to give the reader a romantic experience that's sexy, sweet, and so hot your ereader might melt. Some of her works include the wildly successful Calendar Girl Serial, Falling Series, and the Trinity Trilogy.

She lives in the California Valley where she enjoys her two children and the love of her life. When she's not writing, you can find her teaching yoga, sipping wine with her "soul sisters" or with her nose stuck in a wicked hot romance novel.

Any and all feedback is greatly appreciated and feeds the soul. You can contact Audrey below:

E-mail: carlan.audrey@gmail.com
Facebook: facebook.com/AudreyCarlan
Website: www.audreycarlan.com